Catamount
Bridge

Catamount Bridge

A novel by
Don Metz

Harper & Row, Publishers, New York
Cambridge, Philadelphia, San Francisco
London, Mexico City, São Paulo, Singapore, Sydney

First PERENNIAL LIBRARY edition published 1989.

Designer: Erich Hobbing

Copyeditor: Mary Jane Alexander

Library of Congress Cataloging-in-Publication Data

Metz, Don.

   Catamount bridge.

   "Perennial Library."
   I. Title.
PS3563.E849C38   1988   813'.54   87-17801
ISBN 0-06-09150-6 (pbk.)

---

89 90 91 92 FG 10 9 8 7 6 5 4 3 2 1

For Keita, Luke and Oona

*Thanks to Ellen Lesser
for her clarity and guidance*

Catamount Bridge

One

Catamount, Vermont: September 1967

In moonlight, Leon Woodard limps to his barn. No matter that it's three in the morning; the path he's walked ten times a day for sixty years yields no surprises. He blows into his cupped hands, lifts his shoulders up to frosty air. A sinewy shadow bobs along behind him, down the sloped front lawn, across the lane, merging into darker shadows where the barn roof hides the moon. Leon knows precisely when to stop and reach out for the thumb latch, how to duck in through the tight, low-posted doorway his ancestors found adequate.

Once inside, he shuts the door—from habit, not necessity. His cows are out to pasture, behind barbed wire. At dawn they'll gather at the other door, the cow-sized, barnyard door, waiting to be led inside, collared into stanchions, swabbed and milked. Until then, they'll sleep, some standing, phantom meadow statuary.

Three dark steps in front of him Leon knows he'll find a hay bale wedged against the ladder to the loft above. He nudges it with his foot, reaches down to assess its position, then sits against the ladder rungs and waits. Silhouettes, still black on black, evolve around him; dim grids of light leak through a row of four-paned windows. A grove of posts emerges—eight, ten feet apart in all directions. They stand

1

like forest oaks pressed up against a sagging sky, against the tons of hay above.

Two rows of stanchions, face to face, divide the oblong room. Once, the rows were full. Now, Leon uses half of one side; cobwebs fill the rest.

In the far corner, hidden in darkness, veal calves sleep on sawdust bedding in a wooden pen. Their breathing drifts in puffs across the room, audible smoke shot through with sounds of water dripping in a trough, ripple-ringed across a black-glass surface.

From the open hatch above him, a spill of night air drafts down on Leon's shoulders—old air, filtered through a hundred summers' grasses, scented with the musk of long-forgotten fern and timothy. He closes his eyes. The barn begins to float slowly around him. Rafters, purlins, plates and sills become elastic, weightless, jointless. Shingles melt, walls disappear, the floor dissolves to starry heavens. Leon lets it go; he knows it will return. For now, he listens to the grainy rhythms of his heartbeat, to the sound of time unfolding, rushing and unerring. He hears faint wisps of conversations, morning birdsong, elders rocking on a porch. Picking through a web of thoughts he finds, in time, an image of his wife. The young blond woman's features blur, then sharpen into focus as he reconciles her face with more than forty years of memories.

He shades his eyes and clamps his mouth shut, leans back hard against the ladder. The place and hour are familiar, but tonight his solitude is comfortless. Tonight, the old, secure, enduring smells and sounds of being in the barn are not enough; he needs to speak his troubled thoughts to her as he has never done before. He forms a word that vanishes before it moves his lips. He shakes his head. How foolish. But then he tries again: *Esther?* Nonsense. She's been gone a lifetime. He listens to the silence pressing in on him. He sees her sitting on a wagon filled with bags of grain, rolling past the barn on wood-spoked wheels with iron rims. Her hand brushes her bosom, comes to rest against one hip. He reconsiders: Whether or not she hears him, he will never know. Does it matter? He spits out his frustration, then tries again: *You there?* Each syllable is swallowed by the night. He speaks a sound that is no sound, he hears himself as no one else can, inner voice to inner ear. She smiles at him and turns away, as if to go. He takes a deep breath and begins:

Wait! It's me, your Leon. I know it's early. Moon out straight. Cows still drowsy, waiting daylight. Barn so quiet it seems like death. Could be I'm foolish, thinking you could hear me this way. Nothing lost in trying, Esther. Can't sleep, is what it is. Can't sleep for worrying about what I overheard last night.

Oh, I suppose I should of let them boys know I was so close by. But there it was, all done before I knew it. Now I'm holding questions in my mind that I can't hardly 'cipher. Esther? Hear me. Help me meditate my thinking. You was always clever when it come to helping family. You're up there, ain't you? Through it all? Riding with the angel Gabriel, gazing down on Cat'mount Gore, here—watching us poor foolish devils tending cows and making do with this old rocky hill farm, bony soil leached to hell and gone.

My time's coming. I'll be with you, by and by. Years keep gaining. Ain't complaining. Never did. You know that, don't you? I'm watching more than doing, lately, watching Purdy's boys grow up and turn to men. So quick it happens! You'd be proud, I know you would. I see it twice, two generations. They ain't boys no more, by gorry. Men, I'd call them, men enough for this world.

Esther, hear me. I've took good care of them two, right alongside their mother—seen to their manners and their schooling. Run them to the doctor, kept them dressed in decent clothes. We done all right, Vera and me. I know I should of come to you before, but it always seemed like we was getting by. Till now, there was always answers.

3

Leon suddenly stops and opens his eyes. Is someone there? He adjusts to night-black shapes as pieces of his conversation echo through his mind. Silence. The barn is as it always has been; it comes back in around him.

He closes his eyes and returns to a darkness now animated against his wishes. He winces at the memory of the brilliant orange October day when Esther was buried. He remembers staring at the rude, uncaring dirt beside her grave and thinking how cruel, how senseless, how indecent Esther couldn't witness such a day, let alone the forty coming years that were her due. After the service, he took his infant Purdy home and hired in a neighbor's girl to care for him. With the baby settled in the house, he remembers splitting firewood until long after dark, swinging a twelve-pound maul in cold, mechanical strokes. Beech, rock maple, oak, black locust—even twisted elm was no match for him. Early the next morning and all through the day, his ears were filled with the sound of his chopping, stacking, splitting noises, anything to keep away the sound of Esther's name. At sunset's chill, a pyramid of clean-split stove wood reached up into the woodshed rafters. Then he sent the sitter home and began his long life as a father.

His images of Purdy and Esther are locked in time, unavailable for even the smallest alterations. When he lost them both were younger than his grandsons are today. Each year, he ages; they stay the same. His grandsons and Purdy's widow, Vera, have an ongoing chronology. Vera lives, as Leon lives, without a mate.

She raised 'em with her husband gone to war and dead and me a-huddling 'round the three of them. Too old to play and act rambunctious, I'd take them river fishing, hunt and trap the brooks for mink and muskrat. Taught them all I know about the woods. Taught them how to carpenter and tend machinery, how to fix most anything, you tinker on it long enough. And her, I always wished

4

*she'd take another man, a father to them little boys. Not that I
mean a disrespect to Purdy. Jeesum! He was the best they come, the
best there ever was!*

*Esther, they growed up as good as anyone could ask for. It's plain
they fight like hellcats. Still, they don't mean any harm. It's in the
blood, right through the bone. Twin brothers just as close in looks,
but in their natures just as different . . .*

The barn sleeps on. Memories of boys on horseback
canter across the meadows of the old man's brain. He rubs
his eyes and drops his chin against his bony chest. The hay
bale moves beneath him with a gentle, rocking motion.
Soon it becomes a rowboat and he is fishing the river below
Catamount Village with his barefooted grandsons in the
summer of their fifth year. Harmon hangs a line off the
stern. Bodie lies daydreaming across the bow, trailing shiny
ripples with his fingers. He sees a curved reflection in the
water and looks up.

"Grampy, look! The bridge looks like a rainbow!" he
shouts, pointing up the river.

"Don't go scare the fishes, now."

"It's a bridge, that's all," Harmon whispers. Then,
loudly, "Grampy, I got one!" He jerks his dime-store rod
and reel and pulls a perch into the boat.

"Another one for Harmon," Leon says. "Big one, too,
for such a little tyke."

Bodie watches Leon add the catch to those that lie wide-
eyed and squirming on the rowboat floor. Bodie asks, "Do
fishes drown in air, Grampy?"

"Seems though they might."

Bodie stares up the river. "How come the cars don't fall
off the top of the rainbow bridge? How come they don't go
splashing down into the water?"

"Cause they don't go riding where they oughtn't," Leon
says, watching the cork a-bob on Harmon's line behind the

5

boat. "They ride on the level part that's hung down off'n the arcs . . . Now shush! We got fish to catch."

Leon studies the bridge; a car glides silently across. A tractor pulling a hay rake chugs toward Catamount and disappears behind the maples growing thick along the riverbank.

"Then, Grampy, what's the arcs for, Grampy?" Bodie whispers, still looking at the structure they would soon glide under.

Leon stops his rowing and looks over his shoulder at the thing he still cannot make right. He misses the old wooden bridge, a covered bridge, built long before he was born. The flood of '38 washed it away. Why, he wonders, couldn't it have been rebuilt as it had been before?

A sign at each end of the old bridge warned of a six-ton limit. Although some drivers knew their loads of logs or grain weighed far beyond the posted warning, they crossed it anyway and felt a sense of triumph as the timbers creaked and held. It was understood the bridge would now and then give extra duty.

It had taken years for some to accept that no load was prohibited, no truck was too heavy for the hundred yards from shore to shore held up by the huge new arches. And in this knowledge Leon knew that something good was lost: those two new black-topped lanes, unshakable, string-straight, level and true, eliminated forever the thrill of having crossed the river, the sense of real achievement in arriving safely on the opposite shore.

The new bridge, bossed by out-of-state college boys with their fancy arithmetic, built of structural steel made God-knows-where and trucked to Catamount, ton by ton, for dollars beyond the imagination, dollars that came from strangers' pocketbooks—the new bridge struck Leon wrong from start to finish.

6

There were plenty of men in town, he thought, who could have rebuilt the old bridge: French John, Taylor Gandy, the Martineau brothers (four of them), the McAllisters, Tatro, Jeanrette, Trombley, even Weymouth's bunch. They could have chopped the lumber from the hills within a shuffle of the river—they'd yard it up and skid it down in winter on the ice. Then they'd take and saw it through and through at Lyman Perry's mill and stick it up to dry through spring and summer heat. They'd wait for the drought of August for their caissons and their cribbings. Team the granite blocking down from Barre for the piers. Set their jigs, scribe off their marks and mortice in the trusses. They'd hammer green oak treenails into offset holes; the oak would cure and lock the tenons tight forever, draw it in like iron. If they kept right to it, bulled it through from dawn to dark, they'd have the roadbed bolted tight in time to get their venison. Then finish up the shingling in the spring. And if, by and by, the bridge should sag a little, why, mister, they'd put the oak and threaded rod and gusset plates right to it. It would be built as good as it ever was—by men from Catamount.

"Grampy?" Bodie whispers. "What's the arcs for?"

Leon tends to his oars. "Birds," he says, pulling a heavy stroke. "The birdies take and use it for a place to make their homes. Field pigeons mostly." He pulls another stroke. "Sometimes you'll see a crow, but mostly it's the pigeons."

Leon and Bodie scan the arch together. Sunlight catches the underside of white wings gliding toward the apex. With a few sharp backward flaps the flashes disappear up underneath the mammoth curve.

"Birds don't drown in air. Right, Grampy?"

"I never heard it told they did." Leon rows in silence, rows away from thoughts of drownings.

"Birds can swim in water, right?"

7

"You aim to catch a fish today?"

"I got six," Harmon says. "You didn't get a one."

"Look, you can see the bridge's belly," Bodie cries. The roadbed's shadow cools their faces.

"Your mother's going to have some fish to fry tonight," Leon says.

Harmon stows away his fishing pole, admiring his catch. Leon winks at him and he returns the gesture.

"Who's going to clean these trophies?" Leon asks.

"Harmon caught 'em, Harmon cleans 'em," Bodie says.

"Then you ain't getting none to eat," Harmon shoots back. "You wouldn't even bait your hook."

"I don't care. I like spaghetti better anyhow."

"Looks like we're all done with worms." Leon empties a plug of sphagnum moss into the river and sets the coffee can between his feet. He spins the boat around and starts to row back to the truck at Stebbin's landing. The bridge hangs huge above them for a moment and then diminishes as the boat moves down the river. The sky is blue and the silence holds until they rouse a muskrat around the bend.

The barn roof creaks under the weight of darkness. A veal calf stirs in the corner pen, lets out a sleepy sigh and rolls against the side rails with a thump. Leon lifts his head and squints into the darkness at the familiar sound. The calf returns to deepest sleep as Leon shuts his eyes and recomposes pictures of his wife.

Esther? Listen: Harmon's got a family coming. That ain't what's distressing me. Well, not him having children, gorry! Children's meant to come to us. Been four years now since Harmon and Darlene was married. Now she's carrying, Darlene is. That's Harmon's wife, Darlene, gran'daughter of your old girl friend Millicent. Darlene's mother was Lucile. A Dulac girl. Darlene's daddy's Frank McAllister. Remember him? Him and Lucile run the feed mill. Throwed their Darlene quite a wedding. Oh, we had a merry time! Rented O'Dell Stinson's band and jeesum, how the younguns danced and carried on. Put the booze right to us, too! Come next morning, I done my chores without no help. Ambition? No-sah! Eyeballs just a crisscrossed. Crimus! How my head was ever going to mend. Yessir, we was something gay. You'd of been proud to see Darlene all prettied in her wedding outfit.

Well, I suppose they never got the recipe, her and Harmon. All their friends around here whelping litters left and right. Betsy Judd—she graduated high school with Darlene and Harmon—she's got three already. One more on the way, they tell. Phoebe Dickerson—Pawlet now, she married Howard Pawlet's boy—she's got two I know of. Could be carrying another from what she looked like other day down to the Superette, but all them Dickerson women run so big you never could tell what was what. Sally Munroe's got her two—they say's she's got female complaints and won't be having more.

Way I see it, all the crowd they run with's been bred up for quite some time. Ain't my business, understand, I ain't said nothing, and just as well. Frank and Lucile's been right after her and Harmon—yammering on about grandchildren. Couldn't help theirselves, I suppose, but crimus! What a mis'able way to be! Them kids could of holt back pure in spite. I'd be inclined if it was me! Anyways, she's hatching one. Found out last night, like I told, but then I found out more, and that's the vexing part.

Last week—Wednesday, if I ain't mistaken—papers come for Bodie and Harmon. Papers from the army, there, all official telling how they'd been "selected." Both of them, called up to fight. Harmon's going. Bodie ain't. Bodie says he'll slip up into Canada, cross-lots, need be. He'll take and move to foreign country before he'll shoot another man. Knowing Bodie, I don't doubt it. How you'd like him, Esther! He's got gumptions you'd admire, stubborn as a mule once he's commenced to set his mind a certain way. Him and Harmon been disputing this Viet Nam since it first come on the television. Never did agree on nothing, ever, period. Slander

9

each other up and down and won't neither of them give a fraction. Keep my nose out of it, Esther, ain't my time for such a thing. When I served Uncle I was green enough I didn't know from nothing except when sergeant said to do, I did. Seen too many lay there dead to think but war's an awful thing. Purdy give his life, all drowned in ocean water, trapped inside a battleship. Now Harmon wants to even up the ledger, so he says. Bodie tells him two dead don't make nothing better. Esther, I should judge he's right. Still, how they argue, round and round, but that's not what's tormenting me. It's Darlene's baby's what it is, and who's the baby's father.

Esther, last night, after supper, I done my milking, cleaned my gutters, washed my pails—dawdling like I do come autumn, barn doors open, sun going down. Thought I'd go up in the haymow, throw down two-three bales for my veal calves—six of them, Esther, little critters gaining good.

Just barely I was up the ladder, in come Harmon, down below, with Bodie right behind him. What they come for, I don't know. Could of been for baling twine or burlap sacks or who knows what, but they was at each other like honey bees on a bear. Come to find out I was in for more than I was meant to hear. First, Harmon commences with: "Taking care of Darlene ain't your business, understand?" Harmon's angry, too, sarcastic in his voice. Then he says—forgive me, Esther, this is how he went—he says, "You did your business to her on the bridge that night, and now, for sure, she's got a baby coming." He's riled up good. I like to died right there, Esther, hearing that, not ten feet off from where I stood. Couldn't believe it, shook my head like I was crazy. Bodie barks right back at Harmon, tore into him hammer and tongs. Bodie says there weren't no way he'd fool with Darlene. Never would! Didn't care what Harmon thought! Swore he wouldn't use her that way, and besides, he had his own Loretta. She'd be going with him up to Quebec, need be, anyways.

Then Harmon says, "I'll live with this one, Bodie." "This one" being the baby, if I took the meaning right. "But if I get back from overseas and there's another one crawling around the dooryard, I'll cut your heart out, understand?"

"Cut your heart out!" Jeesum, Esther, he was talking to his brother! Then Bodie told him he'd better make double-sure he come back in one piece, not to leave Darlene and the baby all alone like their mother was. Told him he was foolish for going. That got Harmon raving all over again about Bodie being chicken-livered. Oh, how they carried on—across the barnyard, over to the house still feuding, me gone woozy with the heft of what I heard.

Esther, heed me. These twin boys and Vera's all I got. And Darlene. Darlene's clever, sure enough, good company too, and handy around the place, helps Vera doing housework, cooking, keeping the garden, canning, whatnot. She's all you'd want, I know she is. Treats me good, puts liniment on my shoulder joints, rubs them nice like you did, Esther. Darlene's passing on the Woodard seed. That line goes back, way back. It's all wrote down inside the Bible in the kitchen cupboard. Your name, too, remember that? Old Amos Woodard, first one here, he cleared this christly land when he come back from fighting with the English down in Massachusetts. They claim he knowed General Washington. I don't know. Thing of it is, Darlene's passing on the line. Her baby's meant to keep the family going. If it's a boy, the Woodard name goes up another generation. That can't be wrong. It's only natural.

Leon shifts his weight and cups his head between his palms. The down draft from the loft above refreshes him and cools away the perspiration gathered down his spine. The spinning thread of history pulls taut, then slackens: George Washington and Amos Woodard to Harmon, and now, Harmon's baby—all jumbled together, all stretched apart by knots of memories and voids of unrecorded time. There was a day when Leon and his brother Weymouth climbed the ladder to the loft together, did their chores and

11

played their games in every corner of the barn. But that was all so long ago it could be part of the reverie that brings him back again to Esther.

Esther, what I'm getting at, what's festering in my head is this: Look here, ain't the seed the same? Ain't that what the scientists say? Them boys was born both brothers, twins, and Purdy was their father just like I was father to him, and Bodeman was father to me. All the way back to Amos. Woodards, all of us. Harmon and Bodie was born same batch, same hour. Twins. Identical. Same blood flowing through their veins. So don't it come to reason? Why's it matter which one done the fathering? Ain't seed the same as blood?

Maybe I'm a christly fool for trying to make it come out right. I know, I'm going against common decency. But, Esther, until I make it right, I know I'll never spin a thread, I'll stew and churn until I'm wore out. Harmon off to the military—who knows, maybe gone for good just like his daddy, soldiering overseas, his baby born while he's away. Must hurt a man, not knowing whether he can claim his wife's offspring and then suspect his brother all the while—or worse yet, someone else.

Esther, how I dread this daybreak. Clock keeps ticking, stars move over, chores are waiting, work to be done. Kitchen light'll come on soon; Vera and Darlene putting up dinner pails for the boys. Start their pickup trucks and gone. Be back late this afternoon to help me with the heavy work.

Would I be a fool—would I be meddling to ask Bodie? Suppose I tell Bodie how I come to overhear him and Harmon. Suppose I ask him what went on? Can't be no harm in it. Weren't my fault I overheard. I'll ask him while we're working. Work makes talk come easier. Heavier the work the better.

What I got to do is talk to Bodie. This afternoon when he gets home. It's what you'd do, I know it is.

TWO

Jiggsie Munroe hits a stump and stops. He is clearing land with a Caterpillar D-7 bulldozer, land that will soon be a lawn around a house under construction. The owners live in Massachusetts, a lawyer and his wife—no children. They plan to come here weekends and summers. They are in their early thirties—not much older than Jiggsie—but they seem to have more money than they could have earned themselves. "More dollars," Jiggsie likes to say, "than sense." When they hired him to build their house, they advanced Jiggsie ten thousand dollars for materials, no questions asked. They drive up from Boston on Friday nights in a low-slung, foreign-make automobile. Jiggsie has pulled it out of mud holes half a dozen times. They feed their purebred dog cooked beef liver; it barks at mosquitoes and will not go near the woods around the house.

Jiggsie backs up and drops the corner of the blade under a protruding root. He moves the D-7 forward, lifting the blade at the same time. The stump resists and he tries another angle. His cleated tracks churn into the mulchy loam, pushing against the remnants of the tough old pine. Finally, as the last roots give way, Jiggsie overturns the stump and pushes it off to a gully where it tumbles down the bank and stops in a dry brook bed. He puts his machine in reverse and back-drags his way to where the stump was, smoothing out his ruts as he goes. He looks around; he's almost done—a few more stumps and rocks to move. But they will wait until after dinner. It's noon. He shuts the diesel down.

With the machine noise gone, the beauty of the day rushes in. The sky is flawless. Birds resume their calling. Hardwood trees around the clearing show splashes of red and yellow, hints of cooler days to come. Jiggsie adjusts to the quiet, his ears still tingling from the noise. He crosses the spongy fresh dirt to his truck, picks up a brown paper bag from the seat and walks to the house. Inside, a power saw whines through a cut, followed by a *thunk* as the scrap end hits the plywood floor. He hears a voice say something he can't make out, another whine, another *thunk*.

They'd work all day, he thinks to himself. He wonders who he will find to replace Harmon when Harmon leaves for the army. And Bodie, crazy bastard, Bodie thinks the army will ignore him, thinks he'll hide out up across the border. If both the Woodards leave, Jiggsie wonders if he'll stay in the carpentering trades at all. Maybe he'll look for more work with his log truck and his bulldozer. He knows if he gets drafted they'll never accept him; they don't make uniforms for bodies weighing well over three hundred pounds.

"Time to eat, you scrawny rats," Jiggsie says, coming into the room where Bodie and Harmon are working. They untie their nail aprons and brush sawdust from their sleeves.

"Always count on you for knowing when to tie the feed bag on," Harmon jokes. "What'd you bring today, a buffalo?"

"Nothing special. Just a party snack," Jiggsie says, grinning into his huge paper bag. He pulls out, first, a half-gallon carton of chocolate milk; next, a foot-long Italian submarine sandwich followed by a second, and then three pairs of Hostess Twinkies in cellophane wrappers.

"Going to starve," Bodie says. "No wonder you're so thin."

Jiggsie laughs. He's heard it all. Since early childhood, he has always been the Biggest, but he sees his size as an accessory, a thing apart from him rather than *him*. When he looks into a mirror, he sees a smile he wishes he could—on call—replace with something tougher, but he knows he never will and that makes him smile all the more.

The men sit on the floor, each with his back against one of three walls. The fourth wall holds a fireplace. This room will be the lawyer's living room. His wife wants barn boards on the wall around the fireplace. The boards will come from part of one of the Woodards' old weatherbeaten outbuildings. They will cost the lawyer enough so that the entire building can be resided in tight, new, kiln-dried pine.

Bodie opens his lunch box between his legs and folds the wax paper away from a bologna sandwich. He puts a corner of the sandwich in his mouth, looking at the ceiling. Harmon pours coffee from his thermos, blows across the cup to cool it. Jiggsie holds his submarine with both hands, staring at it as he chews.

"Looks like Darlene's going to be a mama," Harmon says to the window.

"No shit? When'd you find out?" Jiggsie asks.

"Doctor told her Monday night. She went in, feeling sick or something—Doc said she was three months gone."

". . . October–November, December–January, February–*March*," says Jiggsie. "When's the army want your body?"

"Physical's next month. Then, if I'm 1-A . . ."

"Your dink's too big, they'll never take you," Jiggsie says.

"It's true. It ain't my fault."

"Then, shit," Jiggsie pauses. "You could be in 'Nam when Darlene has the baby."

"Shooting up civilians," Bodie says.

"Fuck off."

"You see that sergeant ordered all those peasants shot on TV? Laid them in a ditch?" Bodie asks, scowling at Harmon.

"It happens."

"Christ," Bodie says, flicking a sandwich crust into his open lunch box. "How can you say that? 'It happens?'"

"Happens all the time. And should. You give them gooks a chance, and, pow, they shoot you in the back. Not that you got to worry. You ain't going."

"Somebody's got to keep the women happy," Jiggsie cackles, opening a Twinkie. He glances up in time to see the dark flood spreading up the back of Harmon's neck.

"Bullshit," Bodie says, ignoring Jiggsie. "Those people have a right to do their country how they want."

"You want the world to go Communist?" Harmon says. "See how you'd like living under a dictator, eating fish heads, no paycheck, no truck, no TV. I guess you'd sing a different tune."

"What's that got to do with 'Nam, for Chrissake?"

"You stop them over there—or they'll be over here," Harmon says. "Don't you know nothing?"

"I know your going over there is a fucking waste of time. It won't accomplish nothing. Except maybe get your head shot off."

"You think Dad wasted his time?"

"That was different, and you know it."

"You love your country, you fight for it."

"Viet Nam's not your country. Can't you get that through your—"

16

"Tell Darlene to call up Betsy," Jiggsie interrupts. Political discussions frustrate him, the issues seem so complicated and far removed from Catamount. "Betsy's going through it for the fourth time in November. Could be on Thanksgiving. Dwayne was born the day before Easter. Tammy was supposed to be the Fourth of July but she come two weeks late. Twelve pounds, fourteen ounces. Wilbur Jr. come through one ounce less. Born nineteenth of February. Colder'n a sonofabitch that winter."

Bodie shuts his lunch box as if to close inside the differences he and Harmon will never reconcile. He turns toward Jiggsie and concentrates, dismissing Harmon's presence with the comfort of Jiggsie's agreeable volume. Jiggsie's size suggests a world where there is always enough; he is amplitude itself. And soon, he will be a father again. A miraculous species will be reproduced. Bodie imagines the depth of the creases in the baby's legs, the smothering, mothering hugeness of Betsy, the bed frame deformed beneath Jiggsie and Betsy sleeping, making love.

For all his size, Jiggsie has always had a delicacy of motion seldom seen in men half his size. Bodie had first seen it on the river, the summer they were fourteen and fifteen, before the first of them began to drive legally and fall in love forever. They swam off the banks below the Catamount bridge, all boys—no girls yet dared to break into the boisterous circle. A rope hung from an oak branch spread out above the water. The bank was worn to bare mud now, made slippery from dripping bodies. They'd swing out over the water and stop, suspended in that moment also known to acrobats, then plummet—splash—and swim to shore and scramble back up the bank to wait another turn, to push and shove and banter in the shaded grove, squinting out beneath the trees into the white light vibrating off the river.

As each boy swung, the branch dipped down, then snapped back up like a leafy wing in frightened flight. Winston Gandy, Robbie Tatro, Jean-Jean (French John's crippled boy), Donnie Taylor, Harmon, Bodie and Jiggsie (whose given name was Wilbur Jiggs)—half the boys from Catamount and Pike's ninth grade were there, naked, prancing, dancing colts, squirming with random energy. Some would dive head first at rope's end, some would do a flip or backward gainer, some would tuck and cannonball or belly flop or deadman. For hours the procession continued: up the slope, swing out across the water, splash, swim back and scramble up the slope again.

Jiggsie pulled the branch down so far that patches of sun would appear on unaccustomed spots along the riverbank. The branch would snap back up violently when he let go the rope. Whiplashed leaves floated down to the water in his wake. His style was strictly cannonball, although any other form he chose would give the same appearance. Bodie will never forget standing in line behind Jiggsie, watching him drop into the pendulum and bend his dimpled knees to clear the water's surface, watching him hurtle up the arc's far side, then slow as he came to terms with gravity. At that final moment of equilibrium, twelve feet off the water, going neither up nor down but held in perfect spatial stasis, Jiggsie's pinky fingers pointed straight up, heavenward in pure delight.

Jiggsie works his way into his second sandwich and listens to a room made live with chewing sounds and rumpled wrappers. The three men sit and eat and stare. They stare at their shoelaces, the floor, the puttied nail holes in the chair rail. The quiet is not discomforting; they know each other well enough.

"You got names picked out, now that you're going to be

a daddy?" Jiggsie says. He watches Harmon flick a look at Bodie, then turn to him.

"Thought we'd name him after Dad—if it's a boy. Darlene wants to call a girl Dawn Marie. Something like that."

"Leon must be happy. Christ, it must of tickled the old geezer to know he's going to be a great-granddaddy."

"Haven't told him yet."

"Tell Vera?"

"No, not really." Harmon looks out the window. "Maybe Darlene did today."

"She'll like the idea," Bodie says. "Loves the babies."

"Be nice for her," says Jiggsie. "Especially while Harmon's away." He pauses, thinking of the future. "Can you keep working until you go? You know, more or less full time?"

"I hoped to. Like to put away as much as I can for Darlene."

"Maybe we can finish up here for Simon," Jiggsie says. "Before you get done, I mean."

"Simon's never going to let you go," Harmon says. "He's got all kinds of little goodies for you to do. It's going to be a home away from home around here, you wait. You guys will still be here when I get back."

When Harmon and Bodie were thirteen, they built a small log cabin on a knoll above the barn. They would work on it every afternoon of their two-week Christmas vacation. The sun, that winter, seemed forever hidden behind the grainy clouds; the sky seemed made of purple slate. At the end of the first day's work, they stood inside the waist-high walls as if inside a magic circle, excited by the promise of enclosure. Twilight made it seem that, even then, a warmth was gathered there. Imagination filled the space with tables, bunk beds, chairs and over there—through isinglass windows—a flickering fire in an old box stove. It would be done, it would be built; neither had the slightest doubt.

"This is going to be my cabin," Harmon said. "You can use it, OK? But ask me first."

Jiggsie swallows the last of his lunch and says to Harmon, "Just make sure you do come back. I can't pick on only Bodie all the time."

"You'll have to find him first. Living in an igloo, probably."

"Get off it," Bodie snaps.

Jiggsie wads his paper bag into a tight ball and throws it with perfect aim into the fireplace. He rolls to one side and stands up.

"My goddamn leg's asleep," he says, and limps out of the room. "I'm going to finish up the grading." He walks out into the smell of fresh dirt.

The brothers sit in itchy silence. Bodie pushes sawdust around on the floor beside him, making a little pyramid as Harmon lights another cigarette, staring at the smoke. Outside, they hear the bulldozer start. The grousers slap against the tracks, *clack-clack,* as Jiggsie rumbles the machine across the gound.

"And here all the time, I thought that maybe it was her, maybe there was something wrong with her—she couldn't have one," Harmon says, exhaling smoke.

"Why blame her? You've got no—"

"You saying it was me? There's nothing wrong with me, mister! Ask her. Ask Loretta! She'll tell you. Nothing wrong with this old buck, by Jesus."

"I did ask her."

"Loretta?"

"Yeah. She said it was all smoke and no fire, said—"

"It was in the back of Tinker's frigging Corvair! We were.

20

both knee-walking drunk. Couldn't hardly move. Tinker's christly dog was in the front seat, wanted out. Barked his fool head off."

"So she said."

"So?" Harmon flicks his ashes on the floor.

"So, if it wasn't something wrong with Darlene, it could have been something wrong with you. Takes two to tango."

"If you wanna dance. Darlene and me just don't get together all that much."

"Then why blame her?"

Harmon pauses, inhales deeply. "I'm not blaming her. I only said I used to think it was her. I mean, I thought we got together enough, and if it didn't work, if she didn't get pregnant—it was because of her, that's all."

"You don't have to think it's her anymore, then, do you? She's going to have the baby. That should keep her mother and her girl friends quiet."

The Valley Region slo-pitch league plays once a week in the summer months, from five o'clock until dark. The games are held at the Pike fairgrounds.

It was the night of the summer solstice. Harmon pitched and Bodie played left field for the Catamount Superettes. Jiggsie, Betsy, Darlene and Loretta sat in the bleachers cheering loudly and drinking Genesee ale. The Superettes sat out the last game and watched a 3–3 tie between Quinntown Texaco and the Jordan Giants. After the game, according to custom, the Superettes walked back to the store in Catamount (where they had parked) and gave their uniforms to Randy Jeanrette, who would wash them in the Superette's laundromat before the next game.

By the end of the Texaco-Giants game, Harmon and Bodie were each into a second six-pack. Jiggsie, Darlene and Betsy were perspiring through three games' worth.

21

Loretta drank Fanta orange; she insisted she hated the taste of anything alcoholic. Their group was the last to leave the fairgrounds. Jiggsie was hiccuping uncontrollably, laughing after each eruption as they walked through Pike and turned to cross the bridge. The lamp-lit arches rose like giant arms up into the gathering darkness. Bodie stopped at the base of the left-hand arch and rattled the handle on the access door. The latch broke loose and the door swung open, exposing the hollow core of a huge steel girder. The space inside was four feet wide and high enough to stand in. It rose like a long, dark, airborne tunnel curving up and across and then down to the other side of the river. Foot-square portals in the bottom plates let light—and birds—inside. The sides and top were solid steel.

For years, Bodie and Harmon and Jiggsie had played inside the arches almost every day as they walked home from their classes. On rainy days they would cross the bridge inside the arches; they called their climb "the Cat-walk." When Harmon started smoking Camels in ninth grade, the top of the arch was witness to his first forbidden puffs. Some time later that year, he and Bodie built a planked platform at the top where they stashed their *Playboy* magazines, Budweisers and prophylactics.

As they progressed through high school, the Cat-walk was increasingly forgotten by Harmon and Jiggsie. They had their cars, their girls and jobs. The bridge was kids' stuff now. What if someone saw you coming out?

Bodie never mentioned it, but his visits to the arch continued—always at night. He'd park his truck at the freight depot and enter on the Catamount end. Straddling the port-holes, he'd feel his way up inside, all the way to the top, where he would lie on the platform and listen to the wind and the whooshing noise the cars made as they drove across, sixty feet below. The birds he had frightened upon his arrival would soon return, fluttering through the portals to their perches, cooing comfort in the dappled darkness. The night of the ball game was the first time in years he had approached the arches in the company of others.

When the door swung open, Bodie stepped back and grabbed Loretta's hand. "Come on, you've never been up in there. Come on, 'Retta, you'll like it."

"No way, Bodie Woodard!" Loretta shrieked, half flirting and fully terrified.

"Can't you wait till you get her home?" Betsy said, giggling.

"Come on, Low-Ret-ah." Bodie knelt in front of her like he had once seen a prince kneel down in a high school play. "On bended knee?"

"It gives me the creeps. I'm scared of heights."

"You won't be, up there with me. Come on, please?"

Loretta moved away, slightly out of balance, holding onto Harmon, almost as if she were hiding behind him, as if he would protect her.

"I'll go," Darlene said.

Jiggsie was still hiccuping. Harmon was teasing Loretta. Betsy was looking over the railing at the water. No one heard Darlene except Bodie.

"I'll go," she said, louder, clearing her throat. "I've always wondered what it would be like." She was looking straight into Bodie's eyes, as if Harmon weren't there. Bodie, flushed with Genesee, returned her gaze.

"Go ahead, Darl," said Harmon. His words were slurred. His head moved side to side in search of focus. "Now's your chance to find out." He laughed in nervous bursts. "He's my brother, ain't he?" he said to no one in particular. Another tone, more challenging, almost hostile. "Go on. Do it! Now's your chance." He clumsily pushed Darlene toward the access door. Bodie put his arm around her waist and looked over his shoulder at Loretta, who refused his glance. A car went by with its horn honking, members of the Quinntown team, weaving home across the bridge. Bodie followed Darlene through the door and closed it tight behind them.

The sound of Jiggsie's diesel engine fills the room as Bodie and Harmon sit in awkward silence, waiting for what must be said.

"She liked it, didn't she? I bet she liked it, right?"

"Get off it."

Harmon shifts himself on the floor, pulls his knees up to his chest and locks his arms around them. "You won't tell me anything. She won't tell me shit. You both act like it never happened."

"Maybe it didn't."

"She ain't exactly known to fool around. She's straitlaced as they come."

"So why don't you ask her what went on?" Bodie twists a sliver of wood into a piece of rope. He knows he doesn't have to say what happened. He twists and twists until the fibers break.

"She won't talk about it."

"Women act that way," Bodie says.

"Ordinarily, they tell the truth. Least these ones do, the ones we go with."

"Then ask her, flat out."

"I told you, she's not talking about it. She just smiles, and—and says I give her my permission. I ask her what went on. She says nothing more or less than what I hoped for. I ask her what *that* means, and she says, 'Well, what did you hope for?' "

"She's not dumb, that's for sure."

"Drives me crazy."

"Nothing new."

"I still say she loved every minute of it."

"I still say you're full of shit on the subject."

"How do you think you would of felt if it was you?"

Bodie shrugs, looks at Harmon. "You think I liked the story of you and Loretta in Tinker's Corvair?"

Harmon laughs. "Big deal! She weren't your wife."

"I never put her up to it, either. You asked me how I'd feel? Not good. But I was glad she told me. She was sorry, said she felt like a fool the next day. I can forgive her for that."

"Darlene never told me she was sorry."

"You ever tell her you were sorry?"

"For what? I was pacing around on the roadbed for half an hour while you . . . Sorry for what?"

"For treating her like she was some kind of heifer, waiting to get bred."

"You think that's what I did?"

"Ask her, you don't believe me. While you're at it, ask her how she likes you going off to Viet Nam, you asshole."

Harmon jumps up and crosses the room to Bodie, fists clenched. He stands glaring down at his brother. Words begin to form but disappear as they reach his lips. His body shakes. He punches the wall above Bodie's head, then strides out of the room, holding his bleeding hand.

Bodie slowly gets to his feet and lifts his nail apron from a sawhorse. He ties it around his waist and looks through the living room window. Jiggsie has stopped his Caterpillar and is watching dust clouds billow behind Harmon's pickup as it bounces out the driveway. Bodie sees Jiggsie turn and look back at the unfinished house and knows Jiggsie can't see him through the sun-raked glass, picking pieces of broken plasterboard out of his hair.

The afternoon goes quickly, full of the measuring and fitting that the building of a staircase requires. Following a pattern Leon taught him, Bodie routs a groove for treads and risers into the skirtboards. Underneath, he glues wedges between the stringers and the treads, tapping them tight so that the stairs will never squeak. The lawyer, Simon, is getting more than he will know to appreciate.

Bending over his sawhorses, scribing a perfect line with a needle-sharp pencil, Bodie imagines himself a kind of surgeon. The cut will be precise and clean, the depth and length and width exact. He holds the router like a box of jewels, guiding it with steady hands. The clear pine skirtboard has a tight uniform grain—like smoothly muscled flesh. The router leaves splintery whiskers at the edge of the cut. He trims them with a piece of fine-grit sandpaper and thinks about his brother getting shot to hell. For a moment, the pieces of wood become body parts, perfect in how they fit together. He imagines reconnecting Harmon's leg into its hip socket, tapping in a wedge to make it tight. Nails and glue turn into stitches, the body-boards flop over on the table—here, another incision—there, another limb rejoined. Harmon is in a hundred pieces, waiting to be reconstructed.

By Christmas day, the cabin walls were up above the young boys' heads. They searched along the forest edge for trees suitable for rafters. Bodie soon found a copse of string-straight poplars and began to chop. The first one he cut landed on the stone wall separating the pasture from the woods. As he cut the tree in half, he nicked Leon's ax on a stone. A dull spark fell into the snow.

"Grampy's going to kill you," Harmon said. "Let me chop a while. You lug the others over."

"Wait. I'm almost done." Bodie took another swing and passed the ax head through the remains of the cut. The log parted into two ten-foot lengths and the ax stopped on a rock again, chipping the blade a second time.

"Gonna' kill you double, Dubba. You lug while I cut!"

Bodie dropped the ax, picked up one end of a log and dragged it downhill to the cabin on the knoll. Harmon moved upslope a few paces, limbed a low branch from another poplar and swung at the six-inch girth. After a half-dozen V-cuts to the downhill side and three or four above, a breeze came through and started the tree on its inevitable radius toward the ground. Branch tops swept an arc across the horizon, crashed hard, bounced once and rested, broken in snow.

Bodie ducked and yelled as the leafless tips raked his back and legs.

"Crimus, Harmon! Give a guy some warning!"

Harmon wasn't listening. The tree had back-jumped as it fell; the log butt caught him squarely on the chin and knocked him flat. He lay in the snow on his back, stunned, for a moment, but by the time Bodie reached him he was on his feet pretending it had never happened.

"You OK?"

"Still standing, ain't I?"

At four o'clock, Jiggsie shuts the diesel down and walks into Simon's house. He finds Bodie sitting halfway up the stairs.

"Working hard, or hardly working?"

"Hardly working. Picking crack."

"Tending Tobey's touch-hole, are ya? Time to go home, Goldilocks."

"I suppose."

"Your ugly brother going to show for work tomorrow?"

"Probably. He'll cool off. He's something, huh?"

"Quite a Harmon."

"Rig and a half."

"Seems though he's leaving at a bad time—Darlene pregnant and all. Won't they give him a deferment if he's a father?"

"He wouldn't take it," Bodie says. "He thinks everybody ought to go."

"Screw that."

"I just wonder."

"He'll live to piss on both our graves. Slip through the jungle like a bandit. He's rugged."

Yeah, he's rugged, Bodie says to himself. He's rugged and he's got blond hair and blue eyes. He's six feet tall and plays a good game of horseshoes. He lives on a run-down farm in Catamount, Vermont, with his twin brother, his mother, his grandfather and his wife—who is going to have a baby. He owns a five-year-old pickup truck, a secondhand black and white TV, a couple of good hunting rifles and some pieces of furniture he bought on time. He can work all day and goof around all night and be ready to roll at six the next morning. He's rugged, sure. He looks good, it's true, but he's also a sonofabitch.

Jiggsie bends over and runs his hand along the stair tread nosing. "Not too shabby for an old wood-butcher. Lawyer man should like that good stuff."

"Lawyers are dingleberries," Bodie says as he stands and stretches. "You'll lock up?"

"Yup."

"See you in the morning."

"Same time, same station. Hurry back."

He'll hurry back, that is certain. Despite the absentee owner, despite the friction with Harmon, despite the draw of beautiful weather that would have him roaming the hills instead, Bodie will return; the wood is waiting for him—Douglas fir, spruce, oak and pine, waiting to be made back into something that will live again.

Inside his truck, he tunes the Motorola to the White

28

River station and listens to Elvis Presley singing "Heartbreak Hotel." He turns toward Catamount and follows the narrow road to a left-hand turn, where he downshifts into low and climbs the steep grade, dark with hemlocks. At the top of the rise he looks across a shallow valley—smooth, green pasture—looks at the farmhouse Amos Woodard built in 1782. He slows to a crawl as he often does at this spot on the road and imagines how, for eight generations, a Woodard has made this same trip home and slowed his course at this same point, scanning the fields and buildings for signs: smoke from a brush pile, livestock loose, moving machinery, laundry billowing on the line—signs of progress, signs of trouble, previews of the news to come.

The tin-roofed farmhouse reflects blue sky, metallic in the slanting sunlight. Although he's half a mile away, Bodie sees the kitchen windows open; white curtains stir in the afternoon breeze. Vera's tiger lilies are orange along the house foundation, still bright and hopeful despite the coming frost. Darlene's Pinto and Harmon's truck are missing from the dooryard. Leon's truck, used little now, will be parked inside the woodshed ell.

Bodie sees Leon on the hill above the barn, walking up along the brook with a shovel over his shoulder. His suspenders mark an X across his back. Bodie watches him stop his climb and turn; he tries to imagine what the old man sees as he squints down the hillside toward the sound of the approaching vehicle.

Three

"Grampy wants you to help him up to the water well," Vera says as Bodie comes into the kitchen. "He just barely left."

"Something wrong with the gravity?" Bodie asks, looking at the faucet dripping into the soapstone sink. A buried lead pipe brings water to the house from a well a hundred yards up the hill.

"I don't believe so. He said he had to tend to the stonework."

"Wall probably caved in."

"Could be. He spoke of it last spring. Frost heaves, I imagine."

"There's no stopping frost. When she wants to move, she moves."

"Harmon coming straight home?"

"I couldn't say. He left the job around noontime. Having a fit." Bodie looks out the kitchen window toward the road.

"It's the nerves," Vera says. "I imagine he's worried about Darlene. He told you she's expecting?"

"Yesterday." Bodie shuts the window, keeping his back to his mother.

Bodie knows that Vera is watching him as she folds her

ironed laundry, watching him and knowing there is something left unsaid. "She going to stay on at the Pepper Pot?" he asks.

"They said they'd let her work right up until she has the baby. She'll do the lunch and dinner shift. What worries me is all the standing up they do. She ought to have her feet up."

"They sit around between the busy times. I've been in there when three, four of 'em was playing cribbage in the back booth. Having a hell of a good time."

"She's strong," Vera says. "Good shoes. I'll get her a pair of good shoes."

Bodie turns without looking at Vera and crosses to the kitchen door. "I'll be helping Grampy."

Walking around the corner of the woodshed, Bodie approaches the gate to the upper pasture. Twenty yards to his left is the barn, built into the hillside. Giant haymow doors open to an inclined ramp. Cow stanchions are below, accessible from the downhill side.

Unlatching the gate, Bodie recalls a day when Harmon held the gate shut against him; he remembers the struggle for the right to pass, and the fist fight that followed—ending in a draw by both accounts. It was wintertime, a cold day after a three-day storm. They had been up above the house all afternoon, sliding down the hill on flattened cardboard cartons. A jump in the middle of the run had left them airborne for what seemed to be forever. He remembers the jolt when the cardboard pads reconnected with the snow below the ramp. That afternoon, as darkness drew across the valley, they took their last run and raced for the gate through the knee-deep snow. Harmon reached it first, unlatched it, hurried through, and put his weight against it as Bodie tried to push it open.

The fight that followed took the same pattern it always

did: a wild flurry of punches from both sides (few of them accurate) delivered in a breathless rush of adrenaline. Boxing turned to grappling: headlocks, bear hugs, scissor grips, forms of combat signaling exhaustion, leading to the end. What Bodie remembers now about that gateside fight was looking in the mirror afterwards and finding red wool fibers from Harmon's mittens stuck between his teeth.

Loretta has been through this gate with Bodie on their way to walk the woods. She would wait until they were beyond sight of the house—as if someone were watching—to hold his hand. Loretta Bushway, Tinker's little sister, thin and skittish, wary of men and their motives—she found in Bodie someone she could trust. Despite herself, she felt a pull she never dared call love. Whatever it was, it held her in their partnership, an almost willing communicant.

Loretta: neither beautiful nor unattractive. The impression she makes is one of endless ambiguity, of purpose unresolved. The traits of personality that shape a face and give it form are still in flux, still undecided. When Bodie imagines her face, he can only summon images of photographs. The quote under Loretta's yearbook picture read, "Still waters run deep." The photo showed a girl who looks as if she harbors information too painful to reveal. She is not certain what it is, but it is there, coloring her smile, shading her glance as if dark memories rode relentlessly across her womanhood.

She lives at home with Tinker and her parents. She works at the Pike elementary school teaching first and second grade, spending every day with children as if to compensate for the children she will never allow herself to have. Two or three nights a week she meets Bodie; they go to a movie over in Barre or, in summer, to the stock car races to cheer for Tinker in his rumpled car. They go out for hamburgers—sometimes to the Pepper Pot, where Darlene brings them extra-large portions and they leave her generous tips. Their intimacies are few. If asked, they would blame it on the lack of opportunity—each living among family, each busy with work and responsibilities. They go on. For four years, since they both turned twenty-one, they have met and talked, walked arm in arm, each giving to the other just enough to make the next encounter plausible.

He will see her tonight. He will go to her house for supper. They will probably watch TV until her parents go to bed; then they will turn the lights off and lie on the sofa together, washed in the gray-green light of the little Zenith console. Their bodies will touch—politely. They will talk about going to Canada. Will she go with him? They will talk about Harmon leaving, about Darlene and how she'll adjust to being alone. They will talk about the lawyer's house, his money and his peculiar brand of intelligence. (It is rumored he has never lost a case in court.) They will talk about her children at school, how some of their parents care for them badly—these things and more—but Darlene's baby won't be mentioned.

Bodie follows Leon's route up the brook to where the hill dips into a dish-shaped sag along the waterway. Sugar maples crown together overhead; the understory has been nibbled clean by grazing cattle seeking shade on August afternoons. In the middle of the clearing is a squat gabled roof; its wood shingles are furry with moss. The roof sits like a hat on a low, rectangular foundation of loose-laid stones. The wall toward the brook has caved inward, into the spring pool it surrounds. Leon is on his knees, reaching down into the pool, retrieving shiny stones. His sleeves are rolled up past his biceps, his shirtfront dark with water. Bodie watches Leon's sinews tauten as the old man pulls against a heavy boulder.

34

"Kind of pitiful, ain't you?" Bodie says, kneeling down beside Leon, rolling up his sleeves.

"Crimus, this one's hitched to China." They both tug at it, arms immersed in the cold water. The rock won't budge. "Need a prize bar. Can't get no purchase on it. Maybe we should leave it where it sets and build around it."

"Suits me dandy. My hands are freezing."

"Just like your mother, always shivering," Leon teases.

"That water's cold!" Bodie shakes his hands like propellers.

"I suppose it is. We'll leave it be." Leon reaches into the water and fishes out another stone. "Harmon home yet?" he asks, looking into the dark pool.

"Not when I left the house." Bodie pictures Harmon down at Hubby's Tavern, drinking Genesee, whacking the side of the pinball machine with his palm. But here, on the hill, away from flashing lights and ringing bells, Leon is up to something: Bodie can feel it seeping upward, coming to a surface. He watches Leon stare into the spring pool, as if to ask for guidance. A silence follows: the wind is still, the trees stand mute against the sky. The old man frowns, then quickly speaks his mind:

"Last night, when you and Harmon come out to the cow barn—I was overhead—drawing hay bales to the trap door . . ."

Bodie waits, stiff as a tree trunk.

Leon pauses, studying the glassy surface. "You and Harmon was some riled up."

"Nothing new."

"Course, it ain't my business. You and him has always had your disagreements, but you always got along somehow. Crimus, I felt wicked bad. Should have told you I was there, but weren't nothing I could do, happened so fast." Leon reaches into the pool to his armpits, grasping at another stone. "See if we can't yarn this out," he says to Bodie, gesturing for help.

With their arms stretched down below the ripples, shoulders touching, their faces only inches from the water's surface, the stone feels like a watermelon, long and smooth and rounded. As they begin to free it from the rubble it shifts toward Leon. Bodie slides his hand across the slimy surface, wrapping his arm over Leon's, touching Leon's hand in passing as he reaches for a better grip. He smells his grandfather's Beech-Nut chew. His cheek brushes the sharp white stubble on Leon's jaw. Grunting and pulling, they work the stone loose from its moorings, feel it slide free in the cold clear water, feel the weight unburdened, pulling against them.

"If you don't mind me asking," Leon says, his face a wavy image in the moving surface, "what did Harmon mean . . . by what he said about you and Darlene?"

Bodie pauses. Suddenly, by some intangible signal, both men pull the stone up out of the water and roll it back from the edge. A huge brown lozenge glistens in the speckled light. They rest on their knees in front of their prize, whisking water from their arms. A chickadee lands on the shingled roof in front of them, then flutters off to a safer perch.

"What did Harmon *mean?*" Bodie asks.

"You ain't got no obligation to tell me nothing. I'll keep my nose right out of it."

"It's OK. You couldn't help you overheard us . . ."

"Mister man, I felt some foolish . . ."

"Forget it, Grampy. It's not your fault." Bodie stands and rolls his sleeves down, buttoning his cuffs. He exhales deeply and says, "Harmon thinks it was me that gave Darlene the baby. That's what he was hollering about last night. They just found out she's got one coming."

At first, Leon says nothing; he fiddles with his fingers,

bends them, straightens them in jerky motions. Bodie looks down at the crooked hands, at the stump where Leon's left index finger should be; the finger was lost to a pulpwood saw thirty years ago. Leon's other fingers, thick and horny, have made his life for him, have chopped and tinkered and mended, planted, reaped and brought into being the web of life around him. It must bother the hell out of Grampy, Bodie thinks, to know some things just can't be fixed.

"Another Woodard," Leon finally says. "Another crop." He shakes his head, and with a sigh—or is it a laugh?—he says, "Old Amos, guess he'd have to accept it."

Loretta watches Bodie from the darkened kitchen, through the window by the back door. He backs his pickup quietly out the driveway and turns up Pike's main street, switching on his headlights as he passes her house. When he's gone from sight, she turns the overhead fluorescents on, goes into the living room and straightens out the pillows on the couch. She picks up a pair of empty glasses and turns the TV off, hoping Bodie is not angry with her—although she can't imagine why he would be. She's certain she's done nothing wrong.

He was quiet tonight, quieter than usual. They watched television, watched Vietnamese peasants fleeing from their villages—villages that had been bombed and burned by Americans. The Vietnamese were wearing only shorts and sandals, people so tiny in comparison to the GIs and American reporters that their courage seemed pointlessly heroic, almost pitiful.

"That's who Harmon wants to shoot," Bodie said. "Thinks if you kill them, one by one, you save them from the Communists—except they're too dead to get real saved."

Loretta rubbed the back of his neck. They watched the

rest of the show, hardly speaking. Her parents had gone upstairs to bed soon after supper. Tinker was out working on his stock car at the Pike garage.

The house is quiet and Loretta wonders if that silence would diminish or increase if she and Bodie ever dared to live together. He has told her he will go to Canada—or even jail—before he will answer the summons to the draft. She wonders about Canada, a place she has never been. Is it so much colder? Does everyone speak the Quebecois she hears in French John's kitchen making cookies for the school bake sale? Would they rent a little house or an apartment in a town like Pike or would they be out in the wilds? She wonders about the howling wind, the notorious summer insects, the wolves. She wonders if she could endure the loneliness, the absence of her job and family. She knows her father would not approve of her living with a man unmarried. Would Canada be far enough away so that she could do whatever she wanted—even though she often wasn't sure just what that was?

Bodie didn't kiss her when he left. They hugged, briefly, at the door, and he brushed her forehead with his lips and murmured something about calling her tomorrow. He was in one of his moods again, she thought, and when he acts that way—quiet and distracted—she has no choice but to wait until he has solved whatever it is that's taken him off so far away. He didn't ask her directly about going with him to Canada, just as he wouldn't ask her anything directly about their future together.

She wonders if he is looking for a reason to abandon her, if resisting the draft is just an excuse to get away from her. It isn't likely, she admits, knowing Bodie's way of acting on his beliefs. She remembers how, in eleventh grade, he wrote a report on the beef industry and became, for a year or more, a vegetarian. He answered to a lot of teasing at school about his vegetable sandwiches, but he was steadfast, even then, in doing what he thought was right.

She leaves the lights on for her brother and goes up the narrow stairs. Her father's snoring resonates like the low notes on a roommate's cello at teachers college. Her mother claims she couldn't sleep without her husband's snoring.

Inside her bedroom, the sounds of the sleeping house are comfortable and familiar. The buzz of the yard light outside her window, bedsprings creaking as her father rolls over in the room next door, the bathtub faucet dripping, the hissing radiators on winter nights—these sounds mean *home*, mean all is well. This is her family, the only place where she can imagine she belongs. This room has been her room from infancy. The photographs and mementos Scotch-taped to her walls make her childhood still retrievable. At twenty-five, she feels suspended between the high school drive-in dates and the life she sees her friends involved in— husbands, babies, in-laws, loans to pay off. They tell her of their happiness and share with her their troubles. It seems like such hard work, with such unpredictable results. Loretta doesn't envy them; she feels apart and undefined. Her time with Bodie is not a romance. She knows that, and she asks herself if that is how she wants it. Or, is she just afraid of what would happen if she caught fire, the way she almost did with Harmon in Tinker's car. Harmon ignited something so thrilling and dangerous that she was shocked and then ashamed to think that she could harbor such awesome forces—she, Loretta Bushway, Dexter and Miriam's little girl.

It wasn't Harmon's looks, exactly. Harmon had the same lanky blond good looks as Bodie, their mother's coloring and features. A newcomer to town might mistake one for the other. The difference showed when they were moving,

39

talking, running. The difference showed in energy. Bodie was a steady breeze, day and night, predictable. Harmon was a gathering storm, a dark impervious thundercloud with lightning at the center.

Loretta saw in Harmon's eyes a daring criminality. There were hints of danger in the way he moved, the muscle flexing in his jaw. Even his walk invited trouble. He held himself as if a devilment was waiting to burst forth, as if a time bomb ticked inside him. He had terrified her with that power. She knew he could consume her, swallow her identity, and so she had turned away and clung to Bodie. It would be Darlene's task to love Harmon for all the reasons Loretta could not.

Bodie turns off Main Street and starts across the bridge. He strains forward over the steering wheel to look up through the top of the windshield, expecting nothing in particular, following the arches silhouetted against the star-flecked sky. It is close to midnight; the towns along the river are asleep. To the west, the Big Dipper drags its handle over Woodard Mountain. Dark water stirs the river's edge.

In the middle of the bridge he turns his headlights out, switches off the ignition, shifts into neutral and lets the pickup roll. When he reaches the Catamount end, he swings the truck to the right onto a gravel-topped driveway and coasts to a stop by a loading dock at the back of the railroad depot.

He leaves his truck and crosses the road. He walks to the base of the downstream arch and opens the access door. After looking up and down the empty street, he ducks inside and shuts the door behind him. Slowly, his eyes adjust to the darkness. Above him, a pigeon, startled by the clanking door, flaps out through a portal.

He starts the long climb to the top—for what, the thousandth time? With outstretched arms, his fingertips barely touching the cool steel plates that form the walls, he uses a continuous row of rounded rivet heads for footholds up the steep incline, straddling the portals as they appear, looking down at the hint of light outlining his boots and pant cuffs.

As the arch levels off at the apex, Bodie finds his wooden platform. He feels along the eight-foot length with his hands, brushing off the dust and pigeon droppings accumulated since his last visit. From a duffel bag hung on the wall above the bunk, he shakes out a thick army blanket and a pillow, and spreads them out over the rough-sawn planks.

He lies on his back and stares up into darkness. The summer sun of his fifteenth year intensifies a thousand times, cuts through plate steel and lifts him gently through a glowing opening, floats him silently to prospects over Catamount Mountain. He sees familiar patterns cut across the rolling landscape, sees a barn, a house, a hayfield, sees himself driving a tractor along the side of a field, a towheaded boy on his grandfather's farm. The boy stops the tractor and aims a rifle, steadies it between the soles of his boots propped up on the tractor's hot metal hood. Thirty yards away, a woodchuck sits, unblinking in the brilliant sun. The boy pulls the trigger and the woodchuck flinches, frozen, dumb in instant death. The boy gets off his tractor and walks over to the woodchuck, confused and unbelieving. With the toe of his boot, he gently tips it over. The animal falls, stuffed like a rag into the mouth of its burrow.

The night continues; constellations rearrange themselves against the valley's ragged rim. Bodie wakes, rolls over on his side and looks down through a portal. He hears a truck turn onto the bridge from the Pike Village end. It sounds like Harmon's Chevrolet; it is definitely a big V-8, rumbling thunder across the water. Bodie stretches off the end of the bunk to get a better view of the roadbed but is too late to see anything but the receding glow of taillights on the blacktop.

Four

Darlene stretches her legs out straight and rests her heels on the chair beside her. Vera sits across from her, elbows on the table; her fingers cradle an after-dinner cup of coffee that hides her mouth like a hand of cards. The dishes are done and the kitchen glows with sleepy heat from limbwood coals still lingering in the black iron cookstove. Darlene's cat, a calico named Lady Jane, sleeps curled in a crescent on a rug by the woodbox.

"Harmon says if we start payments now, we'll get a ten percent discount. He showed me the paper. Ten percent off if you get your money in by January first."

"For the double-wide?" Vera asks.

"I guess it's on any of them. But he's set on the double-wide."

"So much more room. I like the way they do the shutters."

"Three bedrooms. And they leave a space for a stair, in case you want to put a cellar underneath."

"If you had a cement foundation, you could have a rumpus room."

"That's what Harmon wants. He has to talk to Grampy about all this. And you, too, of course. I didn't mean to leave you out."

Vera lowers the coffee cup. "You know how I feel about it. We'll be like in the village, live next door to one another." She looks down at the white enamel tabletop. "This place belongs to all of us."

"Still, Grampy is—you know."

"I know. He's got the most put in. His whole life, from the day he was born."

By rights, Darlene is a flatlander, born in Lawrence, Massachusetts. Her father, Frank, left Catamount at the end of the war and went to work in a knitting mill. He earned enough to keep his wife, Lucile, and their baby daughter fed, but nothing extra; every nickel was accounted for. Lucile resented their poverty and argued for a job of her own, but Frank was determined that he alone should earn their livelihood.

Because their rented flat was tiny and her parents argued all the time, Darlene found her only sanctuary in the bathtub. She'd lock the bathroom door, fill the tub to the overflow drain, add strawberry bath bubbles and soak until her fingertips turned white. Sometimes, when the quarrels got bad enough, she would sink so deep that only her nostrils broke the surface and the bitter words from the other room became warped echoes, senseless sounds.

For Christmas, when she was ten years old, Grandpa Dulac sent Darlene an underwater face mask and a snorkel. During her last two years in Lawrence, Darlene's fugitive baths included lengthy periods of lying face down in the tub looking through the glass at patterns in the scratched enamel. Deep grooves became highways, lighter lines were side roads leading to mysterious destinations. A chipped spot was now a hidden lake, now a spaceship at the waiting. She was accompanied, on her adventures, by two imaginary friends: Amanda, with long gold hair—she could shoot like

44

Annie Oakley—and Roberta, dark and beautiful and stronger than the world's ten strongest men.

Their adventures together were of the epic variety—long odysseys to other worlds, rescuing innocents from evil, solving age-old mysteries and discovering buried treasure just in time to save an orphanage from foreclosure. The shouting from the other room at times provided the soundtrack: *Space monsters attacking! Listen to their crazy jabbering! There's one now, Amanda! Fire! And Darlene would blow a raucous burst of bubbles through her mouthpiece.*

Darlene's mother was never bashful about giving her daughter advice. "Don't ever let a man control your life," she would hiss. "You listening to me, Darlene?" Lucile's hair would be wrapped in plastic curlers, dangling against the collar of her quilted orange organza housecoat at three in the afternoon. With her elbows on the kitchen table, an ashtray and a cup of coffee cold beside her, she quickly found her favorite topic: "Men think they know so much, they think they're the only ones who make the world go around. But I've got news for them. They're just big babies, and don't you forget it. Darlene, are you listening to me?"

"Yes, Mom."

"What'd I say?"

"They think they know so much but they're really just big babies."

"And you don't let them push you around."

"Right."

"Don't just say 'right.' I'm talking to you. I'm talking about your future." Lucile lit another Kool and blew smoke into the tropical parrots printed on her wide lapels.

"They think because you're female you can't do the things they do. They think you just stay home all the time and wait for them."

"Mom?"

"What?"

"Where's Indianapolis?"

"You listening to me?"

"Yes, but I was wondering."

"I wish you'd pay attention, Darlene. I'm trying to teach you something. It's over in Maryland."

"Maryland?"

"I think. There's soldiers there."

"Oh."

"See, there's another one for you. Soldiers. Men think women don't know how to fight." Lucile exhaled another plume of mentholated mist. "I want you to remember what I'm saying. You lie around in bubble baths—that's fine for a little girl—but someday you've got to face up to this thing about the way men are and find some way to stand up to them. If you don't, they'll run you over."

"Sure, Mom."

"And the sooner you start practicing, the better off you'll be."

"Okay, Mom."

"Now clean your books off the table and straighten up your room nice and neat. Daddy should be home any minute."

And so it went for Darlene growing up in Massachusetts. When she was twelve, Grandpa Dulac asked Frank and Lucile to come back home to Catamount, offered them a share in the family feed-mill business. Lucile was overjoyed at being reunited with her family—there were Dulacs in every corner of town.

At the Catamount school, Darlene made friends easily, friends she would keep around her for the rest of her life. She quickly forgot Amanda and Roberta. Her underwater bathtub life was replaced by movies at the Rialto in White

River Junction. Her new heroes were Marlon Brando and James Dean.

Their looks were important—they looked wonderful! But more important were the roles they played: drifters, rowdies, rascals, loners, *cowboys*. Women weren't allowed to be cowboys in the movies. Women were denied adventure. As she grew and looked around her, Darlene noticed how precisely movies imitated life.

Vera gets up from the table to pour another cup of coffee for Darlene. Darlene thanks her, watches her at the stove and says to her back, "Guess who stopped by the restaurant today."

Without turning, Vera raises her eyebrows as she asks the question, "Who?"

"Weymouth and some woman. Wasn't Lollie. She was awful. Jeanette sprayed the booth with Lysol when they left."

"How'd Weymouth look?" Weymouth is Leon's younger brother. Vera is afraid of him but she has always relished details of his troublesome life.

"Real old, raggedy. Stunk something awful. Ordered two grilled cheese and coffee. I didn't wait on him, but I was watching. He doesn't have a tooth in his head."

"They rotted out years ago."

Darlene has seen him only once before, a rainy day at the Catamount dump. He was standing halfway down the slope, knee-deep in rubbish, holding a discarded wristwatch to his ear, shaking it over and over again, listening to see if it would tick. When Darlene dumped her bag of bottles and cans over the edge, he looked up at her and grinned a toothless grin. It seemed the corners of his mouth would touch his ears. He held the watch as if to offer it to her.

"He's never taken care of himself," Vera says. "He's barely house-trained."

"He left a dollar tip, though. Jeanette said she earned it, too."

"Money never meant a thing to him."

"You wouldn't believe he was Grampy's brother."

"He's actually younger than Leon. By a couple of years."

"They're so different." Darlene's voice drops off. "Weymouth could die in the Quinntown woods and no one would ever find him."

Vera folds the corner of her apron into a tight little wad. "Cream and sugar?" She reaches for a spoon on the counter behind her. "You sure the coffee won't keep you awake?"

"I could drink it all night," Darlene says. "Harmon says it makes him jittery. Even Pepsi makes him jitter. It's the caffeine, I expect. I wonder what's keeping him?"

"Harmon?" Vera asks. "Maybe we could call him."

"He wouldn't like that. He won't be rushed. He'd probably stay longer if he knew I wanted him home."

"I'm sorry," Vera says.

"I'm not complaining. It's not your fault. I mean, he's usually pretty good about it."

"Bodie said he was upset. He left work early. I think Harmon's worried about you and the baby, that's all. And getting drafted didn't help."

"He's going to ask Grampy if we can put the trailer in before he goes to boot camp."

"You know you're always welcome to stay here in the house."

"He wants to get us settled with something of our own before he goes. It's preying on his mind."

"And he's worried about the baby, of course. Daddies always do," Vera says.

Darlene wants to believe her. She wants to feel pro-

48

tected, but something warns her from it, and instead she feels a need to be brave. "I guess," she says, and marvels how these conversations nourish her, no matter what the topic. She can talk to Vera about all sorts of things and never worry about being rebuked; Vera's maternal claim on Harmon is never wedged between them. And still there are some things that remain unspoken. Some events seem beyond Vera's experience and Darlene can't imagine how they would be taken.

"Purdy fussed over me something awful," Vera says quietly.

Darlene nods and waits.

"Just before he left—I was a month farther along than you—he must have worked fourteen, sixteen hours a day, putting up extra stove wood, fixing the house, mending fences. He put a new motor in our old car because he thought he heard a noise that might mean trouble later on. He made a calendar for me with all my doctor's appointments written in. He wanted everything to go easy." Vera pulls her chair closer to the table and looks intently at Darlene. "You would have liked him." She runs her finger around the rim of her coffee cup. "He was . . ."

"Like Harmon?"

"Partly. Partly Harmon—same get-up-and-go—but partly Bodie, too. He liked to be alone. He'd walk the woods on moonlit nights. Bring me trillium and sawtoothed violets."

Lucky woman, Darlene thinks. The idea of a combination intrigued her since she first saw Bodie and Harmon emerging as distinct personalities. In each of the twins she saw the missing part of the other. She always hoped to combine them, to put them back together. It occurs to her that she convinced herself—four years ago—that marriage to one of them would somehow include the promise of the other. If

49

Harmon had been an only child, would she have married him? She never allowed herself an answer to that question. Staring at Vera as if she were a hundred miles away, she understands for the first time the frame of mind that led her up inside the Catamount bridge with Bodie.

It was dark in there, inside the arch. Harmon slammed the door behind us and I couldn't see a thing except I knew Bodie couldn't be more than a few inches away. I was afraid to move my hands. What if I touched him? They were hollering outside—rude remarks—especially Harmon. I was glad the door was closed. I didn't want to see Harmon; he gets ugly when he's had too many. He was saying, "Do it to her," or something like that, but that didn't bother me. What ticked me off was that he acted like it wasn't my choice, too, like he owned me and could do whatever he wanted to with me. I let him holler out there, let him holler all he wanted.

We stood there—maybe half a minute—and Bodie reached over and touched my arm. I didn't jump. I knew he'd do that and it made me feel better. He slid his hand down to my hand and said come on, he'd help me up the steep part. He showed me how to put my feet on the bolts for traction and then I saw the first hole with light coming up through the floor. He pulled me up to it and as we straddled it I could look down and see Jiggsie and Betsy, lit up from the streetlights on the bridge. Jiggsie had his arm over Betsy's shoulder. I could hear Harmon but I couldn't see him, and I was glad I couldn't. At the next porthole I saw Jiggsie and Betsy again. I saw Loretta, too. It was like looking through a camera. They got smaller and smaller as we climbed up higher. Pretty soon we couldn't see them unless we looked back on a sharp angle. By that time the climb was getting less and less steep, and I didn't care about them because I knew we had to be nearing the top. Bodie's hand felt good in mine. It felt strong, like if I fell through one of the holes he could pull me back up with just that hand. It felt like Harmon's hand, only maybe not so rough, not so much like sandpaper.

All the way up inside the bridge, Bodie is saying be careful here, let me help you, mind you don't slip. Harmon never would do that. He forges ahead and if you don't follow, that's your problem. Bodie led me along at my own speed. I was never scared even though it looked like we were at least a hundred feet up in the air. Bodie wasn't scared either, but I could tell he was getting more nervous as we got closer to the top.

A long time ago, Harmon and Bodie made a wooden floor at the very top of the arch. When Bodie pulled my hand down to touch the boards, I knew that's where we were. He told me to wait a minute and I could hear him brushing the boards off with his hands. Then he was fumbling with something up above and I smelled damp wool and felt air move and realized he was laying out a blanket. He told me sit here and he held my arm again while we sat down on the blanket. There was just enough light coming up through the holes so that I could see his silhouette, but that was all.

I could feel his arm from the shoulder on down, touching mine, and it was hot. Our thighs and hips touched too. We sat on the edge of the platform, holding hands and touching like that for a long time. It could have been Harmon next to me as far as the size and shape of him went. They even wore the same baseball uniforms, but still, it was different. Harmon couldn't have sat still. He'd've been at me right off, breathing hard, undoing my buttons and saying things. At first, I liked Harmon doing that, but after we got married, I got to feeling he didn't even know I was there, he was doing his thing, and if I cared to come along, well, fine, but if I didn't that wouldn't matter any to him, he'd keep right at it anyway. I showed him I didn't like that, but he didn't seem to get it. Or maybe he did: this last year or two he generally falls asleep as soon as his head hits the pillow.

The silence was OK with me. I liked it there with Bodie, holding hands in the dark, but I think it made him nervous. I kept wondering what Loretta thought, wondering if Bodie was thinking about her. She was never a close friend of mine, but we all ran with the same crowd. I didn't have anything against her except she was so mousy.

I liked that it was dark because it made it easier to think I was with Harmon, too. He was the one I was used to. It helped that Bodie looked and felt so much like him. As long as it was dark and we didn't speak, it could have been either one of them. Being brothers made it not so strange. Being twins made it even easier. I guess I felt like I was up there with a combination of the two, the best of both. Being married and secure and having a future with Harmon—and being treated gently, like a real person, by Bodie. The combination is what it was. Up there I had them both and it didn't matter to me what happened.

Darlene looks across the table at Vera and then beyond her to the twisted roll of flypaper that hangs from the ceiling above the cookstove. As the nights grow colder this time of year, insects seek out the warmth of the kitchen and soon are caught in the sticky brown spirals. As Darlene watches, a housefly arcs across the room and collides with the shiny paper, sets it swaying with the impact.

Vera follows Darlene's gaze. "I wish they wouldn't buzz so when they're caught."

"I can't believe they can buzz so long. Their little motors must be something," Darlene says, staring at the pendulum.

Tinker Bushway was flattered when Darlene asked him to teach her how to ride a motorcycle. Tinker kept a half-dozen machines in a shed behind his garage; at least one was always running. The idea of teaching this ninth-grade girl to ride—Tinker had graduated the year before—brought forward uncharacteristic patience and more than a little prurient curiosity.

She made him promise he wouldn't tell anyone about their lessons and he agreed. He thought perhaps she feared her parents would disapprove; this was dangerous stuff, both the riding and the association with a married eighteen-year-old. He thought perhaps Darlene would see him as a hero (a role denied him by his bratty teenaged bride). He liked to think Darlene would fall for him, even though she was barely fifteen. There was something sure about her Tinker found arousing.

For her, the secrecy had simpler purposes: she wanted to be alone. If her friends knew she could ride a motorcycle, they would want to go with her, coax her into teaching them. But she resisted; she knew her independence required solitude.

Tinker started her instructions on a single-cylinder Yamaha, a small-bore, lightweight model, bent and rusty but indomitable. He sent her off around a dirt track worn into the field behind his garage. Creeping along in first gear, trembling with delight, she rode for half an hour until the bike ran out of fuel. On her second outing she learned to shift gears. On her third, she learned to lean her weight into the turns and found an unexpected taste for speed. Within a week she learned to break the rear wheel loose and broadslide through the corners.

Tinker's other motorcycles included a Triumph Bonneville: it was a double-carbureted twin with shiny tapered megaphones and a speedometer calibrated to one hundred and twenty miles an hour. The Bonneville's distinctive howl was a familiar sound along the Catamount cliffs late on summer nights as Tinker "cleaned the cobwebs out," a bullet down the two-lane blacktop, june bug juice stuck to his goggles.

At the end of her first two weeks of riding, Darlene told Tinker she'd give anything to take the Bonneville for a spin. No one had ever ridden the Bonneville but Tinker. The bike was spotless, purchased new and exceptional among

Tinker's possessions for its wholeness. Each part functioned as perfectly as it had the day it left the factory. No one had ever *dared* ask to borrow Tinker's pride and joy, so Darlene's request took him by surprise.

Her first ride was a short one—up to Hubby's Bar and back: five minutes. When she returned to the parking area in front of his garage, Tinker noticed how smoothly she shifted down through the gears, how steadily she pulled up to the spot where the bike was kept, found neutral, turned the key off, closed the petcocks on the fuel lines and dismounted.

Her second ride was longer—halfway up the road to Quinntown to a junkyard where she picked up a distributor cap for a truck Tinker was repairing. From that day on she ran errands for Tinker on the Bonneville, disguised behind a full-face helmet and the studded leather jacket Tinker insisted she wear.

No one but Tinker knew about her secret rides that summer. Occasionally she would pass her friends—walking along the roads or driving toward her in a car—but they never recognized her, barely dared to look at the lone warrior in black leather roaring by on the big machine. Tinker kept his promise and told anyone who asked about the phantom rider that he wasn't certain, but he *thought* the guy was from over west of Jordan Flats.

At the end of her motorcycling summer, Darlene borrowed Tinker's Bonneville and rode to Quinntown Mountain to camp out overnight—by herself. She told Lucile she'd be at Betsy's for a backyard slumber party and she told Betsy she was staying with Grandpa Dulac out at his cabin on the lake, where there was no telephone. She packed a sleeping bag and tarp, took some sandwiches and a flashlight and rode to the end of a logging road that twisted up the mountain along Hall's Brook. She hid the bike in a clump of hemlocks and hiked in to the beaver pond where Frank had brought her hornpout fishing the summer before.

The edges of the pond lay low and damp around several acres of shallow, tannic waters. Sphagnum moss and hardhack hung to soggy islands strung between bleached spars of trees long-drowned by the beavers' ingenuity. The view across the water showed the southern flank of Mooseback Mountain, striped with granite rockslides from summit to base.

With several hours left until nightfall, Darlene made a tidy camp—laid out her tarp and sleeping bag, collected armloads of dead spruce boughs and formed a circle of rocks for her campfire. She used her sandwich wrappers to ignite the branch wood, added bigger pieces until white ashes ringed the fire. Cool evening air drained down the slopes, exchanged for deepening shades of purple rising up the mountain. When finally the heavy night tints overwhelmed the lingering pinks, she slipped into her sleeping bag in perfect equilibrium.

She awoke to men's voices. Ten yards away, at the edge of the pond, two silhouettes stood, wavering. The conversation made it clear they thought they were alone; Darlene's campfire was cold and her sleeping bag was hidden in the shadows. The men had obviously been drinking for some time; each held a bottle, raising it for emphasis, drinking from it during their conversation. Neither used the other's name, but the short one was Canadian. The other, taller figure sounded like he could have been one of the itinerant loggers who boarded at Weymouth Woodard's.

The outlines of their bodies, the downwind whiff of sweat and bug dope, diesel fuel and snuff and stale beer— how the two men stood and swayed, their clothes, their speech, the regularity with which they farted—spelled out their occupation clearly: they were loggers, apparently working together for one of the paper companies. These were men whose hands were reconfigured by their occupation into claws, coarse pincers made for clutching heavy metal objects—pulpwood saws, peaveys, bunk stakes, chains and binders, oversized machinery parts that need repairing late at night in snowfall on a mountainside at twenty-five below.

They talked about a woman named Jolene. It appeared the taller man wanted the woman, but the woman didn't want him.

". . . She didn't drink or smoke. She's good that way. Put up my dinner bucket, coffee thermos. Christ, she'd put the food right to me."

"They take you truck, you don't be careful."

"Kept the trailer decent. You know her sister Ruby?"

"Run with Choquette?"

"That's her other sister, Cloris. Miserable reptile."

"I think Choquette get done with her."

"Fourteen years old."

"Write their name on you goddamn paycheck. Take you money for the goddamn television payment."

"Fourteen years old. Looks twenty, easy. Jolene raised her."

"Pretty soon, they get the babies."

"Maybe Jolene'd put in a word for me, to Ruby. Jolene ain't mad at me. Just disgusted . . ."

"Cry about the trailer be too small. Want the money, money all the times."

"I don't guess Ruby'd like my first ex-wife, Sandra. Bitch told my second ex-wife she liked *her* better'n *me*. Can you believe that?"

"Wha?"

"Ruby's fourteen. She could be lying."

"Could be thirteen."

"*Tell the truth,* that's all I asked the first one for. She didn't know the meaning of it."

"Repossession man, he come and take the chain saw out you hand."

"She'd holler if I fucked her and she'd holler if I didn't."

"They cook the bean and salt pork and you suppose to act like you in heaven."

As the men spoke, Darlene slowly slipped her arm out of the top of her sleeping bag and reached across the few feet to her knapsack. Without a sound, she worked her fingers into a side pocket in search of a bone-handled knife she had packed at the last moment. She found the knife by feel alone; not for an instant did she look away from the men in front of her.

"Jesus Christ a man gets tired working seven days a week. You ever chop for Double Diamond?"

"Wha?"

"Double D. When I holed up with what's-her-face, the one from over Dunbar Heights. Had all them scabby babies. What in hell's her name?"

"Pauline?"

"Shit, no. Pauline? Pauline's from down when we was twitching pulp for Allied Paper. I'm talking the Double Diamond job, that christly freezing country up to Collinsville, the cedar swamp where Jimmy Joozle lost his leg."

"Double Diamond. Bastards owe me still the money."

"Rosanne. Old Rosanne was Double Diamond. Cut my toenails off when I was laying drunk one night."

"Her could of cut you worse than that."

"Claimed my thrashing cut her ankles. Showed me where the blood run through the blanket. Your toenails do that?"

"Wha?"

"Get sharp as razors—curl right over the ends of your toes?"

"You think I am a *animal?* No wonder her throw you out the window."

"That Ruby, she's the one I should of had up to the Double Diamond. Trim her little toenails good. You don't know Ruby?"

"Run with Choquette?"

"Hell with Choquette. That's her sister, Cloris. Ruby don't run with nobody. She's jailbait. Fourteen years old."

"You think her run with you? Ha! Her make you crazy, drop you dead. You too damn old! Her give you the heart attack on top of her."

"You sawed-off little shit. What the hell do you know?"

"First, they take you truck . . ."

Eventually, the conversation turned to fish and then to shotguns. In the middle of a discussion about double-aught loads, the two men stumbled off the way they'd come, still talking into darkness. Darlene heard two distant slamming doors, then the squeaks and rattles of an old truck rumbling slowly down the road, diminishing to nothing.

Stars and frogs took back the night; the terror of being found subsided. Darlene began to breathe easily again, stretched her arms and legs and placed the knife beside her, on a flat rock where she could easily reach it. Jolene, Rosanne, Pauline, Ruby—they tugged at her imagination. Who were they? How did they live with men like these? As compensation, she endowed them with the glamorous lives of Nashville country queens: Jolene with auburn curls and rhinestones, Ruby dressed in shiny satins, Pauline's dress ablaze with gold thread, Rosanne's eyes black as coal. *Run with Choquette?* Darlene found herself smiling, then she laughed out loud. *You think I am a animal?*

Yes, animals: that's what they were. Big, dumb, pathetic

animals! Their brains were feeble, shriveled up from lack of use, too many six-packs. Their brains were run off track by some disease that strikes when whiskers start growing. The storybooks of noble kings and princes must have been written by idiots from another planet. A man should be *expected* to behave like a fool. Any sign of grace is to be viewed with suspicion. The idea left her feeling disillusioned but immensely free. It was simple: zero expectations lead to zero disappointments. A cowboy's credo.

When she thought of all the men she'd ever known and looked for an exception, she was left with none to argue her assumption. Daddy Frank, Grandpa Dulac, her cousins Tim and Tony, all the boys in Catamount (except for Tinker—he let her ride his motorcycles): almost every male she knew was flawed with an irrepressible need to be a fool. Not quite as great a fool as the little Frenchman and whoever the big one was, but a fool nonetheless. And *unreliable.* Unreliable in ways that women were never mean or dumb or insensitive enough to be—like going out for a dozen eggs and coming home at two a.m. Dead drunk. Without the eggs. Her daddy Frank did that.

"Harmon's going to make a good daddy," Vera says, reaching across the table and squeezing Darlene's hand. "Don't you worry. He'll be back—before you know it. He'll be back, I know he will."

Both women know there is no way to tell the future; hoping for the best is their only defense. "He'll be extra careful because he's got you and"—Vera points to Darlene's belly—"to come home to. And Grampy and Bodie and me." She smiles, sincerely, like a mother, like a sister, an optimist.

"If it's a boy, I want to name him Purdy." Darlene spills the words out. "Maybe he'll turn out like Purdy." The idea

59

of a completed cycle excites her: Purdy to Harmon—then, through her, back to another Purdy. She thinks of her science class in high school and tries to remember the semester spent on genetics. All she can recall are jars of disgusting fruit flies and charts that looked like branching trees. "I have this feeling it's going to be a boy. I don't know why. I just can't picture a girl."

"The family runs to boys," Vera says. "Won't that be wonderful?"

It will be wonderful, Darlene thinks, shifting in her chair. The embryo inside her feels important; she feels the weight of Harmon-Purdy's presence rising like a loaf of precious bread. The image of a baby Jesus lying in a manger takes her to the choir loft where she and Betsy sang each Sunday, teenagers in pleated crimson robes. A picture of a Christ child hung along one wall. Darlene knew each detail intimately: Joseph's beard, the sheep, the pristine straw, the shining stars, the Virgin's smile. The Reverend Hall could drone forever; she took her refuge in the pastels of the world around the manger. From there, her Sunday morning imagination could fly off in any direction, returning in an instant at the scraping of the hard-backed chairs, the choir rising to sing "O, Follow Me," Betsy huge and comforting beside her.

"Harmon thought we'd also call him Leon," Darlene says.

"Leon's meant a lot to him. He's raised the boys like they were sons."

"How about . . . Purdy Leon Woodard? Leon could be the middle name." But the middle should also be Harmon-Bodie. Purdy—Harmon-Bodie—back to Purdy again. Darlene sees a diagram shaped like a diamond with the name "Purdy" at the top and bottom points and "Harmon-Bodie" written across the middle. The diamond spins and blurs into a circle like a pinwheel in a fairground breeze. She sees the outside of the circle with "Purdy" written in a repeat pattern, embracing the circle, around and around.

"Leon would be tickled—however you want to do it. Didn't he seem pleased tonight when you told him?"

"He acted like he knew it all along . . . He'll be a *great-*grampy! Won't that be something? I wonder if he'll ever grow a beard? A big white beard like Santa Claus."

"No way, not Leon." Vera laughs. "He thinks people grow beards to hide behind. You'd sooner see him wear a pinafore." The idea of Leon in a dress makes them **giggle**. "Grampy in a bustle!" Vera blurts out, and they laugh and laugh, then suddenly stop to listen to Leon snoring and then laugh again, hands over their mouths like little sisters eavesdropping on some serious grown-up affair.

"Leon calls me Darlin'. Always has," Darlene says. "I think he thinks that's my name. Harmon calls me Sugarpuss."

"Purdy used to call me Sunshine. He said my hair shone like the sun. He said it was a 'golden nimbus.' That comes from a poem."

"I like that better than Sugarpuss. Betsy calls Jiggsie Fudge. Isn't that cute? He calls her Bubbles." And Bodie, Darlene thinks. Bodie called her Baby. Baby, Baby, Baby.

I knew Bodie was nervous, sitting there. We could have been down cellar, anywhere, it was so dark. It didn't feel like being way up in the air. It felt cozy and safe. I put my head on his shoulder and then he said are you cold, Baby, and I made a sound like yes because I knew he wanted to put his arm around me and I wanted him to, I did. I was sitting to his left and when he put his arm around my shoulders, we slid back and lay down on the wool blanket and he clanged his elbow against the steel and said oh shit, and then we laughed and snuggled up. He put his right hand on my stomach and I put my left hand over his and then I felt my wedding ring against his knuckles and it started to burn against my finger like a hot wire. I pulled my hand away and worked it off with my thumb and slid it into my dungarees pocket. Then I put my hand back over his and he started saying Baby to me. It was nice, him holding me, but I was thinking about the ring and wondering if Harmon still made payments on it or if it was all paid off. He never told me what it cost but I always thought it was over three hundred—along with the diamond engagement ring. He would never let me see the monthly bill from Sheldon's. It was funny to be thinking of that while Bodie was saying Baby, Baby in my ear and slipping his fingers between the buttons on my blouse.

"I called Purdy Mr. Skeezix. It came from the Boston Sunday comics. He liked it when I called him that." Vera sighs and looks around the room. "I've got to wash those curtains. You wonder how they get so dirty." She gets up to pour more coffee.

Darlene looks at the curtains and then at the window-panes that sometime soon (she hopes) will shine with head-lights, Harmon's pickup coming home across the valley to the house.

Although she's rarely been with him to Hubby's Bar, she knows the room is mostly filled with men, jostling elbows, talking loud, the smell and tone particularly male. They strut around keeping their muscles taut as if to protect their tender innards. They trade in nouns that sound like clanking metal: *choker chain, rim lock, torque wrench, lag bolt, crankshaft, tailgate, valve ping, solenoid.* They push the words around with obscenities and make them act with verbs like *skid* and *snake, crawl, rig, bite, jam, screw, grind, stick, hammer, snap, crimp, haul* and *ram.* They talk about machines and how to make the cussed things work as if they were a reluctant subspecies of human. If one of the men is sick, another will tell about the illness in terms of where the patient's pickup truck was last seen and how its owner was too weak to get into the cab. They never use a word like *lovely* or *bouquet.* Darlene knows it well. All they are trying to do, she thinks, is say *how are you? I hope you're well, and yes, I'm OK, thank you for asking.*

"Bodie's at Loretta's, right?" Darlene says, trying to remember how many of those male words Bodie uses. She has heard him talk about woodworking. He uses words like *sandpaper* and *feathered edges.*

"He said he'd be late."

"Last week he got here just in time to shave and go to work."

"You think he'll marry her?" Vera's tone is hopeful.

"I hope not," Darlene says, immediately sorry she has said it. "I mean, they don't *do* anything. I think they're bored with each other."

"Lordy, there must be something."

"Maybe so. Don't you think she's mousy?"

"She's plain. But sweet."

The talk of Bodie getting married has made Darlene's fingers tap on the tabletop. She checks the window again for a sign of Harmon and finishes her coffee. "You think we could set the double-wide in back of the vegetable garden? Harmon says the drainage is good. That way, with the barn on the other side of the house, we wouldn't get in Grampy's way—we'd be clear of the animals and everything."

"As long as you're close by," Vera says. "Especially now. I fret so about Bodie. I hate to think of him running from the law. Harmon to the military, Bodie up in Canada and the baby coming."

Back at school, a month after her overnight camping trip on Tinker's Bonneville, Harmon showed Darlene he was interested in her: he put a dead muskrat in her locker. She said nothing about the incident, took the carcass home and skinned it out in the grass behind the mill. The next day, Harmon found the pelt inside *his* locker, pressed between the pages of his history book. As if to prove her theory on the inevitability of male foolishness, he got caught tacking the pelt to the principal's door. He washed blackboards for a week as punishment.

Darlene was impressed when Harmon said nothing about her complicity. The incident gave them a topic they could tease one another about, and soon Darlene was writing Harmon's name on the back of her hand. Aside from Tinker, Harmon was the only male she found interesting. Her theory on men was suddenly deferred to forces not so easily explained. By Halloween, the muskrat was part of their selective history and she was writing "Darlene and Harmon" on her palm in indelible laundry ink.

On Friday, the ninth of November, Harmon passed his driver's test. The next day, with a pocket full of cash he'd saved for years, he bought—at a very high price—Tinker's Triumph Bonneville. (Tinker swore he'd never sell it, but at that price . . .) On Monday morning, Harmon arrived at school early. He parked at the bottom of the steps that led to the schoolhouse doors and worked a rag across imaginary specks of dust on the two-tone gas tank. The Bonneville was tipped to one side on its kickstand, glistening like a rare religious icon undergoing special cleansing rites. When Harmon looked up at his spectators from time to time, he could not suppress the smile that told it all: The thing was absolutely perfect. And, more important, it was *his*. Darlene stood watching from the top of the schoolhouse steps and drew a line through the name on her ink-stained palm.

At morning recess, Harmon asked Darlene if she had seen his motorcycle.

"Tinker's Bonneville?" she said, acting surprised. "I've seen it around, I guess."

"It's mine, now. I bought it on Saturday. Paid cash for it. It's in the parking lot."

Darlene took pleasure in having Harmon believe she had missed the morning spectacle.

"Take you home after school?"

"Too cold," she said. "Daddy said it's going to snow tonight." She pictured herself driving the Bonneville back in August, leaning into turns along the winding Jordan road, surrounded by the scent of chopped alfalfa. How wonderful those rides had been, alone with all that power rumbling dutifully between her legs. "I'll freeze my fingers off."

"So what? Tuck in behind me. You'll be OK."

She would be OK if she were driving—summer sunlight shimmering off the blacktop, hot wind rushing by along the flats and then, dipping down into a shaded gully, cool relief, a brown meandering brook, a narrow iron bridge in dappled light before the climb in grade and temperature back up to heat and open highway surging by in waves of endless space and speed plied thick with summer air. She would be OK if she had *that* again. But it would never happen on the Bonneville while Harmon owned it. With Tinker, she could borrow it and be alone and bring it back with no complications. She ran errands for him in return for rides; the agreement was simple. With Harmon, that kind of equation would be unworkable. And riding as a passenger was almost worse than riding not at all.

"I'm not riding that thing in this weather," she told him.

"You just don't like cycles."

"Right."

"Next summer?"

"Maybe."

"Stubborn."

"Maybe."

"Scared?"

Bodie had me all undressed and I was thinking God, I hope he put my clothes up on the blanket. I could see them dropping through a porthole and floating down and landing on the bridge in front of Harmon. He'd go crazy. But then I didn't care because Bodie's hands felt so good on me. One of his hands, I don't know which, had a cut across the palm. It was rough on my skin but I didn't mind because he was so gentle. He got to taking off his pants with one hand, the other hand still holding me, and all the while he was saying Baby, oh, Baby, Baby. He couldn't get his baseball shoes untied. We both laughed and he sat up and untied his laces as fast as he could and then he just about tore his clothes off.

His skin felt smooth all over and he lay down beside me, holding me for the longest time. We could hear Harmon down below, talking loud with Jiggsie. We heard Betsy's high-pitched laugh and Harmon yelling rude things up at us. We lay there in the dark and I was waiting for Bodie to go ahead. I wanted him. He was holding me tighter and tighter, saying Baby over and over and then his voice got softer and softer, like a little boy's, and then he stopped, just like that. I held him and petted his head until he got his voice back; he was sweating something awful. The wool blanket felt scratchy on my bare back. Then he said he was sorry, we had better go. Funny, just: "We better go."

We found our clothes and he took my hand and helped me down the arch, the Catamount end. I kissed him on the cheek when we got to the bottom and put my wedding ring back on. He squeezed my hand and never said another word. He jimmied the door open and we climbed out on the street. Harmon and Jiggsie and Loretta and Betsy were waiting for us. They clapped and hollered and made a big fuss, teasing us and all. Harmon didn't even look at me. He went over to Bodie with this big leer on his face and

punched his shoulder the way men do and asked him how was it,
was it pretty good stuff, or something like that. Bodie turned
away and started walking toward his truck at the Superette, his
hands in his pockets, looking down at the pavement. He didn't
look back. Harmon was laughing like a madman. I decided
right then I would never tell Harmon what really happened. He
could think anything he wanted. I had this one on him. This one
was mine.

Darlene stares at her knuckles; they feel stiff and un-
wieldy, reluctant to move. In a similar way, her mind is
reluctant to move into certain dimensions; she realizes she
can't talk to Vera about Harmon and Bodie. Sure, she can
talk about the outside things, the parts that everyone can
easily see, but there seem to be different rules concerning
the crucial parts that make them tick. To probe too deeply
risks discovering some awful truth, some contradictory evidence that would spin their lives out of kilter. She senses
Vera knows this, too. Underneath their friendly gloss of
caring conversation she imagines layers of secrets, ledgers
full of little treacheries committed by generations of their
menfolk, harbored safe away within the painful, willing
trust of—hope. She hopes that Harmon loves her, she
hopes he really wants their baby, she hopes he means it
when he says he hates the idea of leaving her, he can't
wait to get back. She hopes it was only a boozy lapse that
led him to the agreement with Bodie. She hopes that
when he falls asleep without touching her, night after
night, month after month—she hopes he falls asleep because he's exhausted, not just tired of her. But how can she
tell Vera this?

How can she tell Vera about Bodie? Each confession
would be a betrayal, an articulation of what, once spoken,
might never be forgiven. Maybe Vera has so many secrets

of her own that she would never be surprised at anything. Maybe she has secrets she could never, ever tell, secrets full of other men from other times, still unforgotten.

Darlene and Vera sit at the kitchen table. Their secrets make a bridge between them, a bridge that forms a safe connection, but one neither can cross.

"I'm going to bed." Darlene yawns. "If Harmon wants to be a bad boy, he'll have to come home to a sleeping house."

"I'll wait up a little longer. I've got some things to tidy up." Vera glances around the room as if to justify her claim. "I'll tell him you sat up for him."

Half an hour later, still awake, Darlene hears Harmon's truck pull in the driveway; she hears as well her thumping heartbeat and pulls her blankets closer to her, moves her pillow. A rusty door thumps shut, squeaks, the way it always has since he bought the truck five years ago. She listens as his footsteps crunch across the gravel and thinks about how much he likes his truck, how he likes to drive it everywhere they go together.

He wouldn't look at me all the way back to the parking lot, even though he had his arm over my shoulder. It was like he was herding me, leading me like a pony, all the while bragging to Jiggsie about the double play he'd made against Jordan Center. Loretta walked the other way, back home to Pike. I felt bad for her and knew I'd have to talk to her, make her believe it wasn't like she thought it was. Or maybe she knew; maybe Bodie was like that all the time and that's why Miss Mouse liked him.

Betsy kissed me good night. When she and Jiggsie drove away, we stood there in front of the Superette watching their lights fade away down the highway. Harmon opened the driver's-side door and sort of pushed me in, in front of him, and then got in behind me. He drove home fast, still wouldn't talk. I didn't have anything to say to him, either, so I watched the headlights in the trees along the curves, watched for shadows making ghosts.

When we got home, he did it again—he herded me into the house and up the stairs, without a word and in a hurry. We used the bathroom, one by one, and when he got in bed I knew this wasn't going to be one of his nights to hit the pillow and snore. He was wound up so tight he shook. His hands went everywhere, not so much like he wanted to touch me, but more like he was checking to see if anything was missing.

Five

Harmon's knife slides in below the breastbone. He works it down the big buck's belly, cuts to the left of the retracted penis, past the downy testicles and finishes at the anus. His hands are greasy with blood; his fingers stain the white hairs red along the edges of his surgery. The buck lies like a broken package, its contents made suddenly public on a cold November day.

"Jesus, he's a good one," Harmon says, pulling his face back from the steam and stench. "I bet he'll go two fifty."

"Two fifty easy," Bodie says. "Look at the fat on him." Bodie kneels and curls the hide away from the incision. A glistening yellow layer lies close beneath the skin.

"He's a fatbacked mother, for sure," Harmon says. "Fatback, fatback. You should hear the spades carry on about fatback. There's this spade from Virginia, Pomeroy Johnson, two bunks down from mine? He's always got the barracks laughing, mister, stories he can tell. He'll eat fatback instead of steak. Eats possum, too. And skunk! Sarge says that's what makes him stink."

Bodie has never heard Harmon use the expression "spade." He can't remember ever having met someone who wasn't white.

"Old Sarge is quite an outfit. They claim he can break

through a man's rib cage and tear his heart out. With his bare hands. They speak as though he did it in Korea. Quite the beast."

Bodie looks out at the Connecticut River. Flocks of riffles dart across the water, ricocheting into barren scrub along the opposite shore. He thinks of flying bullets. Below a huge dead elm, a tangle of sumac holds the season's final colors; each crimson pod becomes a soldier's dying body. Harmon's furlough is almost over, a week spent hunting and telling tales—and lies, no doubt, although he swears it's all true. Tomorrow, Sunday morning, he will board a Greyhound bus in White River Junction and begin his journey to Viet Nam. But now it is a cloudless afternoon in Vermont, made perfect by the stalking and the killing of this animal.

Blood creeps up Harmon's forearms as he probes deeper into the open gut. "Damn, he's stubborn," he grunts, straining to dislodge the deer's entrails. He gives another yank; the last threads yield and a bushel's worth of organs spills out onto the frozen grass. Vermilion, mauve and unexpected blue shine liquid-bright beside the emptied carcass. "Jiggsie eats the heart meat," Harmon says, severing the arteries around it. "Eats the liver, too." He plops it on the ground next to the heart. "I ought to take these back for Pomeroy. Show him what us Yankees eat."

"You think Jiggsie heard the shot?"

"Soon find out." Harmon wipes his hands against his thighs. "In Basic, they have this rifle range. Paper targets, bull's-eyes, little circles with numbers on them. Some guy from up in Maine, he beat me every time. Sonofabitch could shoot the eyes out of a june bug at a hundred yards. Everybody calls him Deadeye. Don't know what his real name is. Helluva shot. Dumber'n shit. Works the woods when he ain't on welfare."

As he speaks, Harmon is skimming gristle from the whitetail's rib cage. "Deadeye told this story, meant to be serious, about this car he had? Dodge Ram Charger, I believe it was. Wouldn't go in winter, so he put the ether to it. Poured it down the four-barrel. Worked slick. She'd cough and fart and start up every time, twenty, thirty, forty below. Then, he says, she got addicted, had to have the ether. Didn't matter what time of year. Liked it better'n high test! Fourth of July, boiling hot, there goes old Deadeye, under the hood, spraying ether left and right. Once they taste ether, he claims, they'll never go back. Can't retrain 'em. Gone for good. Frigging guy believes it! Helluva shot though."

Bodie looks down at his brother's shaved head; the skin between the bristly hairs is white and taut. The idea of bone beneath that skin, of brain pulp held inside that vulnerable shell makes Bodie's stomach heave. He presses his hand over his mouth and runs across the clearing toward a stand of alders. As he runs, bacon grease roils up his throat. Let me make it, please, he begs, his jaw clamped tight against the reflex.

Bacon, eggs, that coffee taste—by god you'd think I didn't chew. Eyes teared up and something caught—a piece of doughnut bridged across the back of my nose. Stomach hurts. Same puffy guts stuffed inside me as stuffed inside that christly buck. Shot him once, clean through the lungs. I got to stand up, wipe my face and breathe. Breathe. *It's not my lungs, remember that. It's not me lying there with all my packings littered on the ground. Did Harmon hear me? No. He's still dressing out his trophy. Listen to him whistle. Christ.*

Bodie straightens up and sees a patch of orange moving slowly toward him through the woods. He wipes his forehead and spits the thickness from his mouth. The orange is Jiggsie, working his way upwind, moving silently through the trees.

He spots Bodie, raises his rifle in recognition and lumbers down the slope to greet him.

"Any luck?" Bodie asks.

"Saw a little spikehorn. Shit. I could of ate him for a sandwich," Jiggsie wheezes, out of breath. "How about you, how about Harmon? You murder up your Bambi yet?"

"Harmon murdered his up good. Twelve-point rack, might go two fifty. Dropped him in his tracks, one shot."

"Decent."

"From six o'clock this morning, all I've seen is tracks and puckerbush. I'd like to get one this year, mister. Last three years I've come up short."

"You ain't holding your mouth right, Dubba."

Bodie remembers the breakfast splattered on the ground behind him and maneuvers himself so that Jiggsie won't see it. But Jiggsie does and looks away. Bodie knows it won't be mentioned.

"Where's old Hor-mone and his trophy?"

Bodie jerks his thumb across the clearing. They walk through smells of sun on fallen leaves. As they approach Harmon and the dressed-out carcass, the air turns thick with drying blood, with viscera and fluids inappropriate to bright daylight.

Harmon sees them coming and holds up the heart and liver.

"Got some munchies for you, Jiggsie. Bring your bib and tucker?"

"Think I'll pass. Trying to cut back. Could go for a Bud right now, though. Drier 'n a popcorn fart." Jiggsie prods the buck's antlers with his boot. "You got yourself an ani-mule."

"Took him through the lungs. One shot." Harmon pauses, leaving room for Jiggsie's further admiration. Re-

74

ceiving none, he looks up and down the length of the deer, wondering if Deadeye could have done any better. "Now I got to engineer a way to lug this critter home. Guess I'll have to cut a pole and ask one of you volunteers to carry half the bounty." He looks up at Bodie, then at Jiggsie.

"Count me out," Jiggsie says. "I come home without my buck, the war department, she'll turn nasty."

"No deer, no sugar," Bodie says, raising his eyebrows.

"You better believe. She likes her venison. Likes the price on it, anyways." Jiggsie giggles. "Old Jiggsie likes his sugar, too."

"Maybe you'll get lucky," Bodie says. "I'll help Harmon. He's giving me half the flank steak, anyway."

"Like hell I am."

"Don't be so mis'able," Jiggsie says over his shoulder to Harmon, walking off upriver. "I'll see you guys tonight at the fire station. We'll get us a table near the band."

"Near the *bar*," Harmon shouts back, staring at the wisps of steam rising from the buck's entrails. "Last night home," he says quietly. Then, "Back to Dix to wait on orders."

"Any idea?"

"You kidding? They're all going over, building up. Need all the grunts they can get. All us Dix guys go. It's like old home week over there. First Cam Ranh, then hit the paddies. Do your tour and re-up."

"You wouldn't."

"I would. You better believe, I would," Harmon says, looking tough. "It's the only way, it's got to be done."

"You sound like one of those recruitment ads on TV."

"Let's get this casualty out of here," Harmon says, irritated. "I'll cut us a pole." He walks off to a stand of young red maples, growing bunched together. Using his oversized hunting knife like a machete, he hacks a ring around a trunk, making slow but steady progress through the white wood. As he cuts, the smooth bark bleeds a watery sap, staining the stump a darker brown.

Bodie uses baling twine to tie the buck's ankles together—first the front pair, then the back. Next, he cinches a line around the belly and draws it closed like an empty duffel. Harmon brings a twelve-foot pole to the deer and they slide it between both pairs of legs. With the pole wedged tight into the ankles, they lift the animal off the ground and rest the loaded pole across their shoulders. The sapling bends with the buck's weight. He hangs upside down between them, neck arched back, tail and antlers scraping high points on the trail.

Harmon walks in front; his rifle is slung across his back, his forearms are russet with dried blood. The buck's head hangs inches from his heels. Its eyes remain wide open but do not see the extra lift in Harmon's gait, the victor returning from the hunt. Bodie sees it. He can feel it through the flexing maple yoke connecting them. He walks in silence, pulled along by Harmon's pride, three steps behind. Or is it three miles? How does it happen, Bodie wonders, that once again he's leading me, I'm following him, at his command, like a shadow with no mind of its own. If he turns left, I'll turn left, if he slows down, I'll do the same. He gets his deer; I don't get mine. But I help him carry his trophy home. He'll be the hero at the fire station tonight and I'll still feel like puking.

They walk for half an hour—quickly at first, then slowly as the deadweight takes its toll. Bodie's view of Harmon's back draws him like a beacon. The hypnotizing cadence of their gait creates quick images for Bodie, images that change with the jolt of a boot against a rock, a twist around a trailside tree. Here, he sees the hanging buck transformed into a man—a man also eviscerated, a yellow man with jet black hair. Harmon is dressed in combat gear, grenades and bullets dangling from his belt. The bloody rings around his forearms extend to his armpits, then to his neck and up the back of his head. Bodie's focus drops to Harmon's spine. The orange hunting jacket disappears and a sniper's telescopic sight aligns its axis on Harmon's seventh vertebra. Bodie blinks his vision clear to find familiar forest and his crew-cut twin in front of him.

Within a quarter mile of their pickup trucks, Harmon breaks the silence.

"MPs been by, looking for you?"

Bodie imagines Harmon in a khaki uniform, white puttees and a wide black belt. "No," he says. "And don't start in on that draft dodger crap. I've heard it all before."

"What are you gonna do if they do come around?"

"I told you. I'm going north."

"Slink off like a fox . . ."

Harmon is suddenly anchored to a stop, pulled downward by the falling weight of the pole as the end behind him strikes the ground. He twists out from under the load and drops the buck over onto its side. Its shiny pointed hooves slap to the ground with a sound like crackling wood.

"You sonofabitch, you kinked my back," Harmon snarls, rubbing at his beltline over one hip. "What the hell's got into you?"

Bodie faces him with his rifle held across his chest, the barrel pointed upward. His right hand holds the walnut stock, his index finger traces the semicircular guard around the trigger. Twenty years of confrontations are suddenly compressed into the space between them. Hearts pound, sweat rises. They stare and recollect their grievances. This time, the terms seem clear: Bodie steps around the deer and walks toward the trucks, just visible in the distance.

"What about my buck?" Harmon calls after him, knowing what the answer will be.

"Fuck your buck," Bodie says, knowing Harmon doesn't need an answer.

The cardboard sign in front of the Catamount Volunteer Fire Department reads:

TONIGHT–6 O'CLOCK
ANNUAL SPORTSMEN'S DINNER
CHICKEN AND LOBSTER FEED $3.00
–MUSIC BY–
O'DELL STINSON AND THE ROMANCERS
–B.Y.O.B.–

O'Dell plays piano. The drums and string base, played by Taylor Gandy and O'Dell's wife, Desirée, sound good behind O'Dell. The sound is part Hank Williams, part New England auto garage. Taylor's backseat gives the band a rhythmic certainty; he lays out time like a steam-run trip-hammer. But it's Tinker Bushway's Gibson Hummingbird guitar that everyone listens to. His fingers flit around the neck like barn swallows at twilight. Notes soar in acrobatic flights across the noisy crowd; base chords flow like water through the folding chairs and table legs. Above the bandstand, Chinese lanterns cast highlights on Tinker's lacquered instrument.

Catamount's fire trucks are parked outside to make room for the occasion. A late November evening's frost has turned the hoods and fenders white. The Ladies' Auxiliary chicken and lobster dishes have been complimented and consumed along with heaps of homemade potato salad, beans and pickled relishes. The red and white checkered tablecloths are damp with blackberry brandy, Black Velvet and beer.

When the musicians take a break around eleven o'clock,

Tinker pulls up an empty chair and sits down with Jiggsie, Betsy, Harmon, Darlene, Bodie and Loretta. Bodie and Loretta clap as Tinker sits down.

"You got it geared up good tonight," says Bodie. "You pick them strings any quicker, they'll put you in jail for speeding."

Tinker grins.

"Look at him blush," says Loretta, and they all turn to Tinker, who accepts a Genesee and tilts his head back; his Adam's apple counts the gulps until the bottle is empty. He wipes his mouth across his sleeve. His fingernails are rimmed with grease, black from the cars he's worked on all his life.

"You hear about the ballyhoo last night?" he asks. "The C.D. si-reen took the radish. Civil defense is liable to be on my ass. I'm heading north with Bodie, here." He laughs, looking toward the door.

"Frank and Jesse James," says Bodie, making an effort to avoid Harmon's eyes.

"You mean that spruce tree outside?" Jiggsie says.

"Spruce tree, si-reen, telephone wires, you name it, I done it. The whole nine yards done shit the bed."

"Looking for pulpwood, were you?" Harmon teases.

"Looking for an allen wrench is what I was. Working after supper, new seals in the portable generator. Had to have me an allen wrench, a big one. Come to find out the tool chest was locked, and all I could find in the chief's desk was two keys. One of them I could tell right away was the key to the gas pumps, got a big plastic disc on the key chain, shaped like a valentine or some such foolishness. The *other* key, I figured it went to the tool chest. Well, I tried it, jimmied it half to death, but there weren't no way that key was gonna open that frigging chest. Then I got to wondering just what that key was for. All the rigs have their own keys left in them and the overhead doors don't have no locks. Chief don't lock his office. Ain't no lock to lock. Ain't no door! I mean to tell you, it had me buffaloed."

"Sounds like you was right to home," says Jiggsie.

"Till I remembered the switch for the si-reen. You've seen the switch for the si-reen. It's one of them locked-up thingamajigs. Red box with a lot of buttons on it. Sets on the wall next to the soap dispenser." He flicks his thumb toward the back wall. "I call it a bear trap. Once you put the key in, there ain't no way you can get it out till you get the all-clear code from the Civil Defense and punch the numbers in." Tinker takes a long swallow of Jiggsie's beer and burps.

"I don't know why, but finding out if that key fit that si-reen switch growed on me till I couldn't stand it no more. Just plain cat-killing curiosity, I guess you'd call it. When I started off, all I was going to do was see if it looked like it would fit." He grins. "It looked like it would. Then, being me, I had to see if I could stick it in. Just hardly a smidgen. And by the jeez, I could!" He rubs his hands together. "Well, it wouldn't take much more to make sure if it was the right key, so I put her in a little farther. Course, about then, the christly thing blew. Mister, that's all she wrote.

"Nine o'clock Thursday night ain't exactly the best time to learn Civil Defense. The instruction book had been propping up the short leg of chief's rolltop desk for nine, ten years now, and I kinda suspected I wouldn't find no comfort there anyhow. I called the telephone operator. She didn't know nothing! The chief was over to Jordan playing Bingo as usual, and the only way I could get a-holt of him was to set off the fire alarm, and that's a misdemeanor. So, I run around trying this and that for fifteen minutes before my eyes lighted on the company chain saw, setting on the running board of the pumper truck. (Meanwhile, that si-reen keeps on a-festering up there on that spruce pole.) I says, Tinker, curiosity got you into this. That chain saw's gonna get you out. So I lug the chain saw outadoors and topple that forty-foot spruce tree. Down she come, si-reen a-screeching and telephone lines strewed six ways to Sunday." He chuckles. "Main trunk line between the border and White River Junction. Them little colored wires was a-twitching all over the hard top like snakes in a skillet. But that ain't the point of it; the noise wouldn't quit. When the si-reen struck the ground, she give out—well, she give out—it was kinda like a *hiccup*. But then she kept right on a-screeching like a banshee. Mister man, she was built *hard*." Tinker clenches his fists and everyone laughs.

"So I says, 'Tinker, get the pumper truck.' The pumper truck weighs fifteen ton, loaded. And she was loaded. I pulled her out into the dooryard and run over that sireen. Stove it all to hell. About time, too. My ears was hurting something fierce. Never did get the allen wrench. Generator's still broke. And Chief said he wasn't paying me nothing for tonight. Can you believe that?"

As Jiggsie laughs, his chair collapses under him. He flattens the wreckage against the floor and laughs even harder. People at the nearby tables turn to look at the commotion, smiling. Betsy gets another chair for Jiggsie. They sit back down and reach into the cooler under the table for another round.

Bodie hasn't spoken with Harmon since the afternoon. The others at the table sense the tension and talk around it, forming conversations that avoid a dialogue between them. Harmon keeps his arm around Darlene at the table and dances with her during the slow numbers, their feet hardly moving on the concrete floor. Betsy coaxes Jiggsie to the dance floor for a polka, which they perform with tiny steps and a kind of grace unique to very large mammals. Loretta won't dance. She and Bodie watch the others, occasionally holding hands under the tablecloth—cold hands, crisp and tentative.

According to custom, the band plays "Goodnight, Irene" at the end of the evening. Everyone knows most of the lyrics; they stand and lock arms and sing, loud and raucous, swaying in three-quarter time. The applause at the finale is aimed at no one in particular but is meant to record a good time. The overhead fluorescent lights come on and a garish green pall breaks the spell like a slap. Chairs scrape the floor, coats are put on and Taylor starts packing his drums. On the way out, shuffling along with the crowd, Bodie holds back, avoiding his brother. But when he glances up to measure the distance between them, he catches Darlene looking at him.

Harmon leaves in twelve hours. Bodie breaks away from Darlene's gaze and steers Loretta toward a side door.

In the truck, Loretta slides across the wide seat next to Bodie; their hips and shoulders almost touch. Bodie keeps both hands on the wheel.

"Wasn't Tinker something?" Loretta says. "I can't believe he's *my* brother. Didn't you think he was funny?"

"Yeah."

"He played great."

"Good picking."

"He's so funny."

"Definitely."

"You never know what he'll do next. You remember the Cadillac?"

"The yellow convertible?" Bodie remembers. Tinker bought it years ago when, at sixteen, he married a girl named Sharon-Ann Deveaux who appeared to be pregnant. For a wedding present, her parents gave them a half-acre lot and a house trailer. After a year of marriage and no baby,

Tinker and Sharon-Ann decided to sell the trailer and use the proceeds for a down payment on a real house. Meanwhile, they would live with her parents. Tinker towed the trailer to a mobile home dealer in Burlington, who gave him forty-five hundred dollars in cash. On his way back to Pike, he stopped for a few beers, then at a used car lot where he traded his truck and four thousand dollars for a yellow Cadillac convertible. A Florida car, the salesman told him. Never seen road salt. When Tinker cruised into the Deveauxs' driveway with the top down and honked, Sharon-Ann screamed obscenities at him he had never heard. Her parents helped her file for a divorce the next day. "Yeah, I remember it. Your brother's something else."

"What's wrong?" Loretta asks.

"Nothing."

"You're sure?"

"Long day. We was up at a quarter to daylight. Hunted deer all over. Guess I'm tired."

"I'm sorry you didn't have any luck."

"It's not all luck." But Harmon got his, Bodie thinks, a twelve-point monster, too. At least he didn't play it up at the Sportsmen's Dinner. At least he acted halfway modest— even though everybody knew about it by the time dessert was served, all the drama, every detail of the kill. Harmon never mentioned the quarter mile before the truck. No one saw the damaged hide, scraped clean of fur where Harmon dragged it through that long last section. It must have been hard, but Harmon would have done it even if the deer had weighed a ton. "Some of it's luck, the rest is . . . I don't know, the rest is knowing how to think like a deer thinks and then outsmart him."

"You're smart," Loretta whispers, putting her hand on Bodie's shoulder. "You're smarter than anyone I know."

Bodie winces at her compliment; her praise makes him uneasy. He knows how little he praises her—how little he finds, in the end, to admire enthusiastically. Her praise leaves him in debt, a debt he has no means of setting. And as for smart, he disagrees: he wasn't smart enough to find the stag before Harmon did, not smart enough to shoot it first and walk out on the front end of that maple pole.

On the way across the bridge, Bodie holds his breath and looks up instinctively at the arches, imagining the wooden platform inside the apex. Loretta plays with the radio, pulling in a Cincinnati station through the impeccable midnight sky. His silence means he won't stay with her tonight. She knows that, he is certain. His silence is one of those signals, long ago agreed upon without ever having been stated; it saves them from questions that might destroy the claim they have on one another. It preserves the fragile union neither would have envisioned when their courtship began. How had it begun? In a way, it really began in Tinker's Corvair, it began because Bodie felt somehow responsible for Harmon's misuse of Loretta.

Tonight will be another night of trying to make up for Harmon—by *not* staying with Loretta. Bodie has made love with her few enough times to remember each occasion perfectly, and what colors each memory is the pushing and pulling of two different instincts: compassion and guilt. Neither emotion, it occurs to him now, makes him eager to repeat the experience. Neither emotion makes up for his brother. The sad embraces, the hard dry kisses, the quietly closing door make it only worse.

He drops Loretta off and drives toward the bridge but dismisses the temptation to stop and climb up to his sanctuary. Without knowing why, he feels in a hurry. He ignores the looming arches and the empty depot, and turns left at the stop sign. Heading south, he looks at the few remaining lights in the row of houses across the river. Bushways' is the next to last. A single bulb shows through the trees, the back-porch light left on for Tinker. Upstairs, Loretta must be in bed, pulling sheets and blankets up around her, seeking comfort. Bodie had watched her watching Harmon tonight at the fire station. She looked afraid. Not so much afraid of Harmon's presence, but more, it seemed, of his departure. She looked to Bodie as if she knew that something more than Harmon, some link, some delicate balance among their lives would also be leaving Catamount tomorrow. But it was only a look. Maybe she was just being Loretta. Bodie shifts his truck into high gear and listens to the sound of night speed.

The farmhouse lights shine across the valley pasture. Bodie can see the gable-end windows of the woodshed ell; Darlene and Harmon must be home. They've left the kitchen lit for him. They've left the floodlight on outside. A gray wash paints the barn's east end, the world behind is left to shadow.

He parks and walks into the house, turning lights out as he goes. At the top of the stair, Bodie's room is to the right. His windows look out onto the vegetable garden. Tomorrow morning, his room will receive sunrise first. Below him is Leon's room, to the rear of the house, and the unused parlor at the front. Pausing to look at the door to his left, Bodie imagines the room beyond, a duplicate to his, used for storage and for access to another room, where his brother and his brother's wife have lived since they were married. He hears the faint murmur of their voices, hears Harmon raise his voice in anger, then Darlene's reassuring murmurs. A silence follows. Bodie goes into his room, leaving his door open an inch. He lies down, fully dressed, and falls into a troubled sleep.

85

Leon's tinny alarm awakens Bodie long before the sun is up. He listens as the old man prepares himself for the day, hears the kitchen door close as Leon goes out to the morning milking. Too restless to sleep, too tired to get up, Bodie lies on his back staring into the black air around him. A mouse scratches at the lath behind the cracked plaster ceiling. Over in the barn, cows stir to Leon's presence. A rooster, crowing prematurely, makes Bodie smile. Then he hears slippered footsteps coming through the storage room and a door swung open. The light switch snaps at the top of the stairs and a yellow blade bisects his room. Darlene taps quietly on his door and asks in a whisper if he's awake, can she come in and talk. He whispers yes and she pushes the door open. Her silhouette seems huge in the door frame, all disheveled hair and housecoat. She snaps the light switch off behind her and closes the door. Her scent makes Bodie think of slept-on perfume, roses crushed by something heavy. She asks if she can sit on the end of the bed. Bodie slides over against the wall and lifts himself up on his elbows, looking for her.

"We've got to talk," she says.

The mattress sags away from him as she sits on the corner of the bed near his feet. "I know," he says. Of course. That was what her eyes told him at the fire station. His must have said the same to her. "It's been eating at me wicked bad."

"I never told him yes or no, that we didn't, you know, didn't do anything," Darlene says.

"I thought maybe you hadn't."

"Did you?" Darlene asks.

"Tell him? I couldn't. He'd never let me live it down. You know how he is."

"It's driving him crazy. Can I tell you something? You've got to promise you won't ever pass this on to anyone."

"I will. I mean, I won't. I'll keep it private, you can trust me."

"Last night, he was begging me to tell him and I almost did, but I kept thinking, I kept thinking about all these things he's done to me, how, one by one, he's taken away all the parts that make me feel like I'm a person." Darlene's voice squeaks against her tightening throat. "He begged me to tell him and I wouldn't and he, he started to cry. Don't ever tell I told you."

Bodie stares at the sound of Darlene's voice but sees nothing, not even an outline of darkest gray on black. He is certain she is weeping and imagines her wet cheeks and runny nose. The collar of her nightgown would be rumpled, her hair matted into her misery, damp against the nape of her neck. He feels the mattress jiggle as she finds a tissue and blows her nose. Perhaps she wipes at her tears as well.

"I won't ever mention it to anyone, I swear," says Bodie. He tries to make a mental picture of Harmon crying, and can't.

"He's had this dream. He's had it for a month now." Darlene gulps for breath. "He dreams he's in a cage. He's surrounded by guys he doesn't recognize. All of them in their own little cages. Prisoners. And to get free, you need to have your son come get you." She sniffs and blows her nose again. "The guards have all these papers to prove if it's your son or not. One by one, all the other guys are freed by their sons and he's the only one left. And he sees this boy walking back and forth, the only boy without a father, and the guards keep tearing up the boy's papers and laughing." Her voice breaks. "In his dream, he's dying in the cage. He wakes up soaking wet."

"Shit," Bodie says, barely audible. "You should tell him."

"I think about it all the time. I know I should. But then it turns into a bet with fate. Or God, maybe."

"A bet?"

87

"A bet about him coming back, about him getting killed." Darlene pauses for such a long time that Bodie wonders if he's imagined all this, if she is actually in the room.

"I don't know where I got it," she says, "but it seems so real. If he knows for sure he's the father, then his life would be complete. God could take him. But if he's still unsure, then his life would have to have another chapter. God couldn't let him die without knowing. He'd have to come back home and find out what was what."

"Then you'd tell him?"

"Then I'd have to." Darlene's whisper breaks into a feeble squawk.

"I don't know. It doesn't sound right," Bodie says. The part about God makes him uneasy.

"I know it sounds weird, but I keep thinking that if I tell him, he'll get killed. And it would be my fault."

"Yeah, but supposing he gets killed *not* knowing? Supposing your fate bet doesn't pay off?"

"I think about that, too. But there's other reasons not to tell him. You, for instance."

"I can handle it," Bodie says.

"And me. I need to keep some balance with him. I've got to keep something for myself. He uses up so much of me. This is the only hold I've got on him. He makes you be that way."

He makes you be that way, thinks Bodie. Isn't that the truth? "You're not the only one, Darlene. He's done that to me all his life. He has to have it all for him."

"So, should I tell him?" Darlene's voice breaks into a sob. The bed shudders with her.

"Telling Harmon won't make him die, if that's what's stopping you."

Darlene sniffs. "I can't," she says.

"Why not?"

"Because he'll think he's such a big deal. It's bad enough already. Listen, Bodie, I shouldn't tell you this, but that night on the bridge with you—it was better doing nothing with you than it ever was with Harmon. It's true, I mean it. Harmon hadn't touched me for weeks—maybe months—before that night. He hasn't touched me since. And here he wants to brag to all his friends, how he's a big bull stud and all."

"That's Harmon."

"I hope you didn't think I was a whore."

"No way!" Bodie says in a cracked voice. Whispering through this conversation suddenly seems ridiculous to him. He raises his voice. "I never thought anything bad of you, I swear. It was me that acted out of line. It scared me, that's all. I never thought of what we did as wrong."

"Shhh," Darlene whispers. "If he finds me here."

Bodie sits up in bed. A pair of rectangles begins to show faintly against the east wall, previewing the dawn to come. He can see Darlene's silhouette for the first time, the slumped outline of her head and shoulders. Her misery weighs enough to drive the end of the bed through the floor. He tries to remember her features, her handsome face, full lips and straight white teeth, high wide cheekbones—but her face won't come to him, won't fit this time and place.

He swings his legs over the edge of the bed and stands up, reaching for her. He finds her shoulder, her quilted wrap, and gently coaxes her to her feet. He pulls her to him, presses her belly against his. The awkward fusion bewilders them, the intimacy is as ambiguous as the twinship that both connects and separates them. She holds him tightly for a moment, then lets go.

"I'm going to name the baby Purdy if it's a boy," she

says, dropping her arms to her sides. "If it's a girl, I don't know, I haven't decided yet," she says. She turns away, suddenly hurrying to be gone, whispers good night and closes the door.

He hears her open the storage room door, close it behind her and then open and close the door to the room where Harmon is sleeping through the end of his last night in Vermont.

Bodie stares at the grid formed by the window muntins against the rising light. It is snowing. Flakes stick in lumps to the pine needles bobbing outside the glass. Each pane frames a different view of the scene beyond, twelve views per window, twenty-four views in all, each one focused on particulars of a landscape shared in common. That one's Harmon, that one's me and that's Darlene. Grampy and Mother are there and there. The muntins keep the panes apart, they hold the panes together. The muntins are like cages. Every view is inside its own cage. The scene outside doesn't care; the garden and the lawn, the barbed-wire fence and the pasture beyond—they go on whether anyone notices or not. Who looks through which windowpane, who lives in which muntined cage doesn't really matter.

He thinks about a day when he and Harmon were twelve years old, walking past Tatro's abandoned mill on the edge of the village. They'd passed the mill a hundred times, but that day something tempted them to twist the flimsy padlock off its hasp and sneak inside. The emptiness of the dusty rooms frightened them, encouraged them to act out some deliverance of their fear. On the second floor, facing the railroad tracks, was a large window. They smashed out every one of its hundred fly-specked panes. When the last of the shards had tinkled like icicles into the sumac below, they swung their clubs at the remaining muntins until their view was unobstructed, framed by one huge rectangle.

90

Running home along the dusty roads, Harmon pulled ahead when they reached sight of the farmhouse. He was standing on the doorstep, breathing back to normal, when Bodie arrived. Through some unspoken understanding, each knew the other would never mention the adventure to anyone. Additionally, Bodie knew that their secrets could no longer be shared but would belong to each of them separately, without the other's complicity.

Six

Leon feels itchy. It's quarter of eleven, but the ten o'clock bus to New York City is still somewhere between Montreal and White River Junction. Leon tells everyone it must be the snow; it's been falling all morning and there could be a foot or more up on the Groveland Heights. He's seen buses stuck in a lot less than that.

The bus station is located in a renovated section of what used to be the Junction Hotel lobby. The dispatcher sits behind the paneled front desk, reading. He tells Leon the lunch counter is closed on Sundays, tells him the only other bus due this morning came and left on time at quarter past six.

It makes Leon nervous, the way Darlene and Vera keep touching Harmon, adjusting this and that, smoothing a crease, picking a piece of lint from his uniform. Any excuse. Leon moves from chair to chair, as if he expects finally to find one comfortable enough. Bodie paces the edges of the high-ceilinged room, stopping short of an elderly couple at the far side of the lobby. The old woman reads a magazine and taps her feet. Her partner dozes, chin against his chest; his snoring is lost to the buzz from the portable heater at the dispatcher's feet.

When the Greyhound fails to arrive by eleven, Leon

announces he will wait in Darlene's Pinto. "Can't stand the heat of this place," he complains, and hurries to the car. Now he sits behind the wheel, studying his hands. This is the third time he has watched men called to war from Catamount, the third generation of Woodards waiting on hard seats in White River Junction.

At seventeen, Leon had volunteered for combat duty in World War One. His father, Bodeman Woodard, made no comment about his choice, but signified his approval by allowing the hired hand to drive Leon to the railroad depot in the fancy gig reserved for Sundays and special occasions. Bodeman never missed a day of milking.

Purdy's departure in '41 was different. Vera was pregnant with the twins and Leon's foot was in a cast. The week before, a tree he was cutting back-jumped and crushed his ankle against a stone. The railroad station was full of families they knew: Munroe, Dulac, Gandy, McAllister, Jeanrette, Bushway, Trombley, Martineau. They sent their boys with no regrets, rough-cut farm boys, scrubbed and eager, filled with dreams of glory.

The day is still clear in Leon's mind. He and Vera and Purdy had kept to themselves, in a corner near the stationmaster's office, while the other families milled about—some even singing victory songs to help relieve the tension. Vera and Purdy didn't say much to one another, but looked instead into each other's eyes—unblinkingly, for such extended periods of time that Leon felt embarrassed and alone, and envious.

Mindful of his father's meager efforts on his behalf a generation before, Leon was determined to convey his love to Purdy, a love made doubly large because of Esther's absence. But what he meant to say and what he said were not the same: "Purdy, you be careful, you're the only son I've got. I love you more than life itself, your death would

94

be the end of me." Words to this effect echoed back and forth in Leon's head and heart, strained to clear his lips full force. But so great was the knot of fear and modesty across his throat that all he managed was: "Keep your head down, boy."

Leon despised himself for that. During the months following Purdy's departure, when no one knew where he was except that he was sailing into danger, Leon spent long hours after the evening milking in his darkened barn, alone with his regrets. During that time, his broken ankle healed awry and left him with a limp he carries still. Layers of calcium and fibrous tissue hardened around the twisted bone and stiffened him as if his wound were choked with all those heartfelt words unspoken. His bobbing gait reminds him still of Purdy at the train depot.

Esther? Hear me, woman. It's happening again, the time for words, and come to find out, I'm no better off than before. Another Woodard going off and me locked up with worrying. There's things I want to say to Harmon, but I can't spit up nothing. How I tried!

He brought him home a buck last night—twelve-point beauty. Feed us half the winter. I told him, him and me would skin it out this morning. Hangs there in the woodshed, Esther, weather's cold, it'll hang a week.

My idea was work and talk. Planned an hour, maybe more, before he'd need to clean up, pack his clothes and drive down here—this miserable hotel bus station. Bus is tardy, so I come out to Darlene's car to meditate the situation. Esther, I don't want to let that boy go—like Purdy went—without my making plain my heart. I got a lot to say inside, but it gets stuck. Never sees daylight.

I tried, while we skun out that buck. But I had trouble coming around to say—you know—to speak it out. It ain't the same as Purdy, Esther; he meant all the world to me. Purdy was—another Leon Woodard, only younger. But, crimus, I don't mean to talk down Harmon.

Esther, hear me, how I sputtered. Discombobulated all my words. He looked at me like I was mental! There I stood, carrying on like a christly fool. I wisht I'd had a lever bar to pry the words out. How they jimmie-jambed acrosst my voice box. Felt as how I'd choke, and all the while my stove-up anklebone a-pounding like a skin-head drum. Can't call it nothing but craven, Esther. Every time I'd have the words laid out I'd see a picture—Harmon dead and wet with blood. Me, I'm standing next to him, trying to explain, but there's no words, like the TV on with the sound switched off.

I don't know if I can say it, say the word I hope to sweet Jesus is what I mean, is what I feel. I can say other words. I can say: this is Darlene's automobile. *I can say* automobile. *And radio and candy bar and comb and mittens and Bodie, there. But I can't say love. I know, I said it to you just now, but I can't say love—out loud. How come? I know you're asking, Esther, hear me. Truth of it is, I don't know.*

You think if I say words out loud where no one's listening I could get the habit of it? It would be like doing lessons. Been so long—I know, I know, I'm acting foolish, but I could try.

*Love. I said it. Love? Out loud. Shh! No one's listening—love— love—*love. *I said it, Esther, did you hear me? I said love out loud. Again, here—*love—*I done it loud that time. Trailer truck drove by and didn't even look. Here. Love, love—*love! *. . . There, Esther.*

How I wish I had the backbone, to stand up, say it to his face. Say, Harmon, I love! *you. Just stand right there and tell him. Harmon, I* love! *you from my* heart!

You see this woman walking to her car, Esther? Looks like a Dulac, but I ain't sure. Parked behind me, going to pass right by my window. I'll set here and practice. Love! *She's coming, Esther,* love! *A loud one.* Heart! *If she was Harmon, I could roll the window down and say it to his face.*

In the bus station, Bodie listens to his brother speaking

and wonders if he should do his best to concentrate, to try and remember every detail, every gesture. Save them as mementos.

"Thanks for breakfast," Harmon says to Vera. "I never had a steak so big. The muffins were the best I've tasted."

"Darlene made the mix."

"It's the double butter and brown sugar," Darlene says. "We wanted you to remember what the cooking's like at home."

"I don't imagine the mess hall's going to spoil me on that account," says Harmon. "I'd sooner eat hog slop than some of what they dish out down at Dix. Probably even worse in 'Nam."

"You remember your envelopes and writing paper?" Vera asks. Bodie hears her asking if Harmon is going to be all right. She strokes Harmon's cheek, brushing away some invisible blemish. "And the picture album?"

Harmon looks as though he doesn't hear her, but he nods his head as if he did. Bodie watches him turn to Darlene, searching her face. She returns Harmon's gaze with the blank expression she seems to show a lot of lately. The skin around her eyes and lips is rosy brown with pigment, an emblem of her pregnancy and a challenge to Harmon's lack of faith. Darlene's strength is appealing, even Harmon must see that. If only it didn't exclude Harmon, Bodie thinks, if only Harmon could enjoy it. She's beautiful, Bodie reminds himself. She'll wait for him, I know she will, she'll stick by him to the end.

When Darlene finally smiles at Harmon, Bodie looks for ambiguity but finds none. She's sincere, she means that smile, at least she's not holding back that part of her. And then, in a terrifying moment, he sees her as Harmon must: a familiar stranger armed with information he will never possess. He must be begging her to tell him the kid is his.

97

Bodie paces back and forth beside the steamed-up windows. For the tenth time in an hour, he looks at the filling station up Route 5. Red and green banners are strung between the gas pumps and the Esso sign; they frame a view of the highway beyond. In the foreground, sitting in Darlene's Pinto, Leon clears the windshield with his palm; for an instant, Bodie thinks Leon is waving to him and waves back.

At breakfast, Bodie wished he'd ignored Harmon's remark the day before and helped him carry his deer all the way to the truck. All through the meal he looked for an opportunity to make it right. He offered to help skin the animal. He asked about the bus schedule, how long the trip would take, joked about bringing the whitetail's heart and liver back to Pomeroy Johnson. Harmon was polite but showed no interest, preferring to compliment the women on the cooking, making a point of being pressed for time. But after his third cup of coffee he changed his mind.

"Hey, Bodie, come to think of it, you want to go out and see where I've staked out for the house? Grampy, can you wait a few minutes? I want to make sure Bodie knows where it's going and all. Don't want to come back and find it up by the cabin, on top of the knoll."

Bodie winced as Darlene looked at Harmon. He could see that last night's conversation was still on her mind as he answered sure, he'd go, and swept a glance past Darlene that was meant to reassure her. He wouldn't tell, she could be sure of it, just as he could be sure that Harmon would give it one more try.

Harmon had put on his heavy winter coat and his cowboy hat. Ordinarily, Harmon thought nothing of standing in a blizzard in his shirt sleeves; cold meant nothing to him. That he had bundled up so purposefully made Bodie realize this would be more than a quick look at four stakes in the ground. Bodie left the house determined to make things better between them in whatever way he could—except for answering questions about the night with Darlene on the bridge.

They walked single file from stake to stake. Their footprints marked the four walls like a full-scale blueprint in the falling snow. The front door would be over here, the kitchen on the corner. The driveway would come over there. Someday, they would build a garage, connected to the house by a breezeway where they would sit on summer nights and watch the sun go down. Bodie was invited.

Harmon talked about digging out the basement, where to put the excavated earth, how to run the footing drains and shape the finished grade to keep the water pitched away from the building. He pointed out the flat area downslope from the house where the leaching bed would be constructed. He waved a line through the air indicating the route the buried water line would take—straight from the old house, tapped into the gravity-fed line from the spring on the hillside above. Electric and telephone lines would be strung to the west gable end, follow the rake and drop down to a meter outside the kitchen door. Bertram Tessier at Monarch Mobile Home Sales had all the dimensions Bodie would need to make the foundation a perfect fit for the double-wide.

"I appreciate your doing this for me," Harmon said— quickly, as if to discharge his thanks as painlessly as possible. "You know I would of had it done myself." And Bodie thought to himself, yes, I know you would have, I'm surprised, in fact, you didn't, but I'll do it, sure, I'll do it, and I'll do it right, you know I will. For that, you trust me, don't you? For that, you don't have any doubts.

"The goddamned bank is supposed to let Darlene know this week. Been dragging their feet for over a month. When they say go, you go, OK? She'll have the money. Soon's the cellar's done, they'll put the home on it and she can move right in."

They had stood there in the blowing snow—what—three hours ago? Stood there hunched against the wind, hands in pockets, side by side, each looking at the stiff brown stalks in the vegetable garden sticking through the cold white blanket, each knowing the other was thinking of Darlene, living alone in her brand-new double-wide. Harmon had pawed the snow with his boot, making ruts and smoothed-out areas with his sole. Bodie had stared at the fence line, counting barbs on the wire as far as the snowflakes would allow.

The long silence before the inevitable question had come. Harmon had finished his arm waving. As usual, the landscape would be altered to suit him. Bodie had listened, recording each alteration step by step, waiting for the threshold. And finally, with all the allowable pauses and fragments of silence dispensed with, the threshold appeared and demanded crossing.

"Goddamnit, Bodie, why the hell won't you tell me the truth?" Harmon had said suddenly, looking squarely at Bodie for the first time. And Bodie had answered with what he'd rehearsed, a question of his own: "What makes you think it's not your kid? You were with her that night, you told me yourself."

"But I gotta know if you were, too. I got to!"

At other times, there would have been a fight; Harmon would have swung on Bodie and they would have poked and jabbed and rolled on the ground until it hurt too much to carry on. But this time it was different—they both knew it. This time neither could win.

"You wouldn't believe me if I told you. You're going to

100

have to assume it's yours." Bodie had started off toward the house. He had finished his part of the conversation. Harmon trailed him and tugged at his arm.

"What about Tinker? Was he nosing around here?"

Bodie studies the condensation on the bus station window. It gathers into droplets, swells into larger drops and finally slips in quickening streaks down the glass to the soggy sill. Behind him, he hears Harmon describing to Vera how his paychecks will be sent to Darlene, what his wages will be if he gets promoted. He sounds like a reasonable person. It seems impossible that he could have raised suspicions about Tinker. This is crazy, Bodie thinks; but Harmon would be suspicious no matter what happened.

' The flags at the Esso station look like a finish line, but when the bus appears in the distance at five after eleven, it appears to be in no hurry. It moves toward them slowly, like an uninspired long-distance runner more impressed with the scenery than the heat of the race. This is the bus that sets the future in motion, Bodie thinks. This gung-ho GI brother of mine, those old folks over there. Where are they going? The bus doesn't care; for the price of a ticket, it will take them away.

During this week of Harmon's furlough, Bodie has tried to look for signs that might convince him how the dice will roll. He looked for signs from nature: If I see a nuthatch before I see another crow, that will mean Harmon will be OK. And he saw a nuthatch, then two more—and never saw a crow for hours. He looked for signs along the road: If we get to the bridge before that truck, Harmon will be safe. They beat the truck to the bridge by a couple of car lengths. He looked for signs in his doughnuts, in his shoelaces, in his shaving cream: If I clean this last patch of shaving cream off my face with one pass of my razor—that will mean

Harmon's whole unit will be wiped out—no survivors. And he studied the fluffy white patch very carefully. A thin stripe along the sides might mean a few survivors. Maybe Harmon would be one of them. He measured—and drew the razor down. His skin was clean. Nothing left! The whole unit, wiped out!

Another time—at the supper table—pouring milk from a big ceramic pitcher: If the milk runs over the top of the last glass, Harmon will drown in Viet Nam. If the pitcher runs out partway to the top of the last glass, he'll swim away to safety. The pitcher gave its last drop with a quarter of an inch remaining to the rim on Leon's glass.

By these accounts, Harmon was to live or die, but none seemed as convincing as the first one, the sign no one was looking for.

With Harmon away at boot camp and the ground freezing up, Jiggsie had decided to start his logging operation early. He had contracted to harvest pine and hemlock from a woodlot on the Blood Brook Road in Quinntown. They would finish Simon's house in the spring.

Bodie cut and limbed. Jiggsie ran the skidder, wheeling the huge machine to wherever Bodie was cutting—waiting while Bodie hitched his choker chains around the butts. With four or five logs attached, he'd winch the bunch in tight against the skidder's log arch until the cable creaked taut against the spool. Then he'd take off, bashing his way through stumps and pulverized slash down to the landing. Each couple of days a logging truck would haul the logs away. It was at the landing that Bodie saw the sign he didn't like to think about.

Harmon had spent his first day home from boot camp around the house with Darlene and Vera. On the second morning, he took his deer rifle and drove to Quinntown, intending to stop at Jiggsie's job to say hello—then hunt the ridge toward Marsten's Gore, away from the sound of the loggers. It was unusually warm when he got to the landing; he could hear the saw and skidder in the distance and decided to wait for Jiggsie and Bodie to come back to their pickups for lunch. He rummaged around behind the seat in his truck and pulled out an old pair of coveralls. He spread them out on the ground, and, using his hard hat for a pillow, took a half-hour nap in the sun.

The sound of the skidder approaching awoke him. He got up and walked over to Jiggsie. They talked for a while and then Harmon left, heading north, on foot, through the woods with his rifle. Jiggsie went back to the woods for another hitch and brought Bodie with him to the landing at noon.

A huge truck was being loaded with logs when they arrived. They greeted the driver—Stub McDermott from Felchville Corners—and ate their lunch in the sun on the tailgate of Bodie's pickup. They watched Stub performing, perched atop the big blue GMC, working the levers, guiding the giant hydraulic claw that loaded the conifers thirteen feet high on the truck. The last log on, a foot across at the butt, rolled over the top of the bunk stakes and off the far side of the truck, out of reach. Stub looked down at Jiggsie for direction and Jiggsie waved "forget it." Stub cinched his load and took off for the mill. It was a few minutes after he'd left that they noticed the body.

Or so it had seemed. Harmon's forgotten coveralls and hard hat had been hidden from view when Stub was loading. When the last log fell off the top of the pile, it had landed dead center on the outstretched garment and crushed the hard hat into jagged pieces. The force of the impact had driven some of the clothing into the soft ground and flipped one trouser leg up over the log so that it looked as if it contained a leg.

Jiggsie and Bodie saw it in the same instant. Later, they agreed they both thought it was Harmon. The red plastic hard hat looked like a broken skull. Jiggsie rolled the log aside and put the hat on Harmon's pickup, a grotesque hood ornament, meant to be funny. Bodie didn't laugh. The dent in the ground made him think of a sunken grave, a troubling sign that won't go away, even now, a week later, in the White River bus station.

Looming close to the window, the bus darkens the waiting room like an unexpected stormcloud. Everyone is suddenly standing; they all gather their possessions and feelings, positioning themselves for the departure. The dispatcher mumbles a garbled message. A few weary passengers disembark from the bus, pulling the depot doors open, shuffling into the room looking lost.

The old couple is eager to get on the bus. They crowd their cardboard suitcases onto a chair near the door and squeeze through at the first opportunity. They're in a hurry, thinks Bodie, they're running out of time. They know where they want to go, and they don't want to miss it. They're Grampy's age. He's never liked buses

Harmon throws his duffel bag into the luggage compartment under the bus and turns to face his family. He hugs Vera first, stooping down to accept her kisses on both cheeks. Her hands cradle his head in one last protective caress. She says I love you, you be careful. We need you back here soon as possible. Her voice cracks but she goes on anyway; tears in her eyes. She asks him to write, tells him to eat healthy food and reminds him he can telephone collect anytime, day or night. He's nodding yes, and sure, I will, pulling back from her in confusion, reaching for Darlene. He gives Darlene a violent hug. His overcoat gets in the way. She grimaces, then kisses him on the lips. He pulls away too soon and tells her good-bye, Sugarpuss.

He stands at the bottom of the steps to the bus. His family watches; snow falls between them. He winks at Darlene and says he hopes it's a boy. He starts up into the bus and remembers Bodie, who moves forward and fumbles an arm over Harmon's shoulder, squeezes him roughly, tells him good luck. Their eyes never meet. Harmon starts up the steps again and stops. Where's Grampy? All of them, at the same instant, turn toward the Pinto.

Leon sits with both hands on the steering wheel; his head and shoulders are moving up and down as if he were driving a bumpy back road. His lips are moving, pronouncing the same words over and over. He grins like an innocent baby, and holding the steering wheel tight with his thumbs, waves with his fingers his grandson's good-bye.

Darlene searches for Harmon through the dark-tinted glass, but each mirrored window is faceless. For all she can tell, the bus could be empty and driverless. It rolls away powerfully through the snow. She waves at the heartless rear window; the others watch with numb curiosity the thing that has taken Harmon away. Southbound on Route 5, it gains speed and diminishes at an inevitable rate until it's a whitened speck, dropping over the horizon.

Gone! Harmon is gone? The weight in Darlene's belly seems unbearable. She reaches for Vera and leans on her shoulder. She walks to the Pinto as if she were walking in wet cement. Her feet drag at her legs, pulling her to the pavement. She stamps her feet to set them free and splashes slush on the hem of Vera's coat. The snow in her face is so gentle it tickles. She looks at the pennants flying above the Esso station. They wave in the wind to the south, waving good-bye to a bus full of memories.

Leon wants to drive. "I'm taking us down to the Pepper Pot, everybody. Don't give me no argument, the treat's on me." He says it so amicably as to invite suspicion.

Darlene searches his face. His expression puzzles her; he appears younger, rekindled, fresher. His wrinkles are overwhelmed by his unusually rosy cheeks. He holds the steering wheel as if it were a precious new toy and announces he's going to order the welched rabbit with russell sprouts.

From the cramped backseat, Darlene holds Vera's shoulder. Vera reaches back and puts her hand over Darlene's hand. They are both thinking of Harmon—separate thoughts but similar, women's thoughts about men: Vera's include a pink baby Harmon, the wonder of his tiny penis, his male parts formed inside of her—include his father, Purdy, shining, chicken pox, pneumonia, clip-on bow ties, haircuts, buying sneakers, ringworm, milk mustaches, the tooth fairy, Christmases, bicycles, a dog named Stink, pies and cookies, 4-H ribbons, hair tonic, pimple cream, baseball games, fistfights, Band-Aids, car loans, late nights, and a wedding, bright with promise, filled with music from an accordion. Her vision orbits her discomfort, sparkling like a prismed chandelier above a muddied floor.

And though their hands connect them like sisters, Darlene sees another side, in monochrome, in shadow. She sees the creases to each side of Harmon's mouth, drawn down in pain the night before, lined with begging for a trust he never should have thrown away. The trouble is, he left too soon. Or much too late. Or he left with not enough. She is confused. Her belly is a stone, pulling her down in her seat. She squeezes Vera's hand and tries to think of Harmon smiling.

Bodie sits behind Leon, his head tilted back, looking up through the rear window. Snowflakes blur into a nervous galaxy, racing by the glass with frivolous energy. The Pinto hits a bump and bounces Bodie's head against the seat. He watches as the windstream changes; chaotic patterns beat against the window without purpose. Each flake, he thinks, is but one zillionth of the storm, one infinitesimal thread of the endless blanket that covers the land, that covers the road the bus travels down, that covers the sunken grave at the Quinntown landing, hiding it there until spring.

Bodie counts the tops of telephone poles, following the wires between them like the lines in connect-a-dot doodles he enjoyed as a child. The poles follow one side of the road and then, at a curve, or for some unknown reason, they appear on the opposite side. The sequence is random, one side, then the other; he watches for signs in the pattern. Six in a row—Harmon will be OK. Four, five, six. Six in a row—best out of three. Play it again, the poles disappear altogether. Here they are back again . . . Best out of three. The car slows down and pulls into the Pepper Pot parking lot at the ninth pole in a row.

"I'm going to have the Fisherman's Platter," Bodie says. The women look away. They have no appetite.

"Welched rabbit, that's my flavor," says Leon. "It's Harmon's favorite too."

Seven

Vera's northwest-corner bedroom is behind the kitchen. Both rooms are adjacent to the woodshed. The bed she sleeps in has no history; it belongs to whoever lives inside this room. It was only during her year with Purdy that Vera has ever slept in something wider, deeper and warmer. Their marriage bed is stored in dust up in the attic. For now, this narrow berth is adequate; this little room is room enough.

When she and Purdy married, Leon insisted they move into what had been his room, the room where he and Esther spent their too brief time together. On the southeast corner of the house, it was once the Sunday parlor. Daybreak lights the windows on the eastern wall; sunlight keeps the room alive all day. But, in that room, the stain of loss for Vera and her husband's father has tarnished any radiance that might ever gather there again. When, from time to time, she dusts the furniture and windowsills, Vera holds her breath until it seems that she will faint. With Purdy gone, the room became a parlor once again, a Sunday parlor in a calendar without a seventh day.

Across from Vera's narrow bed, against the wall that separates her room from Leon's, is a four-drawer maple chest. A cut-glass lamp and a clock below an oval mirror complete the room's furnishings. A shallow closet by the door holds Vera's clothes on wire hangers—plain cotton dresses, the colors faded pinks and grays with little prints of violets and forget-me-nots. Her shapeless flannel housecoat hangs on a hook inside the closet door.

The sound of Leon's rising awakens her. She looks at her clock—four thirty—and turns on the table lamp, gets up still half asleep.

Despite the cold, she stands by the mirror and stares at a photograph of Purdy and her, arms around each other against her father's Ford sedan. The tiny, two-dimensional figure of her husband returns her gaze with a light that warms her belly. She feels his muscular forearm against her hip, her buttocks press against the fender; his odor is all around her. His crew-cut hair, the small flat ears, his narrow nose and dimpled chin excite her. That throbbing neck, that narrow, T-shirted torso, the jeans without a belt, the skinny legs, the worn work boots—everything seems so poised and taut, spring-loaded with energy; his walking seemed more like dancing, sitting still was an agony for him.

And she, that girl beside the boy with secrets yet unaccounted for, she ignores the camera for the pleasure of his handsomeness, absorbs herself in him while some now long-forgotten friend lets light flood through an aperture and captures them in black and white, indelible, against her daddy's car. She wears a blouse, pure white it seems, and a full, dark-colored skirt. Her slender arms and calves are tanned, her nose and lips so delicate as to demand protection. The yellow hair, in natural waves, is pleated in a single braid. Her hand touches his chest as if it were a miracle.

Vera stares at the reflection of her nightdress in the mirror, feeling Purdy's gaze upon her. She stands there for a moment more, shivering. For him. She runs her fingers through her hair, pulls it flat against her skull and shakes it loose. Thirty years ago she'd made Purdy blush when he first saw her hair down.

She listens through the wall as Leon coughs and mutters. Purdy's face in the photograph is the last thing she sees before she turns out the light. Back in bed, beneath the patchwork quilts she lies face down with hands between her legs and listens to the electric clock, its steady turning round and round like some familiar animal in raspy, easy sleep. In little waves, each revolution brings the night back in—and with it come the dreams that lay down clues for her to follow.

Vera awakens a second time at half past five. Outside, it is still dark, but this time she will rise and dress, fill the wood stove in the kitchen and begin preparing breakfast. By the time Leon comes in from milking, the house will smell of coffee and sausages, and dawn will fill the windows with the cold yellow light of winter.

Since the first storm of the winter—on the day that Harmon left—it has snowed at least once a week, so that now, in late January, only the tops of the fence posts show. In leeward gullies, drifts lie deep enough to bury a standing man. The snow has simplified Catamount's rugged topography; shaggy hedgerows, eroded gullies, incidental scrub and rocks—all disappear beneath the seamless white, blown smooth across the landscape.

North of Woodards' garden patch, four wooden stakes describe the corners of a rectangle. The tops are bleached raw gray with weather. Temperatures to thirty below have split the moisture-laden fibers; microscopic particles of ice open cracks along the grain. Four feet below, the tips are held secure in soft dark soil, frost-free, insulated by the snowy mantle above.

It is Monday morning, and signs point toward the three-day January thaw to follow: icicles along the overhangs drip freely, even on the north side eaves. Slush, mixed in with the year's first mud, molds Leon's footprints by the milk house steps. Vera hangs a wash without her mackinaw and mittens on. Her clothesline runs from the woodshed door to an elm tree halfway across the yard. The path she uses to reach the line connects the house and barn. She slides along like a skating boy, pulling a wicker basket behind her on the hard-packed snow. By habit, she hangs the wash in a specific pattern known only to her. The clothes are layered in the basket to make the sequence come out just so. Leon's clothes are on top; they go up first, nearest the house. His overalls, his shirts and pants—dark green cotton, salt 'n' pepper worsted wool—hang heavy on the line. His once-white union suits and socks hang drab against the brilliant snow. They flap and twirl Bojangle feet, dancing without Leon in the breeze. Darlene once embarrassed him with a pair of red long johns for Christmas. He keeps them in their original box, hidden on the top shelf in his closet.

The space on the clothesline next to Leon's once belonged to Purdy. It took some years before that space was used again; the line was long enough to leave it blank. No one had ever wondered at the gap. From her kitchen window Vera felt consoled to see that stretch held in reserve; someday clothing would hang from end to end again, unbroken.

In time, the twins took over Purdy's space. Harmon's clothes replaced his father's first; Bodie's were the next in line. Since Harmon's departure in November, Vera has left a space—one bedsheet's length—between Leon and Bodie's laundry. Today, for reasons she won't think about, she hangs the last of Leon's socks, and next to them—without a gap—puts clothespins on a pair of Bodie's trousers.

The clothes smell good. Still warm, they soothe her fingers as she lifts them to the braided rope. She squints against the winter sun; its unfamiliar brightness warms her face. She finishes Bodie's section with a pair of jockey shorts and pulls a pair of Darlene's panties from the basket. She hesitates, then pins the panties several spaces to the right and hangs a sweat shirt, Darlene's favorite, upside down in the space between.

Darlene's maternity dresses billow on the line like gaudy mainsails, grand against the little pastel flags that fly from Vera's modest row. Hers has always been the last, the farthest from the house. Only Darlene knows that Vera's "underthings" are dried on a wooden rack inside her bedroom.

Vera knows that Leon makes no distinction among the pieces hung along his path to the cowbarn. She wonders if he likes the savory washday scent slapping out at him when sudden gusts poke laundry in his face. Every day, his clothes accumulate a layer of mud and dung; it comes with doing what he does. Once a week, Vera scrubs them clean and folds them neat, in fragrant rows inside his dresser drawers. He grumbles that she does too much, he'd wear his clothes six months, he says. "Crimus, Vera, where's my socks? I barely had 'em broke in good."

In anticipation of the thaw, Bodie has arranged to dig the cellar hole today. After weeks of inaction, the bank finally approved Harmon and Darlene's mortgage and set up an account to pay for the foundation and site work. Bodie left this morning after breakfast to borrow Jiggsie's backhoe. Snowmelt runs along the roadside ditches as he drives it down from Catamount, splashing waves of slush aside from dips between the frost heaves.

At the corner of the house, he digs into the snowbank. Weeks of plowing have formed a frozen wall around the dooryard. With the shovel at the front of his machine, he scoops into the snow, backs up and dumps it to one side. Four feet at a time, he makes his way across the lawn, around the garden to the corner stakes of the house-to-be.

He clears the area within the rectangle, then clears another fifteen feet around to provide maneuvering room. The cleated tires churn the soft earth to mud. Green grass—dormant under the season's snowfall—turns brown in the soupy mix. As he works, the tractor's engine echoes off the farmhouse wall as if to double his accomplishments.

He turns the tractor seat around and faces the knobbed levers that direct the backhoe mounted to the rear of the vehicle. With these eight levers he operates a juggernaut. He begins to dig. A cupped hand fixed to a giant outstretched arm gathers its crumbled payload like a patient, famished beast. Again and again, the arm extends and claws its way back across the cut until it comes up full. Bodie shifts another lever; hydraulic fluid forced against a piston swings the steel boom sideways. Another lever, another piston trips the bucket and dumps the load. The growing piles of fresh brown dirt are fringed with coffee-colored snow.

It will take six hours to dig the hole. Bodie works the bucket as if it were an extension of his body. The levers in his hands move automatically. He choreographs the beast so well his mind is free to wander; he digs a cellar hole while excavating thoughts of Harmon.

The morning after Harmon left, Bodie ate breakfast with Vera before going to work. "What'd you do, Mother, paint the kitchen? It looks different in here."

Vera shrugged and looked around. "I washed the windows, week ago Friday. But there's been no fresh paint in here since you were—what—about ten years old?"

Bodie studied the walls and ceiling, counted the windows, checked each shelf and cupboard, curtains, chairs, appliances. All were there, accounted for, but the house had taken on a new dimension.

Five tungsten carbide teeth across the bucket's biting edge scrape hard against a rock. The friction produces a noise like chalk against a blackboard and a little puff of dust arises for an instant behind the teeth. The rock will be the size of a hay bale, one of several glacial erratics encountered in the hole. Bodie paws at its edges, determining its size and shape. He works the dirt around it and exposes all four sides. Then, reaching to the far side, he wedges the bucket underneath like a spatula and drags the boulder toward him, lifting it out of the hole, back from the edge, out of the way.

Darlene invites her girl friends over three or four times a week. They play cards and cribbage in the kitchen, laughing, joking in a way they haven't done since high school. Leon teases her more each day, flirting impishly with her friends—even pinching Betsy's bottom as she leaves one afternoon. And Bodie—Bodie feels as if he's breathing fully for the first time in his life.

The rock is gone, the hole gets bigger and the digging goes on. Along the west side of the excavation, near the house, the digging has left a plumb-cut wall, a graphic cross-section of geologic time. At the surface is a foot of dark loam. Two feet down it thins out, turns pale and sandy. Root hairs hold the grainy grit together in knotted clumps. Next comes a thick horizon of orange nuggets—water-washed gravel and pebbles running in a perfect horizontal band. A glistening drip falls freely from the seam. Below the gravel, extending down to bedrock far below, dense hardpan slows the digging, strains the diesel's power train. The dripping water forms a growing puddle on the hardpan. Bodie thinks of footing drains, the perforated pipes that will gather water at the basement's perimeter and lead to daylight down the slope below the garden. "Goddamned hardpan," Bodie grumbles, "it's made so tight it's just like clay."

He decides to dig the hole a foot deeper, then cover the bottom with a pad of crushed stone, a porous cushion that will allow groundwater to find its way to the drains. Harmon would like that; it will keep his basement dry. It will keep Darlene's basement dry is more to the point. She'll have a washing machine down there, maybe a freezer and a wall of shelves for mason jars, full of fruits and vegetables from the garden. She'll come down wooden steps onto a concrete floor and do her wash, perhaps her ironing and sewing too—bring the baby with her.

The basement should be dry for her—and warm. A wood stove could do the trick. Or, if they use a hot-air furnace, they could open up a duct or two and make the place toasty. The baby would be in a crib at first, then toddling, walking, running, taking the bus to school. Then a teenager. Maybe playing Ping-Pong down here, maybe playing one of those tabletop ice hockey games. Friends would come over after school and Darlene would make sandwiches for them—snacks on a tray with glasses of cider, brought down to the basement for the kids. The dry basement. Dry because it was built on a pad of crushed stone, because the hole was dug a foot deeper.

Every half hour or so, when he's dug all he can reach, Bodie moves the tractor and begins another section. All in all, he'll move eight times: four positions on each long side of the sunken rectangle. At each new location he begins as if he were beginning another room in the house-to-be, another chapter in his brother's life. The rooms are filled with imaginings of Darlene and the unknown child (whose sex and age seem endlessly variable in Bodie's contemplations), but rarely is Harmon among the players. He stays instead in chapter after chapter of a tale too new to be concluded. The chapters labeled Harmon bubble up without chronology; they assume no logic, none of the compelling story told by layers of sediment uncovered with the backhoe. How clear an account, how dependable a record is kept when time allows the telling: gravel-laden glacial melt washed over lakebed sediment, wind and sunlight, water, plant life—aeon's worth, but steady, steady!—ending with the final foot of topsoil, a thousand years in the making.

Bodie hits another stone, a smaller one, and wonders what the day was like when gravity and ice abandoned this round erratic on its side. Was the valley still unformed? Was it a lake? How cold was it? Vegetation? Animals? Wind, rain, snow, sun? Those parts would remain unknown. How the boulder got there—that question pleases him.

Harmon's story changes with each memory Bodie calls upon. The backhoe's scrape against another boulder stirs an image of the Catamount Grange Hall, Fourth of July, 1954. Harmon and Bodie were twelve years old and spending hours every afternoon up inside the bridge arch. Scores of pigeons nested there, and soon the boys devised a way to catch them. Blocking off all but two of the portals with hen wire, they made up a pair of sliding trapdoors which they connected to a rope strung down to the road-level door. When the rope was pulled, the trapdoors slid into place and the pigeons could not escape. The boys would then climb up inside—one from each end—and catch the birds in bran sacks, held wide open in the eerie light.

That Fourth of July they caught ten birds, six in one sack, four in the other. At first, the pigeons beat their wings against the burlap, furious to be free. But within minutes they lay limp, each a feathered deadweight inside the dusty bags. As he crawled down the arch to daylight that day, Bodie felt the terror of a tiny heartbeat ticking like a racing clock against his palm.

They planned to let the birds go at the Grange Hall Bingo game. They'd sneak in the back and shoo the birds in through the kitchen door. The old ladies would have a fit.

The day was hot, but the trip was short and the birds performed their parts to the desired effect. Bodie's bag was emptied fast, but one pigeon remained in Harmon's sack, stuck or sick or terrified. In any case, it wouldn't fly loose and getaway time was running out. The boys jumped off the back steps and ran into the woods, delighted with the chaos they had left behind. When they stopped, out of breath and giggling behind a huge oak tree, Bodie gestured to Harmon's bag and asked why don't you let it go now. Harmon grinned and swung the bag like a baseball bat—swung it like Ted Williams punching a homer out of Fenway Park— swung it against the tree trunk at a hundred miles an hour. That sickening sound, that hollow *pock* that ruptured every living bird cell trapped inside the twisted sack, comes rifling back. The tungsten-carbide tooth-on-rock sound pulls the image, random, pointless, back again. Bodie casts the rock out of the hole and buries it in the soft brown soil.

Where is Harmon in this house? Bodie can't place him in his imagination. He sees no shop, no table saw, no work-bench—no wall made up with pegboard hung with hand tools, snips and brushes. Up above, in the corner kitchen, dining and living areas—all across the southern wall— Harmon's only proxy is a shadow hovering over a coffee table, lacing up his boots on a bench by the kitchen door. In each vignette his head is hung down, his face averted and his body almost motionless. It could be Harmon. It could be someone else.

As the cellar hole takes shape—a clean geometry imposed upon a geologic order so profound as to belittle "perfect" corners, "perfect" distances between two points—Bodie sees the walls begin to form, sees them growing up from down inside the hole like some miraculous organism. He willfully builds them up and disassembles them again, telescoping in and out of each step of construction, making alterations and improvements as he goes.

In grade school, he and Harmon would spend rainy afternoons "styling" houses at the kitchen table. With their backs warmed by the wood stove and the cookie jar at hand, they drew their latest versions of the world's most sumptuous mansions. Inside-outside swimming pools, rooftop helicopter pads, indoor zoos, sliding boards from floor to floor, soda pop on tap in every room—they fixed in their pictures a life forever perfect, engraved with graphite pencils on a yellow paper pad.

Fixing life forever—does it happen short of dying? Bodie suddenly sees his brother stand smiling in the hole and wonders what is fixed about his life, about their lives, about the lives of those around them. Still smiling, Harmon nods to Bodie's bedroom window. Bodie turns and looks up. Darlene watches him through ancient glass. She moves her hand against her belly and steps back out of sight. He turns back to his brother and finds him gone. The cellar hole seems suddenly smaller, slightly out of square.

He moves the machine to the next position; in another hour, he'll have it done. He looks back at the empty window, then digs hard at the stubborn ground.

Harmon's smile seemed real just then, and with it came a sense of what—permission? Bodie inhales slowly. Traces of the image fade into the hardpan.

The smile was real. He stood there with his palms open

to Bodie, his body loose and easy. What was he wearing? Army green? Civilian clothes? The smile meant thank you? That much would be taken from it. What else? Was Darlene part of the mirage? He turns to look for her Pinto in the driveway—and there it is: dull steel shows through a dented fender where she slid on ice into a tree the week before. She wasn't hurt; he'd fix the dent—he'd keep her Pinto running right.

In high school, senior year, Bodie had gone with Tinker and Harmon for a ride in Tinker's "Combine," an International four-by-four pickup truck. They had driven to the Pikeland Heights, all back lots—paper company–owned and crisscrossed with old roads that every twenty years or so the loggers used for twitching timber. Tinker drove and Bodie sat a-straddle of the floor-mounted gearshift levers; Harmon rode shotgun with a six-pack in his lap, another on the floor between his feet.

The roads were muddy and rutted; water bars and boulders made the going slow. Brush had grown into the roadway, branches slapped through open windows, tugging at their elbows as they passed. Occasionally, they would stop and move a fallen limb from their path, drag it off into the trees. It was black-fly time and the poplar leaves were limp with pale green innocence.

Tinker carried his father's rifle—a thirty-thirty lever-action Marlin—on a rack across the truck's back window. On the dashboard was a box of ammunition, broken open, spilling out. When the ride got rocky, cartridges would tumble to the floor, landing in the clutter of rags and tools at Bodie's feet.

At the Mason Brook crossing, Harmon got out to check the depth of water and mud; even in four-wheel drive, they might not make it. But the adventure was welcome and the truck plunged in and somehow leapt out the other side, dripping like a water spaniel. The jolt spilled Harmon's beer into his lap and cleared the dashboard of its last candy bar wrapper. The next section of road—an uphill stretch through rocky terrain—was so washed out it became impassable.

"Mister, I never seen such sassy going," Harmon said.

"Bony enough for ya?" Tinker shouted. A hidden boulder bounced their heads against the roof liner. "I guess we turn this pup around." He started backing downhill to a turnout near the brook. It was then that Bodie saw the owl.

He'd seen them fly the woods like that in daylight, when they should be sleeping. They'd pick a path or a roadway and fly along it, under the canopy, ready to snatch a mouse or squirrel. Bodie spotted the bird coming down the hill toward their retreating truck at the same moment the bird spotted them; it pulled off to a landing in a rotted elm ten yards off the road.

"Look at that!" Bodie said, and as he did, he wished he hadn't. Tinker was out of the truck with his rifle loaded at the first glimpse of the owl. Two steps off the road put him in a perfect sight line with the blinking bird. One shot, aimed so quickly—how could he have done it?—one shot knocked the creature from its perch. It fell to the forest floor with a fluttery thud.

"Jesus Christ, man, that's an *owl!*" Bodie said, but Tinker never heard him.

Tinker and Harmon ran to the elm and knelt down over the bird. Bodie's feet refused to move; he watched them from the side of the truck. When Harmon yelled come see this monster, Bodie punched Tinker's truck squarely in the middle of the hood, turned his back and pissed on the muddy front tire.

Tinker returned holding the owl upside down by the feet. The pads between its talons were callused and cracked. Its body was huge; its wings hung out a foot and a half to either side, downy and white underneath. Bodie looked at Harmon and believed he saw embarrassment.

"You drive, Harmon. I'm going to hold him so he don't get ruffled. This old hoot-toot's gonna get stuffed." Tinker sat between the brothers and the ride back home began in silence. Mason Brook was recrossed without incident. Tinker talked to the owl. "Take you to the taxidermist. Set you on a white birch log on top of the TV. Two glass eyes. Varnished beak. Want some beer?" He offered it his open can and the owl began to fly.

Later, they decided the owl had been only stunned; the bullet must have passed just inside its feathers and grazed its head. Impact knocked it off the limb and the fall to the ground had left it unconscious. When it suddenly regained consciousness inside the cab, the owl was very much alive. It tried to fly out through the windshield.

Its wings clubbed Tinker's head, its talons ripped into his hands and arms as he tried to protect himself. Harmon stopped the truck; he and Bodie opened their doors and leapt out, leaving Tinker tangled in the gearbox levers, pinned to his seat. The flailing owl made awful sounds in its efforts to escape.

With both doors open, the bird soon darted out and flew into the woods. Tinker stumbled onto the road embarrassed and bleeding, feathers stuck to his curly hair.

"Sonofabitch, I don't believe it! Like to tore me to ribbons! Look what that sucker did to me!" He rolled up a sleeve and showed three gouges, thick red lines sliced across his forearms. "Tore right into the meat, he did." He stared at his arms as if they were strangers. "I don't believe it. He was supposed to be dead."

Bodie had looked at Harmon and seen a smile of relief. The owl was free! How unexpected to see his brother's tender mood. For the first time since the window-smashing spree at Tatro's mill, the potential of their brotherhood seemed possible again. When Harmon saw that Bodie had caught him naked, he glanced at Tinker, suddenly stone-faced, panicked that Tinker had seen it too.

Bodie swings a bucket load of dirt onto the growing pile. The owl is probably still alive—gliding through the woods on the Pikeland Heights. Tinker's pride is long ago recovered; his scars are likewise faded. Harmon's smile that day is exactly the smile he wore down in the hole these minutes past. It signifies what could have been, no more.

He thinks about the muddy truck, how Tinker traded it with blood stains and feathers still on the dashboard one week after the owl was shot. He hears the noise the Corvair made without its muffler. Tinker swapped even—the truck for the Corvair—at Doxie's used car lot in Jordan. And Harmon, how he shunned his old friend Tinker—wouldn't talk to him for weeks. Then, somehow, he had changed his mind—overnight, it had seemed—courted Tinker, charmed him, and borrowed his Corvair for a date with Tinker's little sister.

Tinker's sister—poor Loretta—only Harmon would ask to borrow her. In a single night—with Tinker's beagle dog Geronimo barking in the front seat—Harmon had attempted to make clear to Tinker and to brother Bodie that a sentimental gesture toward a goddamned owl was not a sign of waning manhood. And Loretta? She was the disposable part of his redemption. She would do what women do for men and never know what she was doing it for. Harmon would have seen to that.

Harmon and Loretta and a flock of pigeons, Harmon and

Loretta and a great horned owl, Harmon and Loretta and a barking beagle fly around the hole in an ascending spiral and break out in ever-widening circles in the sky. Bodie stops the machine and watches as the dream dissolves against the snowy hills in the distance. "What in hell was that?" he says out loud, and feels a tingle in his temples.

Bodie excavates the northeast corner last. From this position, he can look across the shallow valley toward the distant tree line where the bank drops down to meet the Jordan Center road. A January palette washes subtle tones against the patchwork white—pearly pinks and ambers tint the snow beneath the hardwoods. He looks up from his work from time to time to watch as airy purples gather under pine and hemlock at the edges of the open fields. Beyond the trees and light and shadow, he watches for a dark sedan approaching up the lane.

The corner he is digging will be under Darlene's bedroom. He takes a second pass at a section already done, tidying a few small clumps of dirt into a perfect plane. Morning sun will strike her room at the same moment it enters his. The same sunlight that warms her floor will warm his floor. As it climbs its arc toward noon and rises to the south—around the corners of both houses—its shadows in the hedgerows to the east will be identical from each of their windows. She will see what he saw from his room. Her light, her shadows—they'll look the same as his. She'd know what kind of day it was going to be as soon as he did: the mist, the fog, the snow, the rain—the "promise" days. Grampy calls them promise days because he says they promise to get better before they promise to turn bad all over again. Today is a promise day; the sun shines down as if there were no such thing as winter, no such thing as snow. And something else: in digging out these tons of earth another substance is removed: It comes up with the earth, like birds released—like owls and pigeons. Unearthed, freed, it flies away.

Behind the noise of the diesel engine, Bodie sings a song he learned in grade school. The song is about a duck and a mouse and a cat named Weethul. The refrain goes: The duck said, Mouse, I'll eat you up / You look so fat and gleeful / The mouse said no, you can't do that / I'm promised to a cat named Weethul.

With the tractor gone and the yard returned to quiet, Darlene opens the parlor door and walks to the window. Piles of earth surround the cavity that soon will be the basement beneath her home. The route of Bodie's backhoe all around the excavation is marked with chevroned ridges, geometrics in the slimy mud. The scene for her is part exciting, part confusing; all this chaos will resolve, she knows, in clean, dependable order. For now, she trusts that the gaping hole and all the mounds deployed around it signify a new beginning. She can't visualize the house, but understands it must begin this way.

Vera comes into the room and stands beside her. "Men," she says, "they love to move dirt. They never seem to like it where it is." She laughs and squeezes Darlene's shoulder. "He dug so fast . . . It looks just right. Can you imagine Harmon's face when he sees it?"

"It's what he always wanted. He was so happy when the bank called and told us the loan would go through. He kept saying, 'Now we got it, now we got it.' At first I didn't know what he was talking about. Remember that?"

"He was jumping up and down."

"Well, he was happy." Darlene bites her lip. "At least, I hope he was."

"No mail?"

"I checked. Just bills and third-class junk. I walked down at ten thirty, thinking this would be the day. It would have been perfect. The cellar hole started—and a letter—both on a sunny day. I stood beside the mailbox—hoping—for a long time . . . before I opened it . . . Didn't do any good."

"Maybe tomorrow."

"I hope so. I miss him much more than I thought I would."

"Let's go inspect Bodie's work up close," Vera says.

"You get your boots—I'll be right there." Darlene pulls the curtains closed.

Vera pauses at the door. "The last letter he sent you sounded good. He's safe. You know he'll watch his step. His letter made it sound OK."

"That was three weeks ago. Every night the TV makes it sound so bad. You heard about Bobby Martineau? Bobby barely graduated high school."

"Let's look at Bodie's sandbox . . ." Vera puts her arm around Darlene.

"They say he'll lose both legs."

"Now, shhh! Let's see if Bodie dug it right."

Looking down at the fresh-dug dirt, Darlene recomposes Harmon's last letter, searching in her memory for messages that weren't there. He'd talked about the weather, his buddies, his health—but nowhere did he mention fear or love, except in passing. The fear of love, the love of fear—the words tumble into the hole and lose all sense of meaning on the hardpan floor. "When I get back," he used to say. "When I get back" we'll such-and-such. "We'll finish the house, we'll get a new truck and drive to Montreal. Rent a hotel room and stay in bed all day."

His letters ended, "Love, Harmon." How inadequate, she thought. But when she tried to compose a fuller sentiment she stopped. "Love, Darlene," meant all of that confused affection she was filled with. More words would not (could not) express the frightened need she had for him.

"The kitchen's going to be right here," Darlene says. "Harmon told me I could have the cherry cabinets with black iron hinges. He's buying me a double wall oven . . . electric, with a self-clean cycle."

In a dirt-walled bunker in Viet Nam, her husband starts another letter:

Dear Darlene,

If only I had a picture of you.
Wish you were beautiful, the weather is here. Ha, ha! My buddy Sippy La Bombard told me that.

It was funny when he told me. Then he took two rounds in the neck and bled to death in my lap. I told him hang on, Medic's coming, hang on Sippy, you'll be all right. Sippy's blowing blood bubbles out of his nose and making awful animal sounds, trying to say something, probably funny.

Sippy, he was always joking.

They stuffed him in a body bag and loaded him in the Chinook. KIA travel bureau took him back to California.

Sippy transferred out. Not enough action, I guess. It's pretty peaceful here. Sometimes we play softball in the afternoons.

When we're not ducking fire from them little motherfuckers. Shoot you morning, noon and night, the bastards, they don't never sleep, too busy trying to blow you away.

Another buddy gave me a radio with a tape deck.

I took it off his bunk when he and eleven others ate the big one on a night patrol.

So I get to play some cool tapes every day. I got Merle Haggard, Tammy Wynette and The Supremes. Tell Jiggs I got an Elvis tape, too.

127

There ain't no fat guys here. Jesus, how these rations rot.

I'm in pretty good condition—for an old timer! Ha ha!

I keep taking pills for diarrhea. Can't sleep more than an hour at a time. I keep having nightmares. I'm up in the bridge with Bodie and the VC throw grenades in through the portals. They weld the doors shut and the grenades fly around and look like pigeons, but we never know which one is real, so we try to kill them all but they won't die, they just fly around us, waiting to explode.

Actually—now don't tell Mom, I got a little skin allergy, but they gave me some tonic for it. It's a little bit like ivy poison.

And a little bit like being skinned alive. My feet don't never dry. I swear I'm growing webs between my toes. Skin peels off. Underneath it's red and raw as beefsteak. Goes right up my anklebones. Sometimes, my socks are soaked with blood.

How's the weather over home? I bet you got some snow by now. Out here, it's rain and sunshine every day. I saw how they grow rice. Under water!

I'll never eat rice again. First day out here, I was under water eighteen hours, up to my neck in a flooded paddy. Bullets splashing all around me, water dyed red with buddies' blood. It smelt like shit and death rolled over. They can have this whole damned country.

They use these buffaloes for tractors. Tell Grampy his old John Deere one-lunger would outpull ten of these rinky-dink critters.

We shoot the fuckers just for giggles, just to ruin Charlie's day.

They got horns like western steers. Hey! We should try us some Buffalo Barbecue! I hope by now Bodie has begun the foundation. Tell me if my checks aren't coming, or if you need anything.

What am I going to send you from this rat hole?

I hope you're getting nice and fat with the baby. Cantrell, he's from northern Carolina, he's got six kids. He says we should name the baby Tiffanee (spelling?) Rose if she's a girl. I don't know. You do what's right. Still Purdy if it's a boy.

Some days I know I'll never see him and he'll never see me, so what's the point of naming him after me.

Or call him Bodie. Ha ha! Only kidding.

Bodie touches you, I'll kill him. Kill him or anybody else. Suits me fine. One thing I've learned: sometimes, I even like it.

Bodie gone up north yet? Tell him hello for me, and Mom and Grampy too. Don't worry about me, I'll be all right. And take care of yourself and the baby, Sugarpuss. Got to go now.

Love,
Harmon

Eight

It is the morning after Bodie dug the cellar hole. He is up at daylight preparing to lay out the footings for the foundation walls. With batter boards and strings in place, he squares up each corner with the traditional three-four-five triangle Leon taught him as a boy. (Once he understood it, the formula became one of those surprisingly reliable truths that seem too simple to be true—like pi in math class unlocking the secrets of a circle.)

Starting at a corner intersection of two strings, Bodie measures three feet in one direction and marks the first string with a piece of blue chalk. Next, he marks off four feet along the second string. With the "three" and the "four" foot sides of the triangle thus determined, the "five" foot side—Leon calls it the "hy-potamoose"—will measure five feet only when the intersection of the strings is adjusted to exactly ninety degrees. Leon waits at the far end of the first string as Bodie gives directions for adjustment.

"Keep a going . . . little more . . . just a tad more . . . whisker . . . Yup, you got it! Spike it right there, Grampy. We got a corner." Leon wraps the line around an eight-penny nail he taps into the batter board. "Three to go. Do this one next, I guess." Bodie gestures to his right. A thin crust frozen into the hardpan overnight crunches under Leon's feet as he walks across to the corner.

"Slave driver," Leon mutters. "Pull a man out of bed at a quarter to daylight." (Leon had been up since half past four, done his milking and all his barn chores.) "Got no sympathy for us old-timers. Make sure she measures ickzackly five. The hy-potamoose don't lie."

With the corners laid out and Leon gone back to the barn—to do some "real work," he claimed—Bodie drags a dozen two-by-tens over from the stockpile in the woodshed and begins the footing forms. He places the lumber on the ground below the four strings, then finds the exact locations of the corners with his plumb bob and starts nailing the two-by-tens together. When he has the basic rectangle formed, he climbs the rickety ladder up out of the hole and goes to the toolshed for his transit, rod and tripod. Back down in the hole he sets the tripod in the center of the rectangle and mounts the transit tight to the top. He checks the leveling bubbles, and after some minutes of fiddling with the threaded adjustments, he is able to swing the transit in a complete circle with no sign of movement off the horizontal plane. He is ready to level up the forms and shouts to Leon to come help him.

While Leon limps over from the barn, Bodie squints through the transit at an upper rung of the ladder. The transit is like a telescope with an X-Y axis across its lens. Or like the scope on a high-powered rifle. As Bodie tunes the adjustment to perfect focus, Leon's foot steps into the magnified circle. His pant leg and an indistinguishable portion of his jacket follow. The next thing Bodie sees is Leon's face, staring straight at him. The transit's cross hairs bisect the old man's nose; his cap and chin are lost outside the brightened ring. His look is one of irritation overcome with puzzlement—as if a hidden camera had caught him in a private moment. Bodie straightens up, blushing, shoves his hands into his pockets, if only to remove them from this instrument that suddenly seems so much like a deadly weapon.

"For a minute there, you looked like Harmon," he says to his grandfather. "Made me sweat some."

"Going to send you up to Waterbury Hospital."

"I'm not saying it was real."

"Put you in one of them funny jackets—jabber to the jaybirds all day long. Stick you full of tubes and needles and take your blood."

"You'll come see me, Sundays?"

"Regular, every Sunday. Bring you posies on Easter day."

"Jeesum, call the Quinntown Taxi." Bodie winks at Leon.

"You got work you want done, or what? I got things to do." He motions back toward the barn. "Got a cow with a twisted stomach." Leon is serious now. "A good one, too. It don't seem right."

Bodie flinches. Without some luck the cow will die within a couple of days, its insides torn apart by the pressures of a blocked digestive tract. "You call the vet?"

Leon shakes his head no. "I seen just as many of these as him. Neither of us has got the money to do a thing about it." He picks up the transit rod and stands it on the top of a form board. "You want this outfit leveled up?"

"We'll find the high point first," says Bodie. "Start over there, that might be it."

"Work an old man half to death," Leon mutters. Bodie knows he loves it.

Looking through the transit, Bodie reads the numbers calibrated up the rod. The cross hairs align with four feet, four; it's fifty-two inches from the transit's horizontal plane to the top of the footing form. They take another reading and work around the rectangle. "Hold it . . . fifty-three and a half . . . Bring her up an inch and a half."

Leon slips a stone under the two-by-ten as Bodie stoops to peer through the transit again. "Close enough for gov'-ment work," Bodie says, and turns to the next location.

Within fifteen minutes, the forms are level. Leon pauses at the ladder, working his plug of tobacco in preparation of what he is about to say. "You're a good one, Bodie. What I mean to say is—" His eyes bulge and he spits dark juice. "What I mean is, you got a lot of . . . heart." He scrambles up the ladder and hurries, mumbling, toward the barn.

The transit-mix dispatcher wants to know if the roads are all right, has the frost gone out and left deep mud for his trucks to sink into. Bodie assures him that the roads are still frozen under the skim coat of slush. Backing across the lawn might be different . . . but he doesn't mention that part. The Allis Chalmers crawler in the equipment shed will pull out anything that might get stuck. Bodie orders seven cubic yards of the five-bag mix for the footings; the chimney pad will take another half yard. An extra quarter yard is cal-culated in as "arithmetic insurance." The dispatcher assures him that the truck will arrive by eleven.

Darlene comes into the kitchen as Bodie hangs up the phone. She puts her boots and coat on without a word.

"Hey, Darlene, the cement's coming. I'll have those foot-ings done by noon," Bodie says, watching her try to close the third button on her coat.

She stands tipped back for balance in the lace-up shoes that Vera bought her. Thick, coarse stockings stop in sau-sage rolls below her knees. "I know—I mean, that's won-derful. I saw you out there this morning with Grampy. I appreciate it, Bodie, I really do." She looks at her watch, then looks at the clock on the wall to confirm what she already knows. "I think I'll walk down and get the mail."

134

"Want a ride?"

She shakes her head. "The exercise is good for me. Another beautiful day." Brave little voice.

"Montpelier station said we're in for two or three more. I won't complain."

"It's just like springtime." She fidgets with her underwear inside her coat.

"At this rate, we'll have the whole basement done by Friday."

For a moment, Darlene looks enthusiastic. She rolls forward onto the balls of her feet and takes a step toward Bodie. She begins some sort of thank-you, but then she appears to reconsider; the gratitude would cost too much. Her inspiration seems to leave her and she turns abruptly to the door. "Vera's out in the barn with Grampy. He's got a cow in trouble."

"I know," says Bodie. His throat feels dry. "Have a good walk. And watch out for the cement truck."

She closes the door on his caring. From the kitchen table, he watches her cross the snow-ringed dooryard and begin the long slope down across the valley. It will take twenty minutes before she disappears into the hemlocks and down the steep cut to the mailbox on the corner of the Jordan Center road. He gets up and pours a cup of lukewarm coffee. Her figure grows smaller. Her dark gray coat against the ivory snowscape emphasizes her aloneness. She walks slowly with her head down. "She's in no hurry," Bodie says aloud. She knows the mailman won't be by until ten thirty. At least it's warm—close to forty. Some mornings she'd walk down there when it was way below zero and blowing hard.

When Darlene finds a letter from her husband she comes back up the hill with renewed purpose in her stride, reading the letter a dozen times over before she stops at the barn to tell Leon the news, then into the kitchen to share the particulars with Vera.

Darlene's mood on these occasions confuses her. The satisfaction she expects is, in the end, elusive, leaves her disappointed. The comfort she seeks in Harmon's sentences melts away between the words, between the letters, through the paper into air. Occasionally, a comfort holds, but thinly; a second reading leaves her tasting only dust.

She feels she should be happy with his letters—and she is when she first sees the envelope, unopened in the mailbox. But what she wants is more than Harmon's scribbled words can give. At night in her room above the woodshed, the baby kicks against Darlene's stretched abdomen and makes the postman's call seem pointless. Harmon's letters? Words on paper. The baby shifts to new positions, ripening on her hidden vine. Here are want and need firsthand, want and need she can respond to.

Down in the hole, Bodie kicks a two-by-ten to test its firmness against the ensuing pour. The plank holds fast—everything looks ready—the concrete is on its way. From across the valley, he hears the truck shift down to make the turn at the end of the lane. He pictures Darlene standing up against a snowbank, nodding to the driver. Perhaps he'll offer her a ride. She'll say no thanks, she needs the exercise. Maybe she's carrying a letter from Harmon—or household bills, or maybe—knock on wood she isn't—maybe there's a letter addressed to him from his draft board, second notice, wanting to know. To hell with that! He climbs the ladder to watch for the truck and rubs his hands together when he sees the top of the yellow drum nudge up over the hill like a toy-box sun.

It's a Mack, the truck is, a big yellow Mack with a Cummings diesel engine. He listens to the driver play the throttle in the distance, hears him keeping constant revs and shifting up, two, three—four times as he crosses the lower portion of the valley, then shifts back down to double-low as he wallows up the slope below the barn. He toots his horn as he passes Leon standing at the milk house door. The final grade from barn to house seems to take forever. A hurricane of air behind the radiator fan surrounds the diesel racket with an arctic howl. Bud, the barnyard tomcat, scats for cover in the woodshed.

A chromium bulldog decorates top center of the radiator cowl. Black and red pinstriping follows the hood contours back to the two-piece windshield. TWIN STATE TRANSIT MIX is printed on the doors in serifed typeface, and above the logo, in smaller script, the driver's name: Dale Wood-ard.

Leon's brother Weymouth is Dale's father, which makes Dale Bodie's uncle even though he's only a few years older than Bodie. He should be Bodie's cousin. In fact, Dale has a half-brother almost twice his age—Weymouth Jr., known as Short-Cord for his practice of selling less-than-promised quantities of firewood.

Just after the First World War, the Woodard home place was deeded, half share each, to Leon and Weymouth when their widowed father died. Weymouth had always balked at farming; he jumped at Leon's offer to buy him out. Five hundred dollars cash and the team of Belgians seemed like a fortune to Weymouth. Within a year, the money was gone and the horses shot and eaten. Leon kept the farm up and helped his brother when he could, but eventually refused when every dollar went for foolishness.

Weymouth's cabin on Quinntown Mountain was home for logging camp itinerants, out of work and often violent. Starving hogs patrolled the place, rooting up the rock-strewn soil in search of grubs and tubers. Rotting hulks of cordwood—stacked for market but never sold—loomed high against the one-track road that ended dead against the cabin door. By dimmest lantern light, frigid winter nights were filled with sounds of brawls and haunting fiddle dirges played in stubborn repetition by Weymouth's woman Lollie's simple brother. Guns were fired, faces bloodied, drunken bodies and empty bottles flung through broken windows. In '53, the cabin burned to the ground and Dale came to stay in Catamount while it was rebuilt. Leon's charity was neither repaid nor acknowledged. Weymouth still accuses him of stealing his share of the farm.

The circumstances of Dale's life were never discussed during that summer, but Bodie had sensed something bad was happening on Quinntown Mountain. From the start, Dale seemed so much older, much more worldly, tougher and cunning. He introduced the twins to sex, showing them a pack of lurid Mexican playing cards that depicted men and women in unbelievable situations—some were even doing it with dogs and donkeys. He taught them all the dirty names for the dirty parts of the body, what you called it when they went together in certain ways. And the things that people did to each other—it was unbelievable! Dale knew it all. He told them how his little sister let him do it to her whenever he wanted. He also knew a guy who actually fucked a chicken. Once, when they were looking at the pictures, Dale pulled his pants down to show them what a great big hard-on was. Bodie refused to believe what he saw. "It can't be real. It's plastic or something." Dale had laughed and made him touch it, told him he'd have one just as big someday.

Dale stops the Mack against the snowbank; air brakes hiss. He leans out the window to greet his nephew.

"Hey ya', Harmon, what's going on?" Dale is missing most of his front teeth. Lumps of wen decorate his bulbous nose. Bodie thinks of a potato.

"I'm Bodie. Harm's in 'Nam."

"Shit! I thought you was your brother." Dale's eyebrows walk around his forehead. "That your woman?" He jerks a dirty thumb toward the end of the lane. Cold flame burns behind his eyes; a feral darkness shades his grin.

Bodie looks around the front of the truck—protectively—for Darlene. He sees her far off, standing still in the lane across the valley. She could be watching something in the meadow—a bird perhaps, or animal tracks zigzagged across the snow. "That's Harmon's wife," he says, still looking at her as if to be sure. "You know Darlene . . . Darlene McAllister?"

"Darlene Mister-licker?"

Bodie shrinks. A scene from the grainy playing cards flashes through his mind.

"I never would of recognized her. She's grown up good, by the looks of it." Behind sealed lips, Dale's tongue counts missing teeth around his mouth. He shreds off a rumbling from his lungs that ends his part of the conversation.

"When you get this thing turned around," Bodie says, "just back up right through here. We'll shoot the whole shebang from over by the ladder." He waits as Dale revs up and checks his mirrors, finds reverse. The truck moves slowly, like an ocean liner leaving port. Bodie stares and wonders at the things this man has seen.

The Mack looms large against the clapboard farmhouse, inching backward toward the hole. Out onto the lawn, the sod gives way, then holds as the soil compacts enough to resist the crushing weight. A slowly rolling wave of turf precedes the giant tires like the bow wave on a river barge.

Six feet from the excavation, Bodie signals Dale to stop. Together, they unclip sections of the chute from a rack beneath the drum and assemble them into one long slide, hung from the rear of the vehicle. They work without speaking, each conscious of the other's silence, each unprepared to break it. With the chute in place, Dale climbs up to a narrow catwalk and stands at the tipped-up mouth of the drum. Two levers within his reach control the flow of concrete down the chute.

"How wet d'you want it?" Dale shouts down.

"Four slump—I want it stiff," Bodie shouts back, squinting up at Dale from the bottom of the hole.

Dale's grin cuts his face in half. *Buncha assholes, goody-goodies. Wet concrete's ten times easier to slush around. Christ, you barely need to tend it—runs like water wherever you want. Assholes like this Bodie, here, think they got to have it stiff because some mucky-muck wrote down somewhere that stiff mix comes out stronger. Let him shovel, no skin off mine. I'll run the slump to one if that's what he wants. Run it dry. See how he likes it, frigging dub. Look at him, Jesus. Here's your four slump!*

Bodie's heartbeat quickens; he moves the end of the pendant chute and guides its shiny snout to the formwork by his feet. He gestures to Dale to begin, and steadies the chute between his calves; the cold steel is alive with the truck's vibrations.

On top of the catwalk, with the sun behind him, Dale peers into the drum to check the mix. From down in the hole, his silhouette resembles a ragged bird peering into its nest—a molting hawk, a mangy crow or even a turkey vulture. A fringe from a tear in his jacket sleeve becomes a broken feather. His nose offsets his pointed chin to form an open beak. His arms move winglike to the controls. The drum turns faster, churning, louder. Bodie looks up at the tons of noise and energy, enchanted.

Tentative gray clumps appear at the orifice above the chute; they hesitate. Random bits of aggregate skitter down the polished trough. Next, a spill of cold gray water and then the mud slide starts, slow and deliberate, one hundred and forty pounds per cubic foot. Now it vomits down the chute and bullies its way into the formwork, then flattens out and slows its flow, a lumpy, sullen glacier. Its rounded leading edge sniffs out each crevice, every cranny. Here and there it finds a crack or knothole and a minor tributary forms, then clogs shut.

The concrete glacier fills its banks, and Bodie, working quickly, coaxes the current with his shovel. His back and arms will ache tonight, but now his muscles serve his purpose. Sweat stains through his shirtfront; a dark stripe spreads out from his spine. Breathing hard to the rhythm of his shoveling, the last few feet to closure are finally in sight. He motions up to Dale to stop the flow and sees Darlene beside the truck, staring out across the valley, a thousand miles away.

Dale climbs down and says something to Darlene; she makes no visible response. Dale shrugs and walks to the truck cab. He will move his rig out to the dooryard, stop and carefully hose it down. He revs the engine, finds first gear and looks in vain for Darlene in his side mirror. With the chute hanging limply from the rear of its body, the truck creeps away like a sad, spent lover.

Bodie grabs a piece of one-by-three and screeds excess concrete from the top of the forms. Working along on his hands and knees, this final shaping gives him pleasure. Already, the liquid mix is forming, assuming its final anatomy. No telltale puddles forming on the surface, no soapy bubbles, no lactic glaze—the four slump was none too stiff; this house will stand forever. Or, as need be. Anyway, it's started off right, he assures himself.

As he finishes, he pauses to imprint the date in the chimney pad. He thinks about adding initials alongside the date. Whose? He looks up for Darlene but she is gone. He scratches a ragged W into the surface with a ten-penny nail, adds the date, and climbs the ladder to the world above.

Across the dooryard, Dale is hosing splattered concrete off the Mack's impeccable paint job. Leon stands beside Dale watching the brittle stream of water ricochet off the sheet metal. A dozen tiny tributaries sneak out from beneath the chassis and form a muddy rivulet, gaining momentum down the lane.

Bodie joins Leon and Dale; he has receipts to sign. He stands outside their conversation, waiting.

". . . Mister, I heard *something* coming, heard you turn off Jordan Road and drop her down to corner gear."

"I guess so. That little hill's a sonofabitch." Dale lisps through the *s* sounds.

"You teamed her up through pretty good. By the Jesus, mister boy, you drawed up quite a freight." Leon surveys the Mack as if it were a twenty-hand draft horse.

"Thirty-ton gross," Dale says. "She weren't loaded full. I run forty ton if I want. Shit, I'd just as soon run overweight. Fuzz don't bother me. Don't pay to diddle with the Quinntown Woodards." A smirk zigzags into his cheeks.

The three men stand next to the hood of the idling diesel. Dale instructs Bodie exactly where to sign the delivery receipt. "Spell your name out by the X," he says like a schoolmaster. "Push down hard—there's carbonated copies underneath. Some of 'em don't push hard enough. Kinda ignorant, but, what the hey, I can't do more than tell 'em, right? Copies come out shitty. Office hollers, but it don't bother me."

Bodie hands the clipboard back to Dale and motions toward the truck's front end. "You got a bearing going in your water pump."

"Tap, tap, tap," Leon says, in time with the clicking sound. "Little man with a hammer."

"That ain't no bearing," Dale says, spitting into the mud. They listen again, six ears together. Tap, tap, tap. The sound insists.

"Them diesels make an awful racket anyways." Dale defends his engine. "This rig don't owe me nothing." He swings up onto the running board and pulls the door open. The floor of the cab is more than five feet off the ground. "They can buy me a new one any time they want." He closes the door behind him and sticks his head and shoulder out the open window. His wooly black hair compresses against the frame. He stares at Bodie's feet and runs his eyes up Bodie's frame. Stopping at his neck, he asks, "How come you ain't in Viet Nam?"

"I don't go in for . . . wars. Like that."

"Is that right?"

"Harmon's gone," Leon slips in, as if to defend his branch of the family. "He's gone eight weeks now, doing good."

"I would have went but my back throwed out. Never mended right. You hear about that guy run into me?"

Leon and Bodie nod. The accident happened late one Saturday night four years ago. Dale had left Hubby's on rubber legs at one A.M. and driven along the River Road toward Quinntown. According to the *Valley Herald,* he had stopped his Nova in the middle of a curve, turned out the lights and was opening a pack of cigarettes when the next car around the curve cue-balled him into the river.

"Frigging guy was barely scratched. Me? I still wear a goddamned corset. Stinks like hell come summertime." He rumbles off a cough—or laugh—it doesn't matter. He's goosing the throttle, itching to go. The Mack starts rolling furrows through the slush.

"How's Weymouth?" Leon calls up to him, walking alongside the moving cab.

Dale looks down at Leon, then throws his head back,

mouth wide open, laughing way back to his ears. "He's—I don't know. Last time I see him we got to drinking and scuffling." Dale stops the truck and unbuttons the cuff on his left sleeve, holds his bare arm out the window. Raw skin bracelets halfway around his wrist. "Pressed me up against the wood stove, hard. Tried to take car keys off me." He laughs again. "I let him burn me. I told the old sonofabitch he was much too drunk to drive . . ." His laughing mingles with the engine sounds. "*My* car, anyways."

The truck free-wheels downslope into the valley. Leon watches it until it hits the flat, then he starts off for the barn. Halfway there, he stops and turns to Bodie and says, "Cow."

Bodie nods. That single word is so much of Leon. His working life is woven with the thread of "cow." He talks to them more than he talks to people. He scolds them, he doctors them—like this one now—he knows each nuance of their moods. Their feed, their bedding, their body weight, their freshening cycles and butterfat tallies—each cow's history is part of Leon's. Ultimately, he neither loves nor hates the animals. His pigs amuse him more. His ducks are easier to care for. Horses are more useful. He'd rather scratch old Bud behind the ears. But the cow is the only animal that ties the hill farm together, the only one to provide the steady creamery check each month. The cow thrives on the prickly browse spread out across the upper pastures, endures the heat and keeps the barn so warm in winter that water never freezes in the trough. Without the cow there would be no farm and Leon would be—what? A carpenter? A mason? A mechanic? It wouldn't be the same without a cow somewhere in the middle of it.

At the kitchen table, Bodie watches Dale's truck disappear at the far side of the valley. The yellow orb lowers itself down behind the incline, into the softwood boughs. He pictures Dale going home tonight to his rusty trailer in Quinntown—empty bottles, brawls, raw garbage, dirty kids half-naked on the floor. Chaos. Dale is frightening. Most frightening is the part of Dale that should be crushed but isn't. His evident rapaciousness for life slaps out at Bodie, challenges him. How could Dale have anything left? How can he keep it up, keep mocking his poor fortune? Bodie wants to talk to someone, make some plans, create some logic in his life that protects him from the eerie pull of irresponsibility that Dale endows with such excitement. Tinker has it. Winston Gandy—Taylor's boy—had it most of all until they sentenced him to two life sentences for killing an elderly farm couple in Weatherby. And Bodie senses deep down *he* has it—*he* could make the valley shake, give Lucifer a merry chase, if only—if only he could see the sense to it.

Vera and Darlene come down the stairs from Darlene's room and sit across the table from Bodie. Darlene has been crying. Bodie knows immediately the letter folded in her hand must be from Viet Nam. She sniffs into a soggy Klee-nex, balls it up and stuffs it up her sleeve. Her wedding band indents the puffy skin around her finger.

"I saw fox tracks down in the meadow," Darlene says. "Mouse tracks, too. The fox must have eaten the mouse. There was a drop of pink on the snow—and that little green sack the foxes won't eat."

"Cats won't either. I believe it's the spleen or the liver," Bodie says. "Must have a bitter taste to it."

"Of course, beef liver's altogether different," Vera says. "Pan-fried beef liver and onions is one of Leon's favorites."

"Jiggsie—he'll take and eat the heart meat."

"Jiggsie?"

"Honest! Harmon saved it for him when he got his buck."

"Poor little thing," Darlene says, about to cry again. "Jiggsie?"

"The mouse. It was out looking around on a sunny day and, wham! Mr. Fox."

"Fox has to eat too," says Bodie, and an image of Dale's lips, drooling, floods his mind. Dale's few remaining teeth are huge and shiny, pointed and indiscreet. His tongue hangs wet and shameless from the corner of his mouth.

"It's nature's way," says Vera. But Darlene won't be comforted. Her jaw jerks back and quivers. Dimples dot the flesh around her chin as she hides her mouth with the opened book of her hands. Vera puts an arm around her shoulders and hands her a fresh Kleenex. Bodie looks to Vera for a sign. Vera closes her eyes to him and shakes her head slowly, back and forth, squeezing Darlene closer as the sobs increase.

"He's going crazy!" Darlene bursts out, and now her sobs become a wail. "He's going crazy! I can tell. He'll never be the same again." She buries her head in Vera's embrace, burrows into Vera's clothes as if to quench her pain in threadbare cotton.

As her sobs subside, Darlene reconstructs herself with handkerchiefs, nose-blowing, deep inhaling and, finally, a sheepish "aren't-I-stupid" grin. "I'm sorry," she says. Vera and Bodie protest.

"It's all right. This is what family's for," Vera says.

Darlene slides the letter upside down across the table to Bodie. "Read it," she says. "Tell me what you think—if you think that's your brother writing."

Bodie looks at her—asks her does she mean it.

"Read it, really. I want you to." Her jaw jerks back. She calms herself with a few deep breaths. "It's just not Harmon. See what you think."

Bodie unfolds a dirty piece of airmail paper and holds it up between him and the women across the table. They watch him as he reads:

> Bink says good day and shine his flashlight on you. For the foolish, one vexation kills another. Him who envies shall take root and be annointed with abiding fear. Over the wicked trembling unto wandering darkness. Bespeak Jehovah! In the earth hell fire burns around their evil throws, flesh of my flesh, the viper strikes and smites . . .

Bodie looks up at Darlene and Vera. This can't be Harmon. The words make Bodie wince, they turn his guts to talcum.

> . . . My enemy shalt run assunder me, three wise men taketh care of my revenge . . . but who shall sip the blood of new builted heavens and also new earths in mine eyes? oh Isreyel? . . . cast off thy rebuke and inquire, lordship, forsaketh me to disentary vines and souls.

The writing runs off the bottom of the page. The other side is blank but Bodie studies it from several angles as if a new perspective might illuminate a hidden text. Nothing. His brother is crazy, the letter is proof.

How was the letter written? he wonders. Was the blank side pressed against a tabletop, the hood of a jeep, a dog-eared magazine with pouting bimbos on the cover? Who's "Bink"? What kind of day was it? The weather? Was it in a jungle? In the paddies? TV shows a lot of paddies. What kind of trees and bushes were there? Were there birds squawking overhead? A scrawny camp dog mooching scraps? Was Harmon's body OK, was his physical health OK? Does he have buddies like Jiggsie and Tinker? Do they like him? What's he say about his family, what's he tell them about Catamount? Some of his buddies could be from

Chicago. Or Wyoming or Texas. Where the hell *is* he? He never even signed good-bye, just folded it and tossed it at us. Here: I'm crazy. You figure me out.

"I don't know what to say—it's wacky—I don't know what's going on. I never saw a letter like that," Bodie says.

"Couldn't we call somebody—some general?" Darlene knows it wouldn't work but tries it anyway. "How about Dexter Bushway—wasn't he in the navy or something?"

"He went with Purdy," Vera says. "He got assigned to a typing pool in Maryland." She says this without a trace of envy. "I'm glad he did. He came home and married Miriam. Tinker was going to kindergarten."

From opposite sides, Bodie and Darlene push Harmon's folded letter across the white enameled steel tabletop. It moves a few inches one way, then a flick of a fingernail jigs it a few inches back. Neither wants the letter. They poke at it as if it were a dirty dying thing.

Craziness: Vera's thoughts stray off beyond the letter, beyond the kitchen—back to the 1930s when she and her mother took a train ride up the White River Valley on the Boston and Maine Railroad, all the way to Waterbury. They sat on wicker seats and ate their cold chicken lunch, packed under a towel in the same woven basket they used at home to gather eggs from the hen house. She remembers the heavy black soot from the locomotive—remembers *hearing* the smoke hit the Pullman car roof in waves of gritty showers. At the Waterbury station they hired a taxi—the first time anyone in their family had ever hired a taxi—and they'd been driven to the institution to see Uncle Carl, who would spend his whole life in that place. Carl was her mother's only brother. He was older, quiet and portly and wore wire-rimmed glasses. She recalls he was wearing a peculiar hat even though he was dressed in pajamas. She

148

was too young, at nine, to consider his position: he was, he insisted, Ulysses S. Grant.

From that day on, Vera has thought of Uncle Carl whenever she feels strange, and wonders if there isn't some of him in everyone. In her moments of confusion—times when reason has no application—she find her hands plucking at the air above her as if her hatlessness will verify her sanity.

Nine

The Valley Region Draft Board meets in White River Junction on the second and fourth Tuesday of each month. The meetings are held in a squeaky-floored room with bare green walls—one flight up from Menard's Men's Apparel. Four chairs and an oak-topped table occupy the center of the room. A lockable four-drawer file, an American flag and a steel wastebasket complete the room's decor.

Today, the meeting began a little after nine A.M. As usual, Bixby Judd was late; his cows had wandered off through a gate left open by the new hired hand. Daryl Hutchins, a retired policeman, and Clayton Foss, first selectman from Canaan Depot, discussed the weather and the bus fare rates to Nashville while they waited for Bixby to appear. At nine forty-five, they heard his footsteps on the stairs. Redolent of the barnyard, he bustled in and took his place at the table. For the next hour, the board considered a 4-F candidate, dismissed a conscientious objector's appeal and pondered how to find an orphan's missing birth certificate.

Bodeman Woodard's file came last. It was noted that Woodard had been sent two letters requiring him to appear for a physical examination, but had failed to present him-

151

self. The Selective Service Handbook was consulted: instructions for dealing with this type of infraction were unclear. Bixby thought they ought to run up to the farm and talk to Woodard. He knew Leon from cattle auctions. Maybe Leon could explain why his grandson hadn't responded. Maybe it was something beyond their control. Better to go ask firsthand than send the state police, they all agreed. At eleven forty-five, Bixby and Clayton left for Catamount in Bixby's pickup. Daryl had a lunch date at the VFW Legion Hall.

For the last two miles on the state road into Catamount, Bixby crept along, stuck behind a highway department truck. Taking advantage of the thaw, the highway crew was pushing back the snowbanks. From a wing plow hung out to the right, a steady stream of slush flew over fence posts onto virgin snow in the fields beyond.

At the Jordan Road intersection, Bixby swung his truck into the turn and shifted up through the gears. He drove quickly through the familiar curves, crisscrossing the winding brook that splits the valley north from south. It felt good to be moving again. He was telling Clayton about his daughter's awful doctor bills when the yellow Twin State Transit truck came around a turn, straight toward him in the middle of the road.

Except for a bent exhaust pipe, Bixby's truck sustained no damages. The snowbank he chose as his escape route left him stuck, but that was all. Meanwhile, the cement truck continued down the middle of the road as if it owned it.

"Never looked back, the crazy palooka. Couldn't see who was in it, could you?" Bixby grumbled.

The lane to Woodard's place was just a quarter mile away. Maybe after they spoke with Bodeman, Leon would bring his tractor down and pull them out. They started walking, squinting in the bright winter light. The sound of trickling water met them everywhere.

"That's strange. There's two men. Walking up the lane," says Vera, dismissing thoughts of Uncle Carl. Bodie and Darlene turn to look. Bodie gets up and goes to the window. These are no idle winter hikers. They walk as if they have a purpose, and there are several purposes for which their presence won't be welcomed.

As the pair draws closer, it becomes clear that neither is in military uniform. "It's not about Harmon," Bodie says. Darlene squeezes Vera's hand as Bodie shifts to another window. "I think I've seen one of them before. Looks like they might be friends of Grampy's."

They don't stop at the barn; they walk as if they know exactly where they are going, coming toward the kitchen door.

Bodie opens it before they knock. Vera and Darlene peer out from behind him.

"What can I do for you?" Bodie asks, watching the thin one look down, making designs in the snow with his boot. The other looks up at the faces in the doorway, eyeing Bodie, assessing Vera, lingering a little too long on Darlene's belly, then shifting past them all, across the front of the house, taking in the new foundation, the tracks on the lawn, everything. Maybe they're from Tessier's, coming to check on the concrete work. Maybe they've come to visit with Leon.

"We're straddling a snowbank down the way," the big one says.

"Transit truck squoze us off the road," says the other, still working on his footprint patterns.

"Had his half of the road in the middle. Never even waved good-bye. Up here, was he?"

"Yup," says Bodie.

"Wisht I knew his name. I don't suppose you caught it?"

Bodie shakes his head. All they have to do is call the dispatcher. They can do that if they want, but they have something else in mind.

They try to hold Bodie's gaze, but can't. "Any chance you'd pull us out?"

"I'll collect my jacket," Bodie says, and moves across the kitchen to the coat hooks on the wall.

"Leon around?" they ask Vera in unison, looking pleased for the first time.

"He's in the barn with a sick cow," she says. "You know Leon?"

"I do," the big man interrupts. "I've knowed him from way back. Bought some heifers off him once. I'm Bixby Judd from White River." He smiles. "Farm down on the flats by the Tigertown Crossing."

"With the blue painted house?"

"That's it. My daughter lives in the silver trailer alongside the road. She's had three operations this year."

As Vera and Darlene express their sympathies, Bodie slips between them and down the steps. "I'll get the tractor," Bodie says and walks off to the equipment shed.

"I'll just stick my head in the barn and say hello to Leon," Bixby calls after Bodie. Bodie answers help yourself without turning around. There is something too apologetic about these two, something sly and squirmy.

Bodie puts a couple of grain shovels behind the tractor seat, drops a twenty-foot length of chain in the tool pocket and drives over to the barn door. They hear him and immediately come out—without Leon. Bodie gestures to the tow bar pinned to the three-point hitch behind him. They step up onto it, holding the back of the tractor seat, a pair of strangers holding on.

154

"This here's Clayton Foss," Bixby shouts in Bodie's ear. "Lives out to Canaan. First selectman."

Bodie nods and wonders what Bixby expects him to say.

To each side of the road, the snow is sparkling bright, like fine white beach sand. Along the flat, Bodie looks to his left for fox tracks and the spot of pink where the field mouse was eaten. He misses it but doesn't care. His passengers are troubling him. He turns his head to see if they're still with him. Clayton's ear is six inches away. He notices the whorl of hairs that spiral out of the old man's head. He wonders if he ever cuts that kind of hair, if everybody grows ear hair when they reach a certain age. He wonders why his passengers won't look him straight in the eye. The tractor putt-putts down the lane and turns toward Catamount without an answer.

The thaw has melted all the snow and ice from the Jordan Road macadam. Bodie's tires get good traction and he pulls the truck out easily.

Bixby unhitches the chain from his truck and drags it back to the tractor. "Much appreciate it. What do I owe you?"

"Nothing. Wasn't any trouble."

"You're Bodeman, aren't you?"

"Yup."

"Brother Harmon in the army?"

"Went last November. You know Harmon?"

The two old men exchange uncomfortable glances, each one hoping the other will speak first.

"See, that's part of what we do . . ."

"It's part-time," Clayton adds. "Keeps us out of trouble, ha ha."

"We meet on Tuesdays. Twice a month."

"It's not like we get paid to do it. It's volunteer."

"Like being a selectman."

"Only different." Clayton laughs another pitiful note.

Bodie looks from face to face. They might have known Harmon, but do they know he's writing crazy letters? Do they have any idea of what's happened to him? They couldn't know. Or even care.

It hits him in the stomach and it feels like liquid lead. These guys are from the draft board. That's where he's seen the name Bixby Judd, on the notices they've sent him. Bixby Judd, the chairman of the Valley Region Draft Board, came up here today with his goofy sidekick to talk about the . . . "You're from the draft board, right?"

"Valley Region. Down to White River." Clayton's voice is squeaky with gratitude. The subject of their visit is finally at hand and he was not required to bring it up.

"Whilst we're on the subject," Bixby says, "I don't know if you ever got your notices."

Bodie feels himself staring at Bixby's truck, the goddamned truck he just pulled out of a snowbank. Harmon's going crazy. Leon's cow is dying. Darlene and Vera don't know what to make of Harmon. There's an unborn baby. There's a hole in the ground that wants four walls built up inside it, wants to shelter Darlene and her baby. Jesus Christ, Loretta Bushway. What about tonight, Loretta? All this melting snow is going to bring the brooks up over the top of the culverts, wash some roads out, take this Bixby's half-ton pickup truck and fill it full of brook-bed gravel, bend it around a tree trunk way down river. Some fisherman will find it come springtime. What about it? Loretta?

". . . We send 'em registered," Bixby drones.

"Course, we got return receipts. Selective Service makes us do that. Taxpayers' money," Clayton adds with an apologetic wink.

Bodie says nothing. He can see his silence scares them and he decides to wait until they speak again. What could they be thinking? What do they make of the pregnant woman up at the farmhouse? Do Darlene and the thousands

156

like her make them proud to serve their draft board? When they saw Leon in that dank old barn, kneeling beside a moaning holstein, up to his shins in shit and sawdust—did that convince them they were doing something useful? Bixby says he knows Leon from way back. Lucky Leon.

"You could go for a 1-Y, conscientious objector. Get a letter from your church and all," Clayton says hopefully.

Bodie's reveries of rushing brooks and Loretta Bushway are finally surrendered to two foolish men who wish they were somewhere else. Clayton is saying something about alternative service, working in a hospital or a mental institution. Bixby nods, ever agreeable, adding that by good old-fashioned horse sense they can avoid unpleasantness, avoid the kind of scene they had last year in Jordan Center with the Maynard boy, the state police, the sirens and the guns a-waving but thank god not a one was fired.

"We never were church people," Bodie says. "My reasons aren't church reasons. They're personal. There's no way I can see it."

"You don't think Harmon could use your help?" Bixby asks. "What's he say on the subject?"

Bodie is stunned by the question. Harmon use his help? In ordinary times the answer was at best conditional. He'd take his help if offered, but the need? Harmon's need was never such that anyone would ever worry about him. You helped him because you wanted to, not because he was in need. But now the letter. He sounded like a television preacher gone berserk. And add to that the darker side, the secret he and Darlene held against Harmon. She calls it pure survival and it's true, she needs the leverage, but the answer to the secret is still held hostage by the two of them. If ever Harmon needed help, yes, this is the time. How Bodie might provide it isn't clear to him, but the question jabs and pierces, leaves his knees wobbly beneath him.

"We don't hear from Harmon all that much. He tells

157

me it's a dirty lousy war and we should be ashamed to be there. He tells me it's against the law. He tells me it's driving everybody crazy. That's what he says on the subject." Bodie whispers the last part and realizes he's done something unusual, for him. He feels a flush and sees a fleeting image of Dale, his rubber face stretched into a gleeful grimace as he bears down on the two old hypocrites in their pickup truck, crowding them into a snowbank without flinching.

"We'll have to talk to Selective Service, Bodeman." Bixby is all business now. "They have their rules. I hope you understand this isn't personal." He smiles. "I always liked your grandpa."

Bixby and Clayton climb into the truck and close their doors gently, as if to buy back Bodie's respect, as if to indicate their love for peace and reasonable discourse. "You'll be hearing from us. I hope you change your mind," Bixby says, turning the ignition, hearing the motor purr.

"Thanks for the tow," Clayton calls out across Bixby's face, through Bixby's window. " 'Preciate it," and he waves bye-bye as if he's waving to a child.

The truck is pointed toward Jordan. They'll have to go up to Woodard's lane and turn around, then pass Bodie again on their way back to the highway. Bixby would give anything to have it otherwise. He hastily imagines a map of the roads between Jordan and White River Junction, but the only reasonable route back home is the one they took to get here.

They drive up the road and turn around in Woodard's lane. When they get back to Bodie, he's driving the tractor with his head held back; his hair shines yellow in the sun. His left rear tire rolls its chevroned imprint up the road like a mill wheel turning, two feet over the center line. Bixby squeezes by with his shoulders hunched together. He's too busy steering to notice if Bodie returned Clayton's frightened little waves.

When she was thirteen years old, Loretta Bushway insisted—through long, impassioned sessions with her mother—that Miriam buy her a training bra. The women in the family, Miriam's side as well as Dexter's, were, every one of them, pencil-thin. Hips and bosoms were provided to other women, but not them. Among her budding robust classmates, Loretta felt inadequate, sometimes downright embarrassed. "I'll die if you don't get me one," she told her patient mother. "Even Susan Tatro has one. She's only in sixth grade."

Miriam agreed at last, and on the morning of her debut, Loretta carefully selected a blouse that would subtly but unmistakably reveal the evidence of her passage into womanhood. Or, as some were quick to observe, her illusion of that passage.

One such cynic was her father, and as it is with closest family, his remarks would wound her deepest.

"What're you wearing under there?" he asked as she sat down for breakfast.

Miriam kicked him hard under the table.

"Ow!" he said. "What the hell's going on?"

Loretta bit her lip.

Miriam decided to stop Dexter before he did further damage. "She's wearing a training bra and you can keep your big trap shut!"

Some men would have quit there. Apologized, and meant it. If they were truly sincere, they might make efforts to erase the incident entirely. Other men, the majority, perhaps, would have let it go with an intolerant shrug or a gruff disclaimer, seeing no need for an apology. Dexter took another route:

"You shouldn't have no trouble training them," he said.

Loretta stayed home from school that day and from then on took to wearing pullover sweaters, her training bra secure underneath, a meager consolation.

Tonight, as she dresses after her shower, memories of the incident recur. She avoids looking at herself in the mirror and slips on her brassiere and panties, then a pair of tailored wool slacks and a cotton turtleneck—a blue one, Bodie's favorite color.

He sounded happy when he called this afternoon. His invitation to go out to dinner was a surprise; she has seen him very little since Harmon left in November. The reasons are not clear, they never are. She flips through a magazine as she waits for Bodie, intermittently talking with Dexter and Miriam eating supper at the kitchen table.

"C'mon, eat something with us," Dexter says, pointing to an empty chair with his fork. "Noodle casserole. It's good, for a change."

"I'm going out with Bodie, Dad. Out for dinner."

"C'mon. A little appetizer. You can use it."

Loretta knows by heart the coming routine. First, he'll tell her she's so skinny she's going to blow away in the wind. Next, he'll tell her she's so skinny she has to run around in the shower to get wet and then he'll say if she closed one eye she'd look like a needle.

"You've got to gain some weight, little girl. Big wind's gonna come along and—"

"Dexter, would you *please*," Miriam hisses at her husband.

The smell of burnt cheese mingles with the saccharine scent of Dexter's Vitalis hair tonic. Before each meal, he combs his hair, looking into a tiny mirror nailed to the wall above the kitchen sink. His parabolic pompadour is perfect every time. Loretta stares at the architecture swirled across his forehead and tries in vain to picture Bodie with her father's hair.

Dexter is a machinist, thirty years with Northfield Tool. His shift lets out at three thirty and he spends his spare time "dubbin" (as he calls it) on his wood-frame house and quarter-acre lot along Pike's main street. In summer, he tends his garden, mows his lawn to carpet grade and freshens up the paint job on his clapboards, doors and trim. At Northfield Tool, he works with tolerances expressed in thousandths of inches. At home, he does his best to overlook less rigorous standards.

Aside from helping Tinker with his race car, and his Elks Club evenings out, Dexter has a passion for mathematical conundrums. He savors them over and over in his mind, tastes them patiently and, like hard candy, lets them melt into his senses. For six months now, the impossibility of determining the square root of minus one has kept him pleasantly baffled. With Miriam's reprimand at the supper table, he retreats to the shrine of numbers, works some calculations in his head and smiles at how the figures move about for him in perfect order.

Loretta has never been certain whether she loves or hates her father. The thought of hating him seems too treacherous to consider, but loving him, *loving* him makes her feel dirty and incomplete. Instead, she puts her feelings off, imagining that someday it will all, somehow, become clear.

Bodie puts the tractor away and goes to the barn to talk to Leon. He finds him sitting on a hay bale in the shadows near the prostrate holstein. Leon hears Bodie enter but does nothing to acknowledge him. These are his chambers. Here, he owes no courtesies. The low, beamed ceiling dips in places, brushing Bodie's head. He ducks by habit, knows the low spots by heart.

Bodie stands outside the circle drawn invisibly around his grandfather and waits.

"Critter's dead," Leon says. And then, after the briefest pause, "You see Harmon's letter?"

"Yup."

"Doozy, weren't it?"

"Wouldn't have believed it was him."

"Carrying some of Carl's blood, I s'pose. Works that way. Pops up like poison mushrooms, strangest places."

"War don't help. Can't say I blame him," Bodie says.

"Jeesum, no. Weren't his selection. Better he'd be here with Darlene, building his house." Leon stands and puts a foot on the dead cow's flank. "Dig a hole for this old girl. We going to have Jiggsie's rig back?"

"Next week. We'll be backfilling."

"Cold enough. She'll keep good till then. I'll tow her out with the tractor." Leon lifts his cap and smooths his hair. "What'd farmer Judd want? Army business?"

"Him and Clayton are on the draft board."

"Figures."

"Looks like I got to make a choice."

"Q'bec?" Leon winces at the lonely sound.

"Or jail. Or 'Nam," Bodie says, surprised at himself. He knows it makes no sense, but since Harmon's letter arrived today he has entertained—in tiny parts at first and then, full-scale—the notion that he could bring his brother back. Somehow, he would find Harmon in a remote jungle camp and lead him home to sanity and safety, home to Catamount. Military regulations, borders, travel, money, passports—these are unimportant details. Bodie the Redeemer would overcome all obstacles.

"You don't want jail," Leon says.

"I know I wouldn't like it. That's why I got to thinking."

"You'd join up? Go over there with Harmon?" Leon

scratches his stubbly cheek in disbelief. "Fickle pickle, ain't you?"

"I just got thinking, since this morning."

"Going on a rescue. Like a cowboy picture."

"Kind of."

"Kinda foolish, you ask me. There's quite a piece of country over there, so they tell it on the TV. I should judge you'd never find him."

"It's just an idea." What good would it really do? Bodie wonders. Harmon was crazy enough when he left. Hard to get along with, anyway.

"It ain't my business," Leon says, and spits against a rusty stanchion. "I'd rather see you living up in Canada than you-know-what in Veet Nam."

"I'm thinking about it."

"I s'pose I'll yarn her out a'doors," says Leon, looking down at the cow. "Died hard, she did."

Back inside the house, Bodie telephones Loretta, then the Densmore Lumberyard in Canaan. He orders plywood, two-by-fours, snap ties, nails, form oil and perforated footing drainpipe, for immediate delivery. He'll begin the formwork for the walls as soon as the material arrives. They promise early tomorrow morning; work on Darlene's house is stalled until then.

Two or three hours of daylight remain. Sun still shines on the kitchen floor.

"I'm going rabbit hunting," Bodie says to Vera. "I'll take my snowshoes, see what I can rustle up." It occurs to him that he has never deliberately hunted rabbits before, but this sudden impulse seems perfectly natural. Harmon did it all the time. He kept a beagle hound for just that purpose, a clever little tan-and-white. She'd run a rabbit to Jordan and back, stay out all night if she struck a scent.

163

Today, Bodie tells himself, is a perfect day for hunting rabbits. Why shouldn't he? He rummages in the closet for one of Harmon's shotguns, picks a double-barreled twelve gauge and stuffs a dozen shells into his pockets.

"Let me make you up some sandwiches," Vera says.

"That's all right."

"Wait. You haven't eaten since breakfast." While Bodie paces the smooth linoleum she makes two bologna and mustard sandwiches and wraps them in wax paper. "Take these along, you may get hungry." She knows he'll eat them. She pats his shoulder. "Darlene's staying home from work. I've got her lying down upstairs. That letter hit her pretty hard."

"Wish it didn't have to be that way."

"Go get a rabbit," Vera says, and gently shoves him out the door.

Above the farmhouse, hardwoods follow the contours to the crest of the first rise. Bodie walks it to the top, then down the other side into a sag where open water lies in puddles, caught between two frozen slopes. He skirts one end of the dip and walks again in a northerly direction, up a series of hills that flatten at random intervals into brief plateaus, then rise again toward the summit. As he climbs, the vegetation slowly changes from beech and maple, ash and oak to white pine, spruce, white birch and hemlock. Lustrous needles replace bare twigs, the open hardwood canopy gives way to dense, compacted thickets. Rabbit tracks crisscross between the snow-draped bowers; the animals are never far from cover. In places, heavy traffic has left a miniature, hard-packed roadbed, six or seven inches wide, sculpted deep with oval prints. In other spots, a single trail of the tell-tale, two-plus-two pattern punctures the snowy mantle like a row of random bullet holes.

Bodie knows each rise and fall, each rock outcrop and

gnarled tree. They are all familiar beacons, totems from his boyhood years of solitary roaming. He stops at a hollow oak and listens to the mountain. The only sound is distant wind in branches far beyond his reach. He looks up for the pair of flying squirrels he once startled here—sent them soaring down the hill to a broken bull pine, airborne rodents, gliding slam-bang through the trees.

To the west of the oak, in a jumble of boulders, he picks his way to a shallow cave. Fox scat crowns a lookout rock that overhangs the opening. Oak and beech leaves line the bottom, gold coins in a chest of January sunlight. He slept there once, when he was small, scratched B.W. into the granite, left his kerosene lantern burning all night as he dreamed of stealthy Indians.

Half an hour from the cave, he reaches a promontory he and Harmon long ago named Bigboat. A shelf of rock configured like a ship's bow sticks out from the slope, rising close to forty feet on the downhill side. From the highest point, at the upturned tip of the rough stone prow, a panoramic view unfolds, framed by spruce tops from below and endless china blue above. To the west, the steeple tip at Jordan Center spikes through folds of piedmont. To the south lies the frozen Connecticut River and its flanks of fertile bottomland. Above the river, tumbling to it, hills hold back a blue horizon. To the northeast, almost invisible through the trees, the pale green arches of the Catamount bridge hump up above the Piketown Flats.

Sun and wind have bared the rock. Bodie takes his snowshoes off and walks to the point, slowly scanning the whitened landscape. A breeze blows from the northwest, chilling his sweat-damped undershirt. He stands with the butt of the shotgun on his boot top, holding the barrel off to one side like a clumsy walking stick. Harmon's gun has not once figured in his consciousness since he left the house. The scores of tracks he has passed, the half-dozen rabbits he has seen zigzagging across the snow have not once re-minded him what the gun was meant for. The gun is simply something he has carried in his hand. He has used it like a stick, to push snow off an overhanging bough, or for bal-ance, arm outstretched, as he jumped from boulder to boul-der. He won't shoot a rabbit this afternoon, he won't even think of aiming at one. He hasn't needed a rabbit—just as a fisherman doesn't need a fish to justify an afternoon of floating on a river.

Sitting crosslegged on the cold stone, he puts the shotgun down beside him. He unwraps one of Vera's sandwiches and eats it in three bites. The soft white bread compresses to paste around the mustard and bologna. He eats the sec-ond sandwich and still feels hungry. Bread meal sticks like suet between his teeth and he wishes he'd brought some-thing to drink.

In the distance, against the purple slopes of the massive Canaan ledges, a thin chalk line of woodsmoke rises straight toward heaven from an unseen chimney. Is that what hap-pens to our lives? What is it that the fire burns, where does it go from here? Bodie sits and stares at the frail transpar-ency until it fades into the ledges, until it seems his body has abandoned him. In time, a cold dark curtain falls and tells him it is time to move. He stands with his shotgun, snaps open the breech and pulls out a pair of unspent shells. Stepping to the edge of the port side bow, he tosses them into a deep white ocean. Then he laces on his snowshoes, buttons his collar and heads down the mountain. As he threads through the trees he is thinking of fire and heaping on fuel; Dale is laughing and dancing, silhouetted in front of the great friendly flames.

Loretta watches her father chew his food and wonders where her boyfriend is. Dexter chews ten times each side, fifteen for steak or pork chops. He tried to teach his method to Tinker and Loretta, but he gave up when Tinker reached his teens and retaliated with an unflattering imitation of a cow chewing cud. My father eats like a machine, Loretta thinks. She tries to picture Bodie at the table but she can't. She'll watch tonight, she tells herself; he can't be like her father.

Before she hears his truck she sees the reflection of Bodie's headlights on the bird feeder outside the kitchen door.

"I'm going now. 'Night, Mom, 'night, Dad."

"Tell Bodie to watch for icy patches. It's dropped right down to twenty-some." Dexter points his fork toward the floor.

"Don't be too late," Miriam adds.

"Mom. Am I ever?"

"Tell Bodie hi."

"Same here," says Dexter. "Tell him there's a sale on diamond rings at Sheldon's."

"Dexter, I swear." Miriam throws her napkin on the table. "Go on, Sissy, have a good time."

As she closes the door behind her, Loretta hears her mother tell her father she could kill him.

Bodie's truck is warm inside. The dash lights twinkle pretty greens and reds. She notices he's cleaned the interior; she smells a trace of Windex. All the surfaces—the vinyl seats, the door panels, the steering wheel, the molded dashboard—are lustrous and voluptuous with curves and highlights, smooth as satin, slippery dry. She slides across the seat until she touches him. He smiles and waits until the song ends before he turns the radio volume down. George Jones and Tammy Wynette are singing, plaintive yearning in every word. A pedal steel guitar anneals their passion as their voices fuse and cool around the words "eternal love."

167

"Hi, 'Retta. You look good tonight."

"Thank you, sir. You're pretty handsome yourself." She touches his freshly ironed shirt, a red plaid, cowboy-cut with a row of pearl buttons at the cuffs. "Pretty fancy for a Tuesday night."

"I'm feeling fancy. Been a long, fancy day."

"Tell me."

"Poured 'crete this morning. Saw uncle-cousin Dale. He's still crazy."

"Drunk or sober?"

"I never thought about it. Could have been either. He crowded two old buzzards off the Jordan road."

"He's nuts."

"He may be smarter than I ever gave him credit for."

"No way."

"He got me thinking. He acts crazy, but then, there's crazy and there's *crazy*. Dale's not *crazy* crazy."

"Just crazy."

"You want to eat at the Four Roses?"

"You *are* feeling fancy."

"Fancy. Crazy. I don't know." He backs out onto Main Street and heads north to the restaurant, ten miles up toward Quinntown, on the river, overlooking the Quinntown falls. As they pass the Catamount bridge, Bodie glances at it protectively, like an off-duty night watchman passing by his place of work. "But I decided it would be a waste to shoot myself."

"You're wacky," Loretta teases. "You sound like Harmon after he's been drinking."

"Harmon's crazy too."

"I know."

"I mean *crazy* crazy."

"I know. Tinker's crazy too."

Bodie looks at her. A passing car illuminates her face. She

168

feels Bodie staring at her and she passes her hand defensively across her shallow bosom.

"Remember Winston Gandy?" Bodie asks.

"That killed those old people?"

"He was *crazy* crazy when he did it, but he was OK crazy the rest of the time—in a way that didn't hurt anybody."

"Until he did that."

"He went too far, it's true. What I'm trying to say is, you can be completely un-crazy and be worse off than, say, Dale."

Loretta thinks of her father chewing venison. She looks down at the speedometer. The truck is moving north at seventy-five miles an hour. She leans her head against Bodie's shoulder and closes her eyes. Voices from the radio are lost behind the sound of pavement rushing by. She hums to herself a nursery rhyme she plays for her kids in school. She wants the truck to roll like this forever.

"Grampy lost a cow this morning."

"Leon did? I'm sorry."

"He takes it OK. Nothing new. He's crazy, too. You know that, don't you?"

"Bodie."

"I mean it. He's OK-crazy, not the kind that Winston came to. Grampy's in his own world, back in history, out with his cows. It gives him strength."

"Strength . . . ?"

"It's how some people collect their power. Get it from the inside, in their own way. Then people call them crazy but they're not. Their power makes them different, sure. All that power is—is being what you really are. Nobody has power over you if you collect your inside strength and use it how it's meant to be used."

"Where'd you get this, from a book or something?"

"I got it from my uncle Dale, from Grampy, Tinker,

169

Winston. I got it from my mother and her uncle Carl. He was U.S. Grant. I got it in a letter Harmon sent Darlene. Harmon's off the deep end but it came to me up on the mountain he's finally come into his power. He's burning something all his own at last. He's not showing off for other people. He doesn't have to squeal his tires or shoot the biggest buck anymore. He *is* the big buck now. Horns all over. I think he's better off *crazy* crazy than he was when he was home, just being hard-assed Harmon and all that crap."

"Bodie, don't."

"I'm serious.

"You scare me."

"You like spaghetti? They make the sauce real spicy. Big meat balls, too."

"Bodie, you seem funny."

"Me?"

"It's scary, all your 'crazy' talk." She searches his face for familiar signs but finds only vague hints. Restless, mercurial—his mood flicks on and off within the shadows of his features. "You had a fancy day, all right."

"You know Bixby Judd? Clayton Foss?"

"I know some Judds from down by White River."

"Same outfit, probably. Bixby, he's the draft board honcho. Him and Clayton came to visit me this afternoon."

Loretta slides down into the seat, slips off her loafers and puts her feet up against the dashboard. Her white socks glow against the glovebox door. She looks at them as if she were observing icebergs from a ship. She suddenly feels at hazard; she is drifting in uncharted waters, her compass gone, her course obscured. She's wanted not to know about this topic for so long. She's kept it hidden deep, submerged along with all those questions that demand but won't succumb to resolution. She has not dared wonder during these

170

last few months if Bodie would be forced to action, knowing that some day, inevitably, he would have to make a choice.

And so, she thinks, the day has come. At last. He's taking me out to supper in his fresh-pressed shirt to tell me he's leaving for Canada. He'll beat around the bush until dessert and then he'll tell me and I won't know what to say if he asks me to go with him. If he doesn't ask me . . . I won't know what to say then, either.

"They're the buzzards Dale ran off the road. I pulled them out. Should of charged them."

"Did they have papers and things? You know, legal things, court orders and all that?"

"Not yet. They said they'd be back to me. It's like they gave me one more chance to mend my ways. Weren't too awful mad about it. Kind of embarrassed about the whole thing."

Loretta slides down further into the seat until her chin digs into her chest. Over the dashboard she sees two scratched arcs in the windshield glass made bright and then invisible with the passing of a southbound car. "I don't want spaghetti," she says. "I don't know what I want."

For dessert, Bodie orders apple pie with ice cream. Loretta orders coffee and puts her paper napkin over her untouched plate of fried haddock. Picking at the tartar sauce with a couple of french fries was the best she could do. Her stomach is a dustbin; her mouth tastes of the residue. She's spent most of the evening looking out the plate glass windows at the spot-lit waterfalls while Bodie talked about concrete and parts of motors, pistons, pumps and fluids—man talk, power words like Tinker and her father use, now inexplicably adopted by a man who knows each wild flower by name.

She waits for him to finish dessert, certain he will tell her something, good or bad. It almost doesn't matter now. She wants to get it over with, go home to the familiar, the faces and the things she can depend upon.

"How was the ham steak?" she asks.

"Good. Hey, listen, it's early yet. How about we ride over to see Simon's house, the one we built last fall."

"Tonight?"

"They won't be there. They only come up weekends, maybe once a month. I know where Jiggsie keeps the key. C'mon, you've never seen it." He smiles at her and looks, for a moment, exactly like his brother Harmon.

"I told Mom I'd be home early."

"She'll wonder, won't she?" He smiles again. "You're not going to get Miss Goody Two Shoes on me?"

"No," Loretta says like a witness under oath, lying to the prosecutor.

"I'll show you Simon's barn-board paneling. Came from Grampy's chicken house. Looks good. He's got it set off with these antique brass lamps."

Bodie pays the waitress and leads Loretta out to the truck. He smells of after-dinner mints; a toothpick dangles from the corner of his mouth. "You weren't real hungry," he says as he pulls out onto the blacktop.

"Guess I'm not too big on food." She thinks of Dexter's constant harping and hates him for it. "But thanks. I liked it, what I ate." What she ate wouldn't feed a bird, she hears her father say.

They drive the road to Pike in silence. She sits a yard away from Bodie, upright, staring straight ahead, holding the door handle as if it were a lifeline. He drives with his head cocked back, his left elbow on the windowsill. He holds his toothpick daintily and probes between his molars. As he turns right onto the Catamount bridge, he swings the truck abruptly into the corner, and Loretta slides across the seat against him.

"Come over, Rover," he says. "I won't bite, I'm harmless." He puts his arm over her wooden shoulders, feels her stiffen to his touch. "They leave the heat turned on to fifty," he says. "It won't take long to warm it up."

"How's Darlene?" Loretta asks as they reach the far side of the bridge. She has never asked Bodie about Darlene and whatever purpose her question is meant to serve will not be part of Bodie's answer. Her question is, more than anything, rhetorical, a tart reminder of an offense never to be forgiven.

"Coming good," Bodie says, ignoring her innuendo. "It set her back today, the letter, but she'll do OK. She'll come around."

"It was that bad?" Loretta moves a fraction out from under Bodie's arm.

"It was different, I'll say that. It wasn't Harmon like we know him. He's a hurtin' pup." Bodie gently pulls Loretta back toward him, turns left and then, a half-mile south, turns right onto the Jordan road.

"Simon still owes Jiggsie seven thou. You'd think he'd pay, with all he makes." He feels her nodding in agreement, still rigid as a stick. "He's got a bathtub built for two. Wait till you see the bed they use. It's half the size of Grampy's cowbarn." Under his arm, Loretta's shoulders shake as if she would break in two.

The bed, indeed, is bigger than Loretta could have imagined. But first, she is shown the barn-board wall, the brass lights, the stairs and the butternut kitchen cabinets. Upstairs, Bodie shows her how the linen closet doors retract into hidden pockets, points out the tub, the special imported tile and how the makeup lights around the mirror brighten and dim on rheostats.

173

Standing at the foot of the Massachusetts lawyer's enormous bed, Loretta clenches her jaw to stop her teeth from chattering. She looks down at her trembling hands and wonders whose hands these could be. Her body won't behave. She watches as it moves itself in unexpected gestures.

Behind her, without warning, Bodie turns the light off and the unexpected darkness hits her like a tidal wave. We're going to do it, here, tonight, in these strangers' room with pictures of their children framed in gold beside the bed. She feels panicky. What if they arrive unexpectedly and find us here? What if Bodie is just using me and never wants to look at me again? Where's he been all this time, anyway? Will my students see it on my face tomorrow morning? God, my father would have a conniption fit if he knew what we were doing. He wouldn't believe it anyway. He thinks no one would have me. Bodie. Why the strangeness leading up to this? Why couldn't you be more like you, the night you plan to do this?

Bodie stands behind her with his hands on her shoulders. He kisses her neck behind each ear, then wraps his arms around her and sways her slowly side to side. He hums a nameless tune and drops his arms around her waist. His hands caress her hips and when he moves to work her buttons loose he feels a teardrop on his wrist.

"Hey, 'Retta, it's OK. We don't have to." He assures her with a hug. "You want to go home?"

She shakes her head. No, she doesn't want to go home. She would tell him that, but her throat is frightened shut. She would tell him that her needs are not the same as his, but she wouldn't know how to say it.

She can't explain why she will go through with it except that, somehow, she feels she should. Images of her friends and family hover over her as Bodie lowers her to the mattress: her bathrobed father in a shower cap; Betsy, pregnant

174

at the county fair; her mother shelling soldier beans; brother Tinker shaving, naked, at the bathroom sink; a movie starring Steve McQueen. What odd spectators, she thinks, to witness these encounters, these hollow episodes which never measure up to expectations.

What place is this? Where are the violins? The numbers on the bedside clock are glowing green. She touches Bodie's face. His features feel familiar, yet there is so little proof of who he is.

"Bodie, can we turn a light on?" Her throat un-husks a brittle voice. "Just something I can see you by?"

He rolls aside and switches on a bedside table lamp. They flinch at the harsh assault of light and avoid looking at one another, relieved still to be dressed. He turns the lamp off, gets up and turns on the bathroom light, closing the door partway behind him. "That better?"

"Better," she whispers. "Bodie, I have to ask you something." He lies down beside her. She stares to find his features, puts her finger on his chin as if to focus. "After the ball game, on the bridge that night. If I had gone up to the top with you. Would you . . . ?"

"Would I have done what I did with Darlene?"

"I've told myself I should have gone instead of her. You asked me first, remember?"

"I asked *only* you. Darlene invited herself when you said you were afraid of heights."

"Anyways, I've always wondered."

"You think Darlene and me did something special."

"Everybody knows. They think she's got your baby."

"They don't know squat. It's Harmon's baby. All we did was, we just got naked. I swear, that's all."

"You just got naked?"

"We just got naked." He laughs. "The blanket itched like hell."

175

"I don't get it."

"The mosquitoes were something fierce." He tickles her at the small of her back.

"I'll bet."

"Don't ever tell." Bodie crosses her lips with his finger.

"Tell what? That you did, or you didn't?" Her voice cracks against her whisper, comes out squeaky in two octaves.

"Just don't tell anything about it to anybody," Bodie says.

"I won't, I promise. But I still don't know the answer to my question. What if it had been me? Would we be itching on the blanket, all passionate and lovey-dovey?"

As soon as Bodie looks at her she knows that he will lie. The tilt of his face gives him away, even the darkness can't protect him.

"With you, I would have wanted to do—everything," he says.

She thinks how odd it is his spurious answer satisfies them both. She wants to hear him say what he did, even though it isn't true.

"Everything," he says again, whispering his deception to the hair behind her ear.

As he rolls on top of her, she folds her arms behind her head and lets the dance begin. She lies there, strangely comforted in knowing—how, she cannot tell, but knowing full well—this will be the last time, ever.

Ten

Outside his bedroom window, Darlene's cellar hole lies sunken in the ground like an opened tomb. Half-moon shadows hide the rectangle of footings at the bottom, frost highlights the mountain range of earth piled up around the pit.

Bodie fumbles at buttons on his rumpled cowboy shirt. This time, the unbuttoning goes slowly; half the buttons don't need undoing. An hour ago, when he dressed himself and then Loretta, buttons didn't seem important. Not much else did, either. She asked him how he felt, was it all right, and he answered, yes, sure, fine, but he lied again and looked away as if to find some missing truth.

She went into the bathroom then, left Bodie alone with a crack of yellow light between them. She stayed in there for fifteen minutes, maybe twenty; time was turgid, thick and lazy. When she finally emerged, dressed carefully, tucked in, zipped up—she asked, "Do I look OK? I think my face is getting wrinkles. My nose. Don't my eyes look baggy, Bodie? Look at how my cheeks are. Flabby. I think my whole head is changing completely," and on like that until Bodie agreed, without caring what he said, that yes, he thought perhaps she had changed, but it was nothing to worry about, she still looked great. Maybe something around the mouth—or it could be her hair? He couldn't be absolutely sure.

Looking out at the moon-washed snowscape, Bodie pictures Loretta lying limp across Simon's half-acre bed. What was the point of it? Who were they kidding? She lay there with her fingers clasped behind her head. Observing. And Bodie couldn't blame her. There was more fire generated in Darlene's handclasp on the bridge last summer than in all of Bodie's nights with Loretta lumped together. Wanting to make up for the way Harmon used her and dumped her was turning out all wrong. Pity can't serve love. Was there a song that went like that? You need a spark to make a fire. And figuring it all out can make you crazy.

Crazy crazy. Maybe Harmon tried too hard to make his war into what he thought it ought to be. Maybe he saw things out there that he could not accept, period. Maybe the cost of taking those things in, accepting them as part of life, was costlier than life itself. He refused them until the conflict scrambled his brains, left him spewing gobbledygook so that other parts of him could remain intact. Inside, he knew how it should be, but meanwhile so much evidence built up—so much blood-soaked testimony filled his senses and told him his ideas were full of shit—that Harmon probably did the right thing: blew his fuses and saved himself by disconnecting his brain from reason.

Bodie throws his shirt at a chair and shivers in the darkness. He's not in Viet Nam. He, at least, can walk away.

He finds the sweat shirt he sleeps in, pulls it on and feels the comforting warmth of cotton nap against his skin. He begins to unbuckle his belt and stops; sleep can wait. The day's configuration—still abstract, still too intense to reconstruct—has yet another element, another curve or squiggle waiting to be added to the jumbled composition. He opens his bedroom door and crosses the narrow landing at the top

178

of the stairs, pressing down the thumb latch on the storage-room door directly across from his. Under his bare feet, the wide-board floors are smooth and cold as tombstone marble. The room is shapeless without light, but straight ahead, in the center of the gable-end wall, he knows he'll find the door to Darlene's room.

He tiptoes toward it, groping like a blind man, hoping she is awake. Three steps short of the door he stops, convinced he is only inches away. He listens for a sign. But even her breathing is lost behind the wall. He inches forward. Each inch convinces him he must be at the door but somehow it stretches away from him, eludes his grasp until at last his knuckles bump the molded casing and he finds the cold steel latch. With his fingernails he taps the door, then whispers, "Darlene—you awake?" She makes no sound. He taps again and slowly opens the door. "Darlene?"

Two dormer windows in her room look south into the valley. In daylight, sun floods through the glass. Now, the moon is at its zenith, halfway through its southern arc. Its silver light throws deformed shadows, crisscross on the bedroom floor. They lie like elongated trapezoids, two hop-scotch grids across a braided rug.

The room is warm and smells of creosote and sweet, dead mice. An ornamented parlor stove is piped into a coarse brick chimney against the opposite wall. Pencil lines of red are drawn around the warped cast-iron door. A table, chairs, and two chests of drawers hunker in the shadows around the room. In a double bed under the low-sloped ceiling, Darlene stirs at the sound of her name.

"What? Harmon?" She sits up suddenly, wide awake. "Harmon!"

"Shhh. It's me. It's Bodie."

"God, you looked like Harmon. Scared me half to death."

"I knocked. Sorry. Maybe this isn't such a good time."

"No, no, it's OK. What time is it, anyway?"

"Past midnight. Look . . ."

"I'm wide awake, really. I was dreaming awful stuff. It's just as well you woke me up." She smoothes her hair and reaches for a glass of water on the bedside table. Her little gulps sound like a child's. "You want some water? Warm in here." She pulls her sheet up to her throat, then pushes her blankets down around her waist.

"No, thanks. Hey, look, I've been thinking about Harmon's letter."

"Me, too. It's awful."

"It could have just been a real bad day," Bodie says. "I mean, one letter doesn't mean a guy is gone forever. It could have been right after some big battle. Maybe he was so wrung out he couldn't think straight. Going sleepless can screw you up something wicked, especially over there, everybody trying to kill each other."

"I wish he'd send another."

"It would tell a lot. You might get the old Harmon back. Still, I've been turning it over since this morning, since before you got the letter. Ever since Dale drove in."

"Dale gives me the creeps. You see how he looks at me?"

"I know what you mean, but that's part of what I'm talking about. It's part of what got me thinking. The thing about not telling Harmon."

"I thought about that, too, especially since his letter."

"It's been right at me. Hit us both the same, I guess, huh?"

"I've been writing him in my head," Darlene says, "trying to give him something to hold on to. Tell him what went on with you and me. I'm sorry, but I have to, don't I?"

"Yup."

180

"It's gone way past what it used to be. There isn't any balance now. He needs whatever power he can get."

"I'd tell him anyway. That's what I decided. It was Dale that made me see it loud and clear."

"Dale's crazy, Bodie."

"That's what 'Retta said. He's crazy, sure, but he's *direct.*"

"Bodie . . ."

"You see his eyes? You see the way he laughs? He doesn't give a shit. He takes in what he wants and spits out the rest. Doesn't let the poisons put a hole in his guts, never lets it get a hold of him. That's how he made it through Weymouth's loony bin on Quinntown Mountain, all the tales you hear of eating dogs and drunken babies. Jeesum, it's a wonder he can work a steady job."

"He barely does. How long's he been with Twin State? Couple of weeks?"

"That doesn't matter. What looks like 'crazy' can be a person's only way of getting by when nothing else will work."

"That's Harmon. That's where Harmon is," Darlene whispers.

"Sounds like it. And the point is, Harmon—or Dale, or you or me—we got to act the way we feel. Or else it screws us up even worse. I'll write him a letter same as you. Telling him what really went on may be the only way to rescue him."

The floor is icy cold. Bodie moves a few steps to the rug and puts each foot inside the shadow outline of a window-pane.

"You can sit on the bed if you want to," Darlene says, pulling the covers closer to her.

"Thanks anyway. You know what I think?" His voice bends into unfamiliar shapes. "I think with Harmon

181

gone, a lot of things look different than they ever did before."

There is no light inside the tunnel, but Harmon keeps his eyes wide open, straining for a mote, a glint, a particle of contrast in the void of black around him. Smell and touch are the senses of survival here. Taste has taken on the palpable properties of fear; chalk and bile have robbed his mouth of spit. In the tunnels, sight is just another open wound he takes along, another stone inside his boot, another rash between his legs. Smell and touch are all he has. Lame companions, but better than none.

Harmon's lieutenant, Stan Dubinkski, likes his men to search the tunnels. They slither on their bellies in the dark, hoping to find a cache of ammunition or radios or maps or stores of food.

"You blow 'em up before you search 'em—hell, you lose all kinds of goodies." His way, Bink's way, you find things. Some rusty AK-47 Soviet-built rifles, some bags of rancid rice you wouldn't feed your hogs back home, some stone-age radios the French threw out when they departed.

The men call Lieutenant Dubinkski Brightboy, they call him a West Point pinhead. Dubinkski does things by the book. He finds some ammunition, he finds some charts that show who's doing what. He finds things that the books he used to read told him he ought to find, and that makes Bink feel as if he's doing a good job. He also loses men in the tunnels. Good men, too exhausted or scared or dumb to tell him to fuck himself.

Last week, Judd—a pimple-faced eighteen-year-old running a two-week fever and half-wasted with dysentery—Judd went down in a hole and crawled into a booby trap. Bink told Harmon to pull him out, there must be something valuable down there. When Harmon pulled on the soldier's boots, they slipped off in his hands. He threw them out and reached back in for Judd's ankles. He couldn't believe how skinny they were. They reminded him of a whitetail deer, slender bones with such a thin veneer of skin and flesh you wonder how they run and jump without breaking to pieces.

Judd was dragged out easily. A bag of bones. His face and chest were smoking, black, his mouth crammed full of dirt. His fever was gone forever.

In Scranton, Pennsylvania, his mother works at a supermarket checkout counter. She thinks about what she will write him each day when she finishes her work: send him a newspaper clipping about a friend of his, made manager of a liquor store. She mails a letter every day. A week from now, she will get the news, then the visit, the condolences. There will be a flag and, later, a medal—for bravery. She will throw the medal off the Lackawanna River bridge.

Judd is not the only one. On this patrol, a month or more, there have been at least a dozen lost in searching tunnels. Booby traps, grenades, cave-ins, some hand-to-hand, some shoot-outs, snakes—nightmare material. And yet Dubinkski still counts his gains, his bags of rice and radios, as more important than his losses.

Lately, Harmon doesn't care. He has been inside so many tunnels he almost feels a safeness there. At least he can be alone in a place where luck has favored him. Each time he comes out unharmed, he feels a tired, guilty triumph.

They touch him when they can. The few who have lasted as long as he has don't, but the replacements do. They find an excuse to brush against him for good luck, pick up his cast-off possessions and wear them on their helmets or in their pockets. Tunnel talismans.

He stays off by himself whenever possible. He doesn't know and doesn't *want* to know the names or personalities of any of the soldiers brought in for replacements. They will die, too. Out of twenty, four are left of the original platoon. Like Harmon, they stay to themselves.

He carries a Bible. Harmon Woodard, who has never been to Sunday church in his life, carries a miniature, dog-eared edition of the Old Testament in his breast pocket. He reads the Book of Job over and over again and dreams of scriptures chiseled into the granite cliffs above Catamount. In view of the Superette. As long as he is reading Job, some vague rationale insists that no harm can find him: no bullet, no bomb, no flying shrapnel will dare violate the sacred ring around him. As time goes by and the bargain holds, its truth becomes palpable: the Book of Job will save his life.

There is no reading in the tunnels. Instead, his memory turns the pages. *"I shall say to God do not pronounce me wicked. Cause me to know why it is that you are contending with me. Do you have eyes of flesh, or is it as a mortal man sees that you see?"*

Tunnel dirt smells like no dirt to be found in Catamount. No plowed field on Woodard land gives up these pungent fermentations, no barnyard dungheap smell compares with the smell of tunnel rot. Nothing Harmon has ever smelled has smelled like these deep soils.

From the first day he landed, it has been the *smell* of Viet Nam that has tugged at Harmon's senses, kept him mesmerized. The hills, the plains, the flooded paddies, each has its peculiar extravagance of odors: blossoms, tree bark, grass and dust, the sour breath of a water buffalo, the warm night winds, the stagnant puddles in the bomb craters—they leave him dreaming in aromas. Inside the little villages, he learns the spicy scents of open cook pots, bitter tinctures, high-pitched perfumes, titillating scents that pinch his nose, that dart and weave across his brain, tart olfactory ambushes.

Although he can't deny he likes most of these exotic aromas, they also remind him he is lost and far from home. To compensate, he conjures up the smell of woodsmoke on a cold October night. A mountain valley in Vermont: white clapboard houses nestle snug along a winding moonlit road. Kitchen lights are glowing orange, the evening sky so crystalline and pure with stars and oxygen that air itself becomes nutrition.

Inside the tunnel, air is made of heavy matter, sticky mist, a musky fermentation oozed from aeons of a patient earth. Harmon's breath and sweat surround him with a poison he cannot escape. Sweat lubricates his body; a slimy film between his skin and clothes makes slithering forward easier, a pitiful advantage.

If air had color, he imagines, tunnel air would glimmer dark and rotten hues. No soft pastels. Tunnel air would be painted from a somber palette: blood and earth and rootstock dyes, larvae, rotted tooth and bone. Tunnel air is shadow air, no highlights, no refractions.

"Looks like a beauty. Who's going to be my mole this morning?" Bink points his M-16 at the entrance to a tunnel. Dug into the dirt floor of a crude hut, the earth around the opening is packed smooth with wear. The sound of Bink's voice falls into the hole and disappears. "Who wants to wiggle? C'mon, Brownies, who wants to be a volunteer?"

His men are silent, hating him, wishing for invisibility. Those closest to him stop breathing, stop blinking, stop metabolizing the tiniest cell. Their hair and skin and nails stop growing; they postpone life itself in order to prolong it. Those farther out, the lucky ones—Lessard, Antonio, Shiffman, the kid with the harelip: Bunny Boy (his real name is Tzjsis Czaja, double curse)—they are far enough away to pretend they didn't hear. They find a bush, a hut, a hill to look behind for snipers. They are suddenly passionate about protecting the perimeter.

The men in between—too close to feign deafness but once removed from the three soldiers in the hut with Bink the Fink—they begin the "who, me?" shuffle, toeing at the ground, avoiding Bink, suspended until the "volunteer" is chosen. Among them, Harmon stands stoop-shouldered in the broiling sun.

It is only halfway through the morning and Harmon's clothes are soaked with sweat. For breakfast, he ate a tin of rations, pork and beans. He puked it up ten minutes later. Since yesterday, his food won't stick; his stomach is lined with slippery dread, a queasy, indeterminate pall that started with the kid from Scranton, Jimmy Judd, with ankles of a fawn.

It was the skin. When he pulled Judd out, stone-dead and charred like bleeding coal, he pulled against the skin around the poor boy's bootless ankles. The skin felt smooth as ivory, as delicate as the tender parts of a lovely woman's body. The feel of Judd's ankles has stayed on Harmon's hands all week. The first night, after dark, he found a packet of army-issue hand soap—coarse granules of lye and potash with a whiff of disinfectant—and rubbed his hands together, dug under his fingernails and scrubbed off every hint of dirt. As he scrubbed, he stopped now and then to sniff at his fingers, smell his palms, in hopes the ankle scent was gone. He kept the hand soap in his mess kit all week, scrubbed his hands raw but still could not erase that lingering invisible evidence.

Finally, he gave up trying to clean his hands and varnished them instead with grease and mud and animal dung, anything to mask the memory of a bootless boy. Then yesterday, he realized the smell had moved inside him, now was living in his guts, refusing to accommodate his food.

"C'mon, you pussies, who's the mole? What's wrong? You wanna live forever?" Bink looks around; the men avoid him. He will have to give the orders. No one here has volunteered since Judd had his face burned off.

As he does each time his feet stop moving, Harmon opens his Bible and begins to read. He has torn away all but the Book of Job, pruned back the pages to the only parts that still have meaning. *At despoiling and hunger you will laugh, and of the wild beast of the earth you need not be afraid* . . . So spoke Eliphaz, so spoke Harmon, moving his lips with each syllable and glancing up in time to meet the lieutenant's gaze.

At despoiling and hunger . . . Hunger, Jesus, I know hunger, Eliphaz is speaking to me . . . *You will laugh, and of the wild beast of the earth* . . . Down in the hole—that half-pint Bambi—Jiggsie could have ate him for a sandwich. Little whitetail Jimmy Judd, kid from Scranton, Pennsylvania. Didn't know the word of Eliphaz. *You need not be afraid.* Down in the hole the wild beasts of the earth need not be afraid. It says so. Here.

Bink watches Harmon holding up the tattered book he reads at every opportunity. Bink has made a list of men who need a spell of R and R. Woodard's name is at the top. A month ago, Woodard was gung-ho, the kind of willing, raw recruit that country boys so often are. He could scout and track with the best of them, shoot a maggot off a body bag at fifty paces. He saved Bink's life on the river one day, blew three snipers out of a hooch. Dubinkski will never forget that. Woodard had the stuff, all right, but lately he's been doing what too many do a few months out: drugs or religion, religion or drugs, the same cop-out no matter what you call it.

"Woodard! Got your lucky book?"

" 'The wild beasts of the earth need not be afraid,' " Harmon reads aloud. He acts as if the hole weren't there.

"You up to it?" For a moment it seems too easy to Bink. Something is wrong. Bink knows his men, he keeps them going. Woodard has searched the tunnels more than anyone. He is their lucky gopher. He finds whatever there is to be found and stays out of trouble. But just now, it seems like he is too far gone. The Bible stuff again. So much of it lately. But it seems to work, so why not let him? If Woodard wants it, he can have it. No one else will volunteer. Not these boneheads. Not today.

"I like it down there," Harmon says. "My brother, he's holed up like that. Up north. He's got an igloo cave." He tucks his Bible into his breast pocket and walks to the tunnel entrance.

He knows the other men are watching him; he can feel the tension disappear now that he has volunteered. They probably feel sorry for him, but it doesn't matter. He knows how it goes: they're glad they're not the ones to go.

"Good luck, Reverend," Antonio says. "Save the broads and booze for me."

"Hey, Woody, scrounge me up some reefer."

"Take care, man," says Alvarez.

"Watch for snakes, Dude. Two-step Charlie ain't no joke."

"Of the wild beasts of the earth, you need not be afraid," Harmon says to no one in particular.

"Them Cong's a beast."

"Ain't dat some shit."

"Good luck, Woodrow my man."

They watch him strip his pack off, drop his bulky belt and rub his awful hands together. They watch him in the way young children watch a simpleton—part mocking, part afraid of inexplicable behavior. They know the barest details of his life and those are incomprehensible to some. The ghetto blacks and Spanish equate a farm in Catamount with life on Mars. Dubinkski thinks Harmon's speech is strange. He says the way Yankees talk is "like eating toast without butter."

188

"You got the good book?" Bink asks, patronizing.

Harmon pats his pocket. He silently repeats his catechism. The words of Eliphaz will direct him, keep him steady as a gyroscope. He looks around at the faces staring at him. *At despoiling and hunger you will laugh.*

He looks beyond the faces at the deserted huts around the tiny village. Insects fill the air with sounds of tireless machinery. A rim of trees with flayed white bark hems in the scene from all around. A dog barks. Harmon sees the running figure. In one instinctive motion he grabs Antonio's M-16, flips on the automatic selector, flops to his belly and fires twenty rounds into the small brown body.

Bink and the others duck for cover, weapons ready for an onslaught. But in the end, the only sound above the silence is Harmon's whispered monotone: "The beasts of the earth . . ."

They watch the shredded body until the insect chirring starts again. A flock of birds flies overhead. More minutes pass, still no man-sound except for Harmon, off and on, his mantra murmured into the stock of Antonio's rifle.

"Shiffman. Delgado. Take a look." Bink motions toward the body. The soldiers move cautiously out into the open, watching the trees beyond.

"It's a kid," Delgado says, looking down at the crumpled form. "Carrying a grenade."

Shiffman prods the body with his boot. "That ain't a grenade, you asshole."

"The fuck it ain't."

"It's a bottle of pills." Shiffman leans down to pick it up.

"Fuck you."

"Up yours, greaseball It's fucking penicillin." Shiffman drops the bottle on the corpse's head. The bottle cap comes off; white capsules spill like decorations on the blood-soaked ground.

In other circumstances, Harmon would be a murderer. Today, he is a workman doing his job, a carpenter driving home another nail.

"One less dink to make into a Cong," Alvarez says.

"The Rev can shoot."

"Gave the little motherfucker one hell of a headache."

"Ruined his day."

"Another notch on my piece," Antonio says. "Let me have that thing," he says to Harmon.

"No way. That ain't your tally. Reverend did the fancy work."

"Yeah, but he used my weapon, that's what counts."

"Thievin' bastard—it's Reverend's kill."

"It's just a kid, anyway."

Harmon gives the gun to Antonio without looking at him. His eyes are elsewhere, searching the ground for something he can't name. He takes out his Bible and thumbs through Job, and to himself, he reads: *A brother to jackals I became, and a companion to the daughters of the ostrich. My very skin became black* . . . He stops reading and holds his left hand away from him, looking at the dark, cracked skin, first the palm, then the back of the hand. He turns it in slow motion, clutching at the humid air like a prehistoric reptile . . . *and my very bones became hot from dryness.*

"Still my gopher, aren't you, Woodard?" Bink watches Harmon studying his hand.

Harmon folds the Bible into his pocket and smiles at Bink. "I'm going to be a daddy in March," Harmon says. "A baby boy. Call him Eliphaz."

Bink motions to the tunnel. "Probably be twins, a stud like you."

"One for Bodie, one for me," Harmon says as he drops to his knees at the edge of the hole.

Bink hands him a flashlight and his .45. "You want ear

plugs?" Harmon tucks the pistol into his belt and shakes his head no. He snaps the flashlight to the "on" position, but the bulb won't brighten. He whacks the head of the flashlight against his knee; the light comes on. He clicks it off and on again to test it and crawls head first into the tunnel.

They watch him disappear, calling after him with thin encouragements.

"Be cool, little brother."

"Don't take no shit from nobody."

The flashlight beam shows fifteen yards of tunnel, curving slightly to the right. Pushing with his elbows, knees and feet, Harmon snakes himself forward with little room to spare. Here and there, a root thread dangles in his face. The air turns thick, the smell hits hard. The tunnel smell and taste are back, along with the dread of what comes next.

The curve begins to straighten. Careful, this could be a setup. Harmon feels a tingle on the back of his neck. He points the light up at a hollow bamboo tube. An air shaft. These guys are serious. There must be something in here worth the effort.

Harmon's stomach wafts up waves of ankle scent. He wiggles forward and sees, ten feet ahead, the edge of a room. The tunnel opens into a vaulted crypt, eight feet across and perhaps twice as long. The space is filled with stacks of boxes. At a glance, Harmon knows he's found a major cache of ammunition and explosives.

As he begins a rough count of the boxes, the flashlight quits. The tunnel is unconditionally black. He bangs the flashlight against his palm, clicks it off and on. No luck. He unscrews the butt and slides the batteries out, rubs the terminals against his shirt, hoping to dislodge the circuit-shorting corrosive fuzz that grows so fast in humid weather. He reassembles the flashlight, tries it, bangs it again and again. No use. *Where, now, is the way to where light resides?* The verse seizes his brain; he sees it on the soiled page: *As for darkness, where, now, is its place, that you should take it to its boundary and that you should understand the roadways to its house?*

Rather than crawl out backwards he decides to wiggle the remaining distance into the room, grab a handful of samples from the stacked boxes and then crawl headfirst out to daylight.

He thinks of the bridge at Catamount. Even on moonless nights, it would never be as dark as this; the little portals always showed faint squares of light between his feet. And the smell up in the bridge. That made the difference. In spring, the aromatic texture of buds and blossoms, the green-leaf smell that followed rain. River water late at night smelled unlike water at any other time of day. In summer, you would swear the arch was filled with bales of new-mown hay. In autumn, burning-leaf smoke and in winter the peculiar scent of cold painted steel and pigeon dust.

Providentially, these pleasant memories find him now, trapped in the unfamiliar stench of alien soil, slithering toward a stockpile of explosives booby-trapped in such a clever way that even with his flashlight he would not have seen the tiny detonators buried half an inch below his elbows.

It is a commonly held belief that in the moment between the sight of sudden death and death itself a record of one's life is summoned up for instantaneous review. On these occasions, time ignores convention and delivers in one elastic instant what the memory holds dearest, ignoring logic and chronology. A parade of loved ones, places and special events passes by at an almost leisurely pace. And so it is with Harmon.

Before he hears the roar of awesome thunder that will erupt (he hears the first part only), he sees the flash and knows what follows; he knows at last the circumstances of his death and feels the surprise of relief. The terrible anxiety of never knowing how it ends, when every hour new possibilities present themselves in threatening variations, is over. It has taken too long, but putting an end to the waiting makes any outcome, even this, an acceptable deliverance.

The flash uncoils vivid scenes of life in Catamount, in spirals, voices, faces, patches of sky, kaleidoscopic images astounding in their clarity. Vera, smiling; in her hands a laundry basket. Leon, bent over his cutter bar, hay chaff stuck to his suspenders. Darlene in a rowboat, in a bathing suit, a drop of perspiration between her breasts. Bodie with a baseball bat awaiting Harmon's pitch. Jiggsie in his truck with Betsy, Tinker at the speedway, winning. Darlene holding a child whose face is turned away. Darlene holding the child in her arms. Darlene in the kitchen with a loaf of bread. Darlene at the stove, a fire roaring. A flame, concussion, heat, a volcano, spiraling into wider and wider circles, into the universe.

The blast blows a ragged patch up out of the ground, ten feet deep and thirty feet across. Dirt and debris fly high into the air, above the tallest trees. A storm of clumps and pebbles rains on every hut and pathway. Far-flung pieces sound like gunshots as they land on a tin roof across the clearing. Smoke billows out of the burning ground like the smoke from brimstone, burning eyes and nostrils with the clammy stench of nitrates.

The concussion knocks the soldiers over. Even as they are thrown against one another, they know that the inevitable, once again, has happened; lucky streaks come to an end. The Reverend had his number called. And the Reverend was lucky, in a way; it happened fast, no time for pain, no time for self-recriminations. Soon, they would send a replacement for him, a new recruit with shiny boots. Meanwhile, Bink would have them bag what they could find of Harmon's body and send it out by helicopter.

"Gimme a flashlight," Bink finally bellows. "Who's got a goddamned flashlight?"

Darlene watches Bodie against the moonlit dormer window, remembering a story Vera often tells about Harmon and Bodie. When they were thirteen, Harmon was sent home from Boy Scout camp in Valley Forge with the measles. He awoke the next night in considerable pain, but not because of the measles. His shoulder hurt and Vera couldn't comfort him. The following day, Bodie's scoutmaster called with the news of Bodie's broken collarbone, suffered the night before. There were other stories like it: a stepped-on nail, a fall out of a tree, a car crash in which Harmon had broken his nose. In each case, pain was felt by both.

Bodie trembles at the realization of what he is feeling; a wool of dread weaves through his body, his senses liquefy, surrender to events unfolding half a globe away.

"Bodie?" Darlene whispers. "Bodie, are you all right?" She watches him put his palms against his ears and squeeze his head. He doubles over, elbows out like a diving airplane, twisting at the waist against a phantom gravity.

"Bodie, what's going on?" As she asks, she fears she knows the answer. She throws aside her blankets, swings her feet out onto the floor. "Bodie!" She rushes to him and he collapses, drenched in sweat, against her. She drags him to the bed, pulls his limp body against her cotton nightshirt. She comforts him as Harmon-Bodie, as her husband–brother-in-law. Bodie-Harmon-Bodie—all in one, now indistinct one from the other, unified in this one, the one she suddenly knows will be the lone survivor. He breathes heavily against her, huddled against her body. She strokes his hair and talks to him about his brother. Without ever saying it, they talk as if he's gone. They talk until the dawn comes in, until Leon walks the path back from the barn and asks Vera for toast and coffee in the kitchen down below.

Eleven

The thaw goes on, as if it were attending Bodie's work on the foundation. The nights are cold; each morning an inch of frost firms up the muddy patches. For three days in a row the transit trucks come early, crunch across the frozen crust, unload and leave the walls to cure beneath a warming sun. Each afternoon, the ground turns soft and slippery while the morning's pour congeals inside the plywood forms.

Dale drives the trucks. Each load requires little communication between Bodie and him: how stiff do you want it, back up over here—but he senses something loosened in Bodie, a thawing. Dale felt Bodie's eyes on him that first day, felt he was being watched, especially when Darlene was around. For Dale, the watching was more a form of flattery than insult. He enjoyed the attention even though it carried with it the accusations of being a "Quinntown Woodard." If Bodie wanted to watch him, he would play the part expected of him—and he did.

But now, he finds himself to be the watcher. Bodie Woodard, cousin-nephew, has a different walk today, a different way of placing his boot soles on the ground. Dale watches feet, he always has. For him, a pair of feet tell stories by themselves. They represent an attitude that hands and body,

197

eyes and speech and all the rest cannot convey. From self-apologetic pigeon toes to careless duckfeet, watching how the foot connects the body to the ground spells out for him a certain side of character. He has seen in feet the clues that made the difference in the settling of a late-night brawl, in avoiding disagreements over money owed or pride offended.

Bodie's boots today are animated by a sense of certainty. Dale takes it in. He watches Bodie balance on the balls of his feet. The intervals between steps are selective—a pause as Bodie thinks about how far to swing the chute, a rapid sequence, sure and parallel as he moves along the staging to retrieve a fallen anchor bolt. No toeing-in, rolled-over heels, no flat-footed fatigue or tiptoed panic, no stumbling, tripping, shuffling gait but every step put down with confidence, like solid stone.

Dale's observations are intuitive, honed by necessity rather than choice. As a child, his welfare, and sometimes his survival, depended upon his ability to know when to be invisible and when to express his needs. The signs were made of subtle goods, signs of the feet as well as others: the white around an iris, the slope of a shoulder, fingers tapping on a tabletop, a tone of voice across a single syllable. Signs that brought a slap across the mouth were different from signs that led to a bowl of cereal with milk. He learned the nuances early without knowing what he'd learned except that slaps became less frequent and his bowl was almost always full.

"You got her whupped," he says to Bodie at the end of the final pour. "When they bringing the home?"

"I told them Monday. I'll set my sills on Saturday."

"Darlene, she's happy?"

"I guess."

"Still working?" Dale asks.

"She'll quit next month. Baby's due in March."

"She'll have the house in time."

"Hell, it only takes a day to set it on the cement. They hoist it off the low-boy with a great big crane. Put the two halves together so tight you couldn't squeeze a dollar bill between them. Lag-bolt it together. Splice the clapboards across the joint."

"Slicker'n a trout." Dale decides he'll show Bodie his gums, and grins for all he's worth.

"Comes furnished. Pictures on the walls, avocado appliances. Good place to start a family."

"Harmon, he's gonna have it made." As he mentions Harmon's name, Dale suddenly knows he has trespassed. Something about the way Bodie half-turns toward him. Something about the line that subtly tightens the corner of Bodie's lip. Within the next few seconds the signs pile up so fast that Dale withdraws to safer business. He reaches for his clipboard holding the invoice for the concrete. "Mark your John Henry here and I'll get this rig out of your way."

Bodie writes his name, hands the clipboard to Dale and asks, "Your back still bothering you?"

"Rainy days and mornings."

"You married?" Bodie asks. He looks, to Dale, as if he's thinking about something else.

"Shit, I'd sooner run uphill. Been through that good stuff once too often. I'd act a fool again, I guess. But that ain't going to happen this week."

"Girl friend?"

"More than I can use. You want one?"

"Nah, I'm . . ." Bodie kicks a scrap of two-by-four into the hole. "I'm too goddamned busy."

Dale laughs. "Too busy? Christ, that's no excuse! There's women out there *needs* you, boy! You got to do your *duty!*"

"Nah."

Dale sees Bodie's feet come undone. He presses for another clue. "Darlene don't keep you busy, does she?" He says it with an eyebrow raised; the leering grin he tries to hide sneaks out around the corners of his mouth.

Dale squints as Bodie looks over at him. He watches Bodie studying, inspecting, one by one, each feature of his face, his broken nose, his mouth—yes, yes, he talks too much—his chin, the pocks, the pores, the scars—all made into inventory.

"Between the job with Jiggsie and this frigging cellar hole I've got all the busy I can use." Bodie's feet come back under him. "I was going with Loretta," he adds.

"That your truck I see last night up to the Riverside?"

"Could be."

"Heading for tall timber, was you?" Dale knows, this time, the needle won't prick.

"Softwood, every bit of it." Bodie grins, looking surprised at himself. "Doing my duty, I guess." The circle closes and both men smile.

At some expense to Loretta, Bodie has returned to parity with Dale. Did my duty, he thinks to himself, and found out where it stands with her. Part of that I owe to Dale. I owe him for showing me the courage it takes to do what you want to do, even if it gets you something you didn't know you were looking for. The crazy dingus. Running Bixby off the road just for the hell of it tickles me.

Bodie walks Dale to the cab and listens as the diesel comes alive. "Water pump bearing's getting worse," he shouts above the engine noise.

Dale looks down and shakes his head. He'll run it until the pump won't pump and then he'll complain to his boss about the overheating engine. "Them bearings always do

200

like that." He shrugs. "This puppy ain't been overhauled since Big Boss bought it off of Northland. Oil and gas is all I give her." He grinds first gear into place and lurches the rig forward. "Don't work too hard," he says, and guns the ten wheels through the slush. Then, "You going to pour the floor tomorrow?"

Bodie nods yes, then calls after him, "Stay in the shade."

Stay in the shade? Bodie wonders. This afternoon, the sun will set before five; tonight, temperatures will be in the twenties, maybe teens. Shade? This place has shade enough. The trick is to stay *out* of the shade, the trick is to find enough of the sun that heats the earth, grows grass and trees and makes you thirsty, makes you sweat. Like they sweat in Viet Nam.

Bodie has fallen through. Images of Viet Nam are melting Catamount's snowy fields and filling his mind with visions of a sweltering jungle.

The details come from television. Every night at half past five they sit in the kitchen and watch the news, Leon and Vera, Bodie and Darlene—transfixed before the little black-and-white Zenith console propped up on the countertop. They comment freely on the local news, the politics from Montpelier. Leon moans about overspending, Vera writes down the name of a book reviewed, the address for a pamphlet on canning vegetables.

The national news comes on at six, a network broadcast with telecasts from all over the world. Inevitably, a lengthy section covers the war in Viet Nam. As the footage rolls from Saigon—or Tonkin Gulf or any of the endless battle zones whose very names sound painful and too much alike to remember—activity in the farmhouse kitchen stops. Leon stops his rocking chair, Darlene puts her knitting aside, Vera wipes her soapy hands into her cotton apron and Bodie puts his pencil down, stops doodling on his yellow pad. The Woodards stop in unison and search the screen for a glimpse of Harmon.

Like spectators at a race-car track, they want to see their favorite win. They'll settle to see him go by safely. If he must, they want to see his crashes, too. If it must occur, they want to know the details, how the wheel came off, how the roll-bar held. They want to measure the skid marks, they want to see the dent in the wall where he hit, head on, and walked away.

They grow impatient with the foreign correspondents. Leon may grumble, "Quit hogging the show," and wave them off, asking, "Where's Harmon?" They watch the endless footage showing rain-soaked paddies, muddy villages. They watch tall grasses flattened by the turbulence from a helicopter touching down, GIs, hunched over, running to climb aboard. And always, the soldiers' gear and helmets make them indistinguishable from one another.

"Ought to give them numbers like the football teams."

"You'd think they'd show the soldiers' faces."

"That looks like him! See? There! Looks just like him!"

"That weren't our Harmon. Had a mustache."

"Could have been a shadow."

"Possible."

"There! See him? No? Well, it might have been."

"Ever see such awful jungle?"

"How in hell they plow them side hills?"

The images are images of tired, hot, frustrated men. Sounds of gunfire in the background lose significance. A correspondent's blow-dried hair and microphone block out the awful truth of what those guns are meant to do. *Rat-tat-tat-tat. A new offensive, planned for April, seems to have been stalled due to the discovery of* . . . The face, the voice, the rational explanation of pure chaos comes to Catamount as if those bullets had no targets made of flesh and bone.

"Keep ducking, Harmon." *Rat-tat-tat.* "Them bullets can't be meant for you."

Bodie feels he has been to Viet Nam and yet he knows it has only been through television. One night he watched an interview with a wounded soldier bound for home. The pearls of sweat across that black man's face told more than any spoken word; they slid at random off his brow and disappeared, replaced, each one too soon, by still another, then another. How much they were like liquid soldiers, obedient to some incalculable process of selection.

The soldier sweat sticks to him; Bodie wears its dank tattoo and swears he knows the rising swelter of the jungle after morning rain, he swears he hears the clicking of a trigger and the *rat-tat-tat,* the bullet meant for anyman, for everyman, for him, even. The pearls of sweat have become his own; they waken him on snowy nights and strangle him with jungle vines, blindfold him with enormous leaves, enshroud him in hot bedclothes made of writhing snakes and scorpions.

"Keep your head down." To hell with the shade. "I mean it!" he yells after Dale's truck, and wishes for a three-day blizzard.

Early Friday morning, Bodie strips the last of the forms. He pulls the nails out of the two-by-fours and stacks them with the plywood off to one side of the foundation. He'll use each piece again on one of Jiggsie's jobs for studs and decking.

At ten, Dale brings the first load needed for the basement slab. By noon, he's back again. Bodie floats the concrete down and starts at two with the power trowel. By dark, the floor is smooth and hard. With luck the thaw will hold another day and let the slab cure without a deep freeze.

Before supper, Bodie calls Tessier to tell him he can bring the double-wide on Monday. Tessier agrees. He wants his money. With a gangplank over the open ditch—the foundation won't be backfilled yet—Darlene will walk into her new house on Monday night.

At supper, Leon talks about Harmon. "He's laying low, I'd bet it of him. Biding time. He'll show them little stinkers."

"Harmon's clever, all right. Remember Herbie?" Vera tells a story they've all heard, about Harmon sneaking up on Herbie, a stuttering hired hand, painting the barn, clinging to the top of an extension ladder. Harmon climbed the entire height of the ladder undetected and tweaked Herbie's foot. Herbie thought he was being attacked by birds. He dropped the paint bucket and almost fell on top of Harmon, called him a "n-n-nasty lil' n-n-numbnut."

Leon barks a laugh, an old gray fox. He likes the story every time. "The paint pail struck a heifer's backside, splashed two more was standing there. By jeez, they come from miles around to see my red-haired holsteins."

"Herbie swore he wouldn't 'p-p-paint' the barn again until young Harmon was 'b-b-back' in school," Vera says, blushing at her imitation. She is proud of Harmon. She and Leon sit at the table side by side with their backs to the wood stove and *testify.* All through supper they trade stories of Harmon, stories that recall his strength and cunning—hunting, fishing, mischief stories, tales to fill his vacant chair with something more than dread.

Across the table, Bodie and Darlene are silent. They follow each anecdote with polite attentiveness, they laugh and nod agreeably, but each is held away from real participation by the cloying memory of Bodie's vision three nights past, the jolt of moribund empathy that figured Harmon dead. Neither will say it. They haven't talked about what happened, but both have come to a provisional acceptance. If Harmon is gone, the stories across the table tell like eulogies. The mother and the old man are reconstructing the past selectively, endowing it with the best that was and leaving the rest in peace. If, on the other hand, Harmon finds his way back home, the stories need revision. Don't they? The stories are nothing more than fragile hope chests, quickly fashioned from material at hand.

"Darlene, you haven't touched your plate," Vera says half through the meal.

"I'm working on it. Guess I'm slow." She fidgets with the tablecloth.

"That Harmon, he can make the groceries disappear." Leon grins across the table. "Eat twice the 'mount that Bodie eats. Ain't that right, Bodie?"

"It always used to be that way," Bodie mumbles.

"What's that?" Leon cups his hand to his ear.

"I said, he used to eat more than me. But now, I think, we're probably about the same."

"Course, he's got army rations. I imagine they ain't up to Vera's." Leon gulps down a huge forkful of mashed potatoes to prove his point.

Bodie smiles at his grandfather and makes a bet: he bets that Harmon wouldn't know the difference.

As the food on the table is portioned out and enjoyed, so are the stories of Harmon. But appetites for both are soon satisfied, and the sound of cutlery clanking on plates replaces the voices that began so hungrily. Leon now sits in craggy reserve, with the authority of a stern and silent referee. A sinewy old tree? His shade is sparse, sometimes elusive, but worth the search. And never failing. A father? Perhaps, but Leon is most of all an *element,* a combination of earth and stone. He sits looking down at his plate, blinking, eating the last of the mashed potatoes as if to be no part of waste.

Darlene gets up to clear the table; she needs something to do. Vera protests, says it can wait, but Darlene continues, saying she's itchy with all the sitting. As she carries dishes to the sink, she brushes Bodie's shoulder. This brother, who looks more like her memory of her husband every day, is also less like him as time goes by. Could Harmon have been so different? With only Bodie here, it is difficult to remember. Their images overlap—some parts coincide, some blur to uncertainty. When Darlene attempts to call up images of Harmon alone, the picture invariably fades away.

Harmon is Harmon, Bodie is Bodie, Darlene tells herself. Comparisons are worthless. In ninth grade, she had made a list of all the boys she knew, assigned each with a plus and minus column and checked off qualities like "selfish," "handsome," "strong" or "smart." From the results of this list she hoped to pick her boyfriend. She never did. The list got lost. She wonders now and then where Harmon would have ranked, where Bodie would have figured on the list. Just out of curiosity. But what were the criteria? What seemed good then might turn out not to matter. In the end, she realizes, she chose Harmon much as a moth will choose an open flame.

She wipes the table clean and squares the chairs around it. Harmon's place has not been sat in since the day he left. His chair is moved elsewhere and sat upon at times, but no one sits where he sat at the table, on his chair against the window.

"Harmon will need some fattening up when he gets home," Vera says. "We'll fix him good." Darlene smiles gamely at Vera's good intentions.

"Put the meat back on him," Leon adds.

Darlene listens as Leon and Vera discuss Harmon's appetite. They think Harmon is coming back, they won't consider any other possibility. They talk this way as if to *make* him come back. They make him skinny because that's something they can fix. Go ahead, make him skinny as a rail but don't get him killed. They'll put the meat back on him but don't ask them to put his head back on. They're only people. They talk like this because it's the only thing they can do for him. Puny, but talk is all they've got. Until three days ago, she joined the talk, she offered up her hope: "When Harmon gets home," or, "Wait till Harmon sees the shirt I bought for him." She has stopped saying things like that. She has barely said a word tonight, nothing about Harmon—hasn't for the last couple of days and Bodie hasn't either. The unanimity that used to circle the table is in pieces.

"Wish that boy could see you moving in on Monday." Leon is speaking to Darlene, but he sounds so far away. "Still can't believe they do it up that quick. A whole house in a single day. Seems like magic. Course, if Harmon came back for the weekend, he could stay over a few days. Help them build it, him and Bodie."

"It's already built, Grampy."

"I know, I know. 'Modular,' they call it. Modern gizmo."

She watches him scratch through the thick gray hair at the back of his head.

"You'd think they'd bring him over," he says to Darlene. "You'd think they'd let him out for just a day or two."

Darlene looks again at Harmon's chair, finds nothing new and stares into the night-blackened window. The reflection returns an old man's gaze, nothing else.

The telegram comes to Catamount, confirming Bodie's premonition. Darlene brings it from the mailbox to Vera's kitchen. Side by side they stare at it, given over to sounds sprung loose from sources far beyond their known anatomies. There are no words among these thrummings, no satisfactory protocols.

Later, when Vera brings the telegram out to Leon in the barn, she leaves him quickly, as he would wish.

He stands at the foot of the ladder and looks up into a darkened hayloft, his cheek still wet with Vera's cheek. He speaks his thoughts:

Hear me, woman, how I dread this. Esther? It's a telegram. Vera brung it to me, hugged me hard inside the door. Harmon. Army business. I see it, across the envelope. Don't have to look, I know what's in it. Crimus! Tears strung down her face. I dread it, Esther.

Purdy's time, they sent two men in uniform. Shoes was black and shiny. How they shone. Pants creased up so sharp and starchy. Spit 'n polish. Purdy's time, I was up back, bucking cordwood. Snowy day. She clanged the bell, back then she did. Strange. It was, what, still forenoon? Clanged the bell and down I come. What's ailing her? Left my saw half through the log. What's ailing Vera? Time to call Doc Adams? Must be something, all that clanging. Come around the woodshed corner, see two officers in uniform. And Vera, swinging the dinnerbell clapper, round and round. Oh, Esther, it was an awful sight. Her staring off to Timbuktu. Took all the strength we had to pry her fingers off that clapper rope.

Them officers, the flakes slid right off'n their polished shoes. Straight as they stood, you could see they hated what they come to do. She made them stay for coffee and doughnuts, polite and proper. Gave them doughnuts in wax paper. Doughnuts, Esther. All she knew to do, her carrying twins, a month to go. Now, they send a piece of paper.

I knew it, soon's I see them soldiers, felt a shock take holt of me. Black Chevrolet car. Road plowed out good that morning. Purdy's drowned, they told her. Purdy's dead. They stood right there and watched her ring that iron bell till I come down.

She come undone when she got ready. Who'd of blamed her? Esther, she was tore up awful. Broke a china sugar bowl. Crash! Pots and pans six ways to Sunday. Beat on me, she did, poor girl, two fists a-flying. "Why? Why? Why?" she hollered, pounding at me, "Why?" Pounding at a turn of fate she couldn't change. I guess she knowed it. Me, I stood like elmwood, twisted up. I'd of let her pound forever if I'd thought it'd bring him back. Her face swolled up, so red, the tears, they come all afternoon. Your Purdy, Esther, hers and mine, they sent a black car, officers.

Next morning come a heavy storm, snowed all day solid. Bucksaw blade was rusted brown when finally I come back to it.

Esther? I can't read this christly paper! Must of been Darlene that got it. Walks the lane most days at mailtime. Saw her go down by this morning. Looks for Harmon's letters every day, just like we done with Purdy. Vera and me in '42.

All day to buck up half a christly cord! Pitiful! Couldn't keep no concentration, strength drained out, I'd saw and up'd come Purdy's face, our son, all drowned and blanchy. Vera stayed down to the house, flat out, laying quiet on the divan till the boys was born. A month like that, no words could ease us, neighbors by to stand and shuffle shoes across the parlor rug. What could they say?

The Herald run his picture, there. Some letters come. But what's the difference? No grave to mark, no stone, no body. Disappeared is what he was. Sunk to the bottom of the deepest ocean. I'd just as soon be there too, Esther, if I thought you wan't waiting elsewheres. And now, for Harmon, for all he done, they send this paper with a stamp on it. Pocket change, that's what it cost.

She got his letters before he died, Darlene did. That's all she got from overseas. Stopped in here to show me both. "Look, Grampy, see the letter Harmon wrote." First letter, I could see his thinking. Tell her news, but not the bad news. Done the same when I was serving. Bad enough, the things you see. Another letter, what a

209

doozer! Didn't make no sense at all. I don't believe he wrote it, is what I told her. Must be some mistake, it must of. Harmon weren't like that, all flowery words. No sir, second letter, her and Vera— Bodie even—got all worked up, Harmon's off his rocker. Foolish. Harmon's got more sense than that. He's Woodard blood, way back. Well, I s'pose there's Vera's uncle Carl, but still, I don't believe it.

Darlene, how she'll take it I don't know. She's rugged, Esther. Knows her mind. Moved into the new house now, all fixed up perfect, one room special for the baby, decorations on the ceiling. Clinic told her six more weeks. For Vera it was only four. Six weeks, four weeks, twenty years. It ain't enough. A hundred years still ain't enough to give the words it takes to tell a boy he's got no daddy. This one coming, I ain't got the strength to raise him like I done with Vera's. This one needs more'n I got left.

But Darlene, she won't do like Vera did. Vera won't give up on Purdy. She'd barely blink if he walked through the woodshed door. She's kept him up, I know she has. She's made that way. She gave them dressed-up soldiers doughnuts.

Esther? Hear me. It's come back around. Another woman carrying a Woodard baby, left without her husband on account of war. So much the same. Now, there's telegrams instead of dressed-up soldiers, it's Chinamens instead of Kaisers. But it comes out equal for Darlene and Vera, them and their babies. And us that's left, me too old and Bodie—Bodie too set in his ways I suppose. We see it going around and around, like crops and livestock, seasons, moon. No stopping it. It's Nature, how it comes up, new, the same but different, teasing us to keep on watching, always changing, always the same, starting, ending, starting, ending.

How I dread it, walking back up to the house. This barn has hid me more than once. Chores enough to keep a body busy, true, but more than that, these timbers hide my insides when they churn and bother, cover up my thinking when it's back and forth so many times I can't see where I started off.

210

Truth of it is, this cowbarn's probably harmed *as much as it's done good. Slink down here to hide away. Accomplish what? Clean out my gutters? Put down clean bedding? Come in here and mope, leaving* them *to wrassle what I can't stand up to.* Them, *up there, around the table, holding hands together, giving comfort, comfort I ain't got the means to give or take. Comfort this old man has gone his life without. Ain't too liable to start in now, and that's the pity of it.*

How I dread it, seeing Darlene, face tore up. Vera, oh, she'll tend her, that's for sure. She gave them soldiers three, four dough-nuts each, took down their names and wrote them both a letter. Told them she was sorry what their job was, sorry how they had to go around telling such as her the worst news anyone could hear. She gave them comfort, Esther, after they come up here in a black sedan and told her Purdy Woodard's dead. I always wondered how she done that.

This paper don't mean nothing. Once you know somebody's gone, the paper they write about them—phh! Give you flags and medals. Phooey! Poor excuse for living blood. Pocket change for Harmon Woodard? Hear me, Esther, the way I see it, Bodie ain't been too far wrong.

Leon drops his hands to his sides and sits down on a hay bale. He will wait before returning to the house, wait and wonder whether he is heartless or a coward.

Darlene is on her hands and knees in front of her new kitchen cabinets. The doors are open and all the contents—dishes, pots and pans, a blender, napkins, scouring pads, detergents—are piled out on the floor. With a bucket of sudsy water and a yellow sponge, she is scrubbing all the surfaces of something even she can't see.

"This shelf is loose," she complains, her head inside a cabinet. "You'd think a brand-new kitchen wouldn't fall apart the day it leaves the factory."

Bodie and Vera sit drinking coffee at the table above her. "Craftsmanship," says Vera. "They let things go they shouldn't, nowadays."

Darlene hears the comment from a world away, a patch of stupid conversation she has no interest listening to.

"Bodie could fix the shelf for you."

"No problem," Bodie says.

Darlene knows he means it. She knows he'd welcome any task to fix, repair, *construct* something, put something broken back together. She knows they both need something to do.

"What's the problem, track come loose?"

As Bodie kneels beside Darlene, his knee rests on the hem of her maternity dress where it touches the floor. She hates the dress, the way she wallows in it, the way it drapes diagonally down from her collar across the swollen abdomen that draws her spine into a sag. Her elbow touches his as he leans forward to look into the cabinet with her. Shoulder to shoulder, they block out the light. She sits back on her heels as he fiddles with the shelf.

"Would you turn down the thermostat?" she asks Vera. "I can't get used to how hot it gets in here." Her forehead shines with perspiration. She stares at Bodie's narrow hips and wishes she felt nimble, wishes she could drain away the lead inside her veins. The floor pulls at her; she weighs a ton. "This rotten place is filthy," she says.

Like the hands that throw out attic junk, her voice sounds as if it is discarding worn-out word collections, boxes, bushels, dustbins full of used-up words whose absence will eventually make room for one word of enormous size. When occasionally a corner empties and is ready for new tenancy, she looks for little words to fill it, nothing words that make no demands. Harmon's name alone will need ten times the room she has to offer.

"If I had a screwdriver, I could fix it," Bodie says from inside the cabinet.

"Look in there, in the end drawer." Darlene points as Bodie pulls himself upright. As he moves to the drawer, Darlene turns to Vera and asks, "How'd Grampy take it?" She wants a one-word answer.

"You know Grampy," Vera says. "He keeps the barn so dark. He wouldn't read it. But he knows."

"Got a Phillips head?" Bodie clatters through the drawer.

Darlene turns toward Bodie and begins to stand up. As she does, she scans the objects in her kitchen: the opened cherrywood cabinet doors, the row of drawers, the curved Formica counter edge. The details pull her in and hold her, pass across her brain with no residual effect. Her eyes move to the window: snap-in muntins, curtains, pot of ivy, cloudy sky. Another storm? The paneled wall above the window meets the ceiling with a strip of molding, varnished pine. Had Bodie nailed it there? Back to the window. Grainy clouds, a lowery day. She feels it coming. Her body slumps into a long slow arc. She senses Bodie catching her before she hits the floor.

The sensation is one of sinking and ascending at the same time. She's weightless, yet she falls and rises, formless, in a vacuum. Light intrudes, retreats and pauses, blinks again and opens to—what? Heaven? Could it be? More flashes: Harmon's image, walking toward her, dressed in a glowing light. She reaches out to touch him, looking for his features beneath the helmet. As she reaches, he is pulled away, still walking toward her but losing headway, walking faster but fading back. She runs but can't keep up with him. His shrinking figure, half its size, a fraction, now reduces to a small black dot, a speck inside a swirling cloud that opens to the sound of Vera's voice.

213

"She's coming out of it."

Darlene is stretched out on her back. A pillow holds her head up off the kitchen floor. At first, the room is unfamiliar, surprises her for a moment. Then it comes back quickly: this is her kitchen, her new home. The face above her belongs to Vera. Bodie is kneeling, looking down at her, off to one side. The cabinet doors are open. All the contents are out on the floor. And Harmon is dead.

She closes her eyes and breathes in and out deeply. She opens them again and traces her steps: this is her kitchen, her new home, the faces belong to Vera and Bodie, the cabinet doors are open and there's stuff all over the floor. A telegram came this morning with the news about Harmon. What were the words? . . . *in the line of duty . . . a booby trap . . . heroically defending his position . . . sacrificed . . . freedom . . . sympathy . . . further arrangements.*

Darlene closes her eyes again. She reconstructs the day, beginning with the walk down to the mailbox. Perhaps she has left out something, some key element that, once recalled, will rearrange the outcome. If she can find the crucial detail, all that follows might be different. She begins with:

Her galoshes. Bending over her huge abdomen to put them on. A nuisance. Her coat and scarf. Then she says good-bye to Vera, waves to Leon on her way past the barn. Then down the hill. Careful, it's slippery. Betsy fell while she was pregnant and worried she had hurt her baby. OK, down the hill, across the flat. The wind dies down and smells of old snow. Warm enough, she loosens her scarf and unbuttons her coat. What then? Clouds are tumbling by. Snowbanks along the roadside are splattered with mud and slush. A new storm will freshen things up, hide the dirt. Now down through the hemlocks. This part is always spooky. Narrow, steep, between high banks, closed in with branches thick above. Now it opens up again to meet the town road. Here, the details are important.

She sees it: she pauses as she always does, composes her wishes, concentrates. Fifty paces to the mailbox. She sees the postman's tire tracks. The mail is waiting in the box. What's there is there, and yet each day she beams her hopes, X-rays her wishes through the metal shroud as if to change the contents. She counts the steps to the box and waits respectfully in front of it. Before opening the door she gives her wishes "one more chance" to solidify, to transform, by whatever process, the contents to her liking.

She opens the box. Inside, third-class junk mail lines the corrugated bottom. Colored ads for bargain cuts of beef and bread curl up to make a cradle for three envelopes on top. Two envelopes are white. She sees the Agway logo. Leon's grain bill. No airmail envelopes with foreign stamps. She reaches for the letters. What? A doctor's bill and . . . a telegram.

What did she do next? Darlene concentrates, opens and quickly closes her eyes. This may be where the dream can be derailed; this part is critical. Was there really a telegram? Think.

Two envelopes are white. She puts them in her pocket with the junk mail and holds the other. To MRS. HARMON WOODARD. God. It couldn't be!

It is. A yellow envelope, a telegram marked PERSONAL. For her. She holds it up to the clouds but nothing shows through the heavy paper. No clues. She turns and walks the fifty paces back to the lane. She aims her feet at the indentations imprinted in the slush on her way to the mailbox. She can't see her feet. She can't feel her feet or her legs or her hands and arms. She is walking without knowing how to walk, folding the unopened telegram between her stupid fingers.

Turning up the lane, she hurries. The hill seems steeper, her heartbeats hammer at her throat as she emerges under open sky and stops in her tracks. The lane leads across the meadow and uphill to the barn, to the farmhouse. Beside the farmhouse, a surprise in the landscape, a new, white building. *Her* house.

Could it be? Does she open the envelope and read the words: *in the line of duty . . . enemy fire . . . freedom?*

She does.

Wait? How does she open the envelope? Did another telegram spill out into the mud, a second message canceling the first? Is it possible?

No. She clumsily opens the envelope with her fingers, pulls the contents out of the ragged tear. A single sheet of paper. Her name. Clearly her name. She reads it over and over looking for a spelling mistake, the wrong address, a comma wrong. But it all is there. Harmon's name, spelled correctly, too, his rank and serial number. *We regret to inform you . . .*

She looks away, at a row of fence posts. It was here that she saw the fox tracks and the mouse entrails, the drop of blood blushed pink into the snow. Weeks have passed. No sign remains, the mouse, no more, the fox off hunting other mice, waiting, pouncing, trotting off to leave behind another crimson epitaph.

Between the posts, she traces rusted rows of wire, sagging, cold, in parallel defeat. Barbs clutch the strands like regiments of tiny wretched birds. No chirping here. No feathers turning in the wind. The fence ascends the hill, drawn to the buildings huddled at the top. She follows it, imagining her hand gripped tight around the wire, threading the rusty barbs through her palm without a trace of pain.

"She's coming to."
"I'll get a damp washrag."
"She's white as a sheet."
"She's moving. There."

Darlene looks up at a slowing swirl of faces. The motion stops and bounces briefly in the opposite direction like a tired carousel. Vera and Bodie are looking down at her. Their faces seem magnified, unattached to their bodies.

"Let her get some air."

They pull back. Darlene feels a cool, wet washcloth on her forehead. Callused fingers gently squeeze her hand. Harmon's fingers. She moves her head to focus on the hand, the arm, the shoulder that could, if it would, belong to Harmon. The shoulder joins a neck like Harmon's, the jaw, the cheek . . .

"You'll be OK." The cheek is moving, forming words from Bodie's mouth. "You rest a while." He removes her hand from his.

"You want some water?" It is Vera's voice.

"I wish I'd told him," Darlene whispers.

"Just lay quiet, good as gold." Vera strokes Darlene's hair, smoothes it back in time to feel the lines of teardrops slide across her temples toward her ears. "There's nothing we can do but make the best of what we've still got left," Vera says.

"Poor guy," Darlene whispers. She wipes her tears with the back of her hand.

Vera pauses, looks away as if to collect her thoughts and says, "Bodie? See if you can find Darlene a Kleenex." But

Bodie is gone. "I'll be right back," she says to Darlene. "Don't you worry. We'll pull through."

It's true, Darlene thinks, we will pull through. Then, one by one, we go. We all do. It's only the survivors that have to do the rearranging.

Vera hurries back with her box of tissues. Darlene glances up at her and then looks past her, at the grimy clouds beyond the kitchen windowpanes, at the pot of ivy on the windowsill; a fresh green tendril hangs down toward the sink, and at the tip, two tiny leaves.

Twelve

Bodie knows he'll find Leon in the cowbarn. He knows the lights will be shut off, Leon alone with fifteen cows in damp, sweet barn air, ruminating.

The conversation will be brief; he knows that too. But what must be said must be said: Darlene was right. They should have told Harmon while they still had a chance. Now, the chance is gone forever.

Closing the door behind him, Bodie adjusts to the darkness. What little light there is swells in through half a dozen four-paned sashes arranged along the eastern wall. Years of webs and flyspecks turn the snow-reflected gray to amber, washing the first few feet of floor with pale, medieval half-light.

Beyond the light is Leon, leaning against the farthest window, arms crossed on the dusty sill. Bodie knows he's watched him walk across the yard, along the clothesline, across the lane to the low-posted door. And Leon won't look up; the boy will have to go to him.

Bodie's footsteps match the cadence of dripping water in the trough at the other side of the barn. As he draws near, the old man spits on his thumb and rubs the window glass. Through the shiny hole a patch of snow appears, then a portion of the farmhouse. Bodie waits as Leon rubs and spits and rubs again, directed outward, concentrating. Side by side they stand composing how the words will sound.

"Glummy, ain't it?" Leon's tone invites an answer and at the same time asks for nothing.

"Mercury's down. Might see some snowflakes."

"Yes-sah."

False start. Each knows it. They pause and think, unhurriedly, at ease with the silence draped between them. Bodie counts the holsteins tied to their stanchions as Leon rubs the window glass further.

"Someday, I just might wash these windas."

"Whether they need it or not," Bodie jokes. "Once every fifty years?"

"Smart boy. How's your mother doing?"

"Seems all right."

"Darlene?"

"Kinda rocky. Fainted flat out on the floor. She came right back."

"The women, they take it extra hard."

"What about you?" Bodie turns to look at Leon, eye to eye. "It must be hard for you. With Daddy, now with Harmon."

"Gets me thinking."

"About?"

"Doughnuts. Vera's hand-cut doughnuts." Leon rubs the glass with his handkerchief. He rubs again and stands back to inspect his work, says nothing more.

"You know that time we talked? Up at the well?" Bodie asks.

"Fixing where the wall caved in?"

"Right. You asked me, *told* me how you'd heard Harmon and me talking."

"Right over there." Leon points toward the door. "Me, up above with the trapdoor open. Couldn't help it. Weren't my idea."

"I know, I know. But what we *said*."

"About who done Darlene's fathering?"

"Yes."

"It don't concern me. Put it out of my mind."

"Harmon never knew if he—if he was or wasn't."

"Mister boy, I'll tell you something." Leon turns to Bodie with an intensity that surprises them both. "This whole life is made of questions nobody knows the answers of. I don't care how smart, there's always something left to puzzle on." He turns back to his window, pulls out a pouch of Beech-Nut and wads a plug up inside his cheek. "One cow out of fifty gets a twisted stomach. Why? Why that particular cow? Hundred soldiers go to fight and ten come back. You can't predict it, which ones will. You never know."

"I wish I'd told him."

"Wisht I'd said a few things too. There's things I wisht I'd told him ever since he was a baby. Him, and you. And your father."

"But you didn't hold back."

"I did."

"Not on purpose."

Leon spits a brown gob of tobacco juice into the corner. "Makes no nevermind. The fella on the other end, it feels the same to him now, don't it? Thing of it is, even though he's missing something, he don't stop to figure out what. He don't even know what it is."

"Still."

"It ain't your fault. It ain't my fault. It ain't nobody's fault; the way people are is the way they are. You say you should of told him something? By the Jesus, so should I! Set there looking through Darlene's windshield. Done the same when Purdy went. Never told them how I felt. Inside." Leon thumps his chest with his fist, coughs and spits another gob into the corner.

"They knew how you felt about them."

"Says who?"

"Me. You never said so, but I know you loved them. I know you love *me*."

"Ain't you got some work to do? Go on, git! I'm busy. Crimus! Set 'n gab all day, you'd let him."

"I just wish I'd told him, that's all."

"Wouldn't bring him back."

"No, but it might have made it easier."

"Nothing easy's worth a goddamn."

"Still . . ."

"Torment yourself all day, you want to! Won't help nothing." Leon limps past Bodie and picks up a push broom, starts to sweep the worn concrete aisle. After a few deliberate strokes he stops and looks back at Bodie. "Picture it swapped around. I do."

"How?"

"Supposing you got all done—Harmon was alive, you went and died in a—in a automobile accident."

"And?"

"You'd be all done . . . You wouldn't set there asking riddles."

"I don't know."

"Harmon wouldn't have told you everything. He'd feel bad, too."

"But I knew something that Harmon wanted to know, something that was very important to him."

"Swap it around, boy. Can't you picture it? Harmon went his whole life holding back on you—on purpose! Times I see you hurt real bad on account of him. He never give no slack. Just to be contrary! Holding, holding, holding back. Sometimes I'd of whupped him good if Vera'd let me. Made me mad."

"You saw that?"

222

"And more. Truth of it is, he used you bad. That's how he was, how he always was. Made that way."

"I always thought you liked him better'n me."

"Better'n you? Don't be foolish." Leon gives the broom a couple of vigorous pushes and stops. "You boys was wicked different—both had sides of Purdy that was carbon copies . . . half-page each . . . . Mix you two together, there'd be one Purdy, hunnert percent, and one leftover fella walking around—nobody'd know where he come from. Hummph! Like Harmon better'n you? Ain't too likely. You was quiet. Harmon, he'd clamor for attention. Prob'ly got more on account of it, but that don't fool nobody. No-sah, you two boys was always equal to me. Wouldn't make no difference what you done. In here"—he thumps his chest—"you counted equal, salt 'n pepper, rig 'n-a-half, the both of you." Leon returns to scrubbing the worn-out floor with his worn-out broom.

Bodie steps to the window where Leon had stood. He looks out through the cleaned-off pane and watches timid rays of sun sneak through the clouds, sees a sparkle on the snow. "They said they'd notify us of 'arrangements.' What do you think that means?"

"Frigging booracrats. More telegrams."

"Funeral?"

"How'n hell should I know? Purdy, all we got's a flag. Weren't nothing to dig a hole for. Jeesum, ain't you got some work to do?"

Jiggsie tips up his welder's mask and looks at his handiwork, at the gobs of blue-black steel still smoking on the snowplow's corner. The weld looks good: little pea-sized puddles overlap in a long thin line. He strikes off traces of carbon scale with a wire brush, then groans as he rises to his feet. "Mother of Jesus, I'm getting old," he moans. "I appreciate you letting me use your outfit, Tinker. What's the damage come to?" he asks, inspecting the plow for other signs of wear.

"You don't owe me."

"I'll settle up with Helen," Jiggsie says. It's an old joke, taken from a grimy sign on Tinker's garage wall. The sign reads: HELEN WAITE IS OUR CREDIT MANAGER. IF YOU WANT CREDIT, GO TO HELL AND WAIT.

"She'd like that, Jigg." Tinker wipes his hands on a faded red towel. "Roads been bad?"

"Not since the storm. I think that's when I cracked this mother. Slid side-wise and struck a stump."

Jiggsie takes Tinker's socket wrench out of his hand and reaches up to an oil-pan drain plug. He steps aside as a shiny column of oil glugs into a bucket on the floor. Up on the hydraulic lift, the Nova's underbelly looks like a huge, rusted insect undergoing surgery.

"Could of bent your plow frame, too," Tinker says.

The side door opens and Bodie walks into the garage. They greet him with the usual jokes and insults: "Getting any?" "How's it hanging?" "They let you out on good behavior?"

Bodie ignores the friendly banter. "I've got to have Simon's telephone number," he says to Jiggsie. He sounds exhausted.

"The legal eagle?" Jiggsie cocks his head as if he hadn't heard correctly. "You want his office or his house?"

"Office, I guess. Better give me both."

"What's up?" Jiggsie asks as he rummages through the greasy address book he keeps in his breast pocket. "You get caught abusing little girls again?" He laughs, then stops abruptly as he sees Bodie's stony expression. "Something serious, huh?"

"He told me to call him if I ever needed to," Bodie says. "Never thought I would."

Jiggsie scrawls the digits on the back of a folded envelope, wondering if Bodie will say what's bothering him, determined not to ask again.

"It's about the draft board stuff," Bodie says. "I've got to do something, soon. They came to see me, want my ass."

"Jesus, Bodie . . ."

"Simon'll figure it out," Tinker says.

"He's a clever little shit. He'll figure out a way."

"I hope." Bodie's tone is flat, almost futile.

"I don't doubt it for a minute," Jiggsie says. "He's never lost in court, he told me. Regular Perry Mason."

"It's time I got it over with," Bodie says.

Something else is going on, something bigger than the draft. Instinctively, Jiggsie wants to ask about the family— Leon, Vera, Darlene, Harmon—but with each he sees the possibility of disaster. Could Leon have had a heart attack? Darlene lost her baby? Vera sick? Harmon?

Jiggsie suddenly sees the inside of the garage as if time had come to a standstill. Bodie stands like a cemetery statue on the far side of the snowplow. Tinker is under the lift with his arms stretched up into the Nova's innards, listening, saying nothing. His fingers are probably wrapped around an exhaust pipe clamp; the threads will be long gone, the hex nut rusted to a rounded lump. In a minute, if the world will ever start turning again, Tinker will pick a cold chisel out of his toolbox and drive it into the clamp with a two-pound hammer. The ring of the hammering will fill the garage: *womp, bang, womp, womp.* And Bodie will tell a sad, sad story.

Tinker grabs the cold chisel and starts pounding. Time resumes its course and Jiggsie decides he must be wrong about Harmon. He must.

"How's the pickup running?"

"Good," Bodie says, preoccupied, dreary, uninspired.

"Dale still driving for Twin State?" Jiggsie is embarrassed this time. His respect for Bodie's privacy has led him to absurdities; his attempts to cheer him are pathetic. Made-up questions; *bang, womp,* in the background.

"Harmon's dead," Bodie says, looking at Jiggsie for the first time. "They sent a telegram this morning." His voice is as dry as winter husks.

The banging stops. Tinker puts his hammer down and walks around the truck to stand near Bodie. No one knows what to do. The three of them have known each other for more than twenty years. This is the worst thing that has ever happened to any of them. This is the first time they have felt, together, totally helpless. They stand by the salt-stained plow searching for a phrase, a word, but each prospect seems too trivial, too clichéd to serve their awful needs. Saying "Harmon's dead" out loud has opened up a cold, dark crack. Jiggsie wonders: Will the crack heal in, or leave him split in two forever?

He breaks the silence with a whispered "Sorry, Bodie," shrugs his massive torso and turns away to gulp his throat clear, blinking, straining against a stone laid heavy on his heart.

"I can't believe it," Tinker says. "I just can't picture Harmon . . ."

The wedge drives deeper, the truth retrenches. The music on the garage radio is suddenly hateful, rude, absurd. Bodie looks at the folded envelope in his hand as if remembering what it's for. "I've got to go," he says. He tries to smile, a useless crinkle across his lips. "I've got to call Simon and get my status figured out." He leaves the door ajar behind him, starts his pickup and backs slowly out onto Pike's main street.

A milk truck coming down the highway brakes hard, swerves to miss him. The driver hunches over, looks through his rearview mirror at the pickup truck, at the driver who never noticed what had almost happened.

Jiggsie watches through the garage windows until Bodie's truck is out of sight. He pulls the door shut, hears the latch snap. Closure. The hopeless sound of a door locked tight has never sounded quite so loud. "Rough," he says.

"You better believe it. This might sound goofy, but I almost think Bodie had it in mind, like he knew something would happen to Harmon," Tinker says. "Been keeping to himself, near as I can tell."

"Been working on Darlene's house. Got her moved in good. Told me he was coming back to work next week. I've got all kinds of it waiting for him."

"Scarce around Loretta. Mother said she hasn't seen him two-three weeks. Hasn't even called. Loretta's all tore up."

"Won't help it any, she hears this."

"She was stuck on Harmon, way back. Even though he used her bad, she thought he had it all over Bodie. For a while, anyway."

"A lot of them did. He had that look." Jiggsie pictures Harmon on the Bonneville in dark glasses, his blond hair slicked back, a pack of Camels rolled into his T-shirt sleeve.

"I can't see him not being around. It's going to take some getting used to," Tinker says. "You can't just close him off like tap water."

"Darlene, I pity her right now."

Tinker says, "At least she's still got Bodie."

Physical examinations for the Selective Service draft inductees are held in the Colrain National Guard Armory. Candidates are drawn from a fifty-mile radius that includes most of the communities in the sparsely settled northern halves of New Hampshire and Vermont.

The armory consists of a huge central hall—as big as an airplane hangar—surrounded by smaller rooms. Lines of men in their underwear move slowly in and out of the little rooms, submitting to blood drawings, hearing tests, vision tests, height, weight and posture, urine samples, bend over, spread your cheeks. They are measured and prodded, interrogated and lectured on their way to qualifying for the armed services. And like anyone stripped of control and clothing and stuck in an interminable line going nowhere, they feel apprehensive. There is no conversation. They stand and they shuffle forward a step at a time and stare straight ahead at another guy's back.

On the phone two days ago, Simon told Bodie to report for the exam. He would probably pass, earn a 1-A classification, but at least he would stop the local board from initiating legal action, get them off his case for a while. Meanwhile, Simon told him, there were appeals that Simon would work on—an agricultural deferment, or, conceivably, a head-of-family classification. Also, he said, be sure to ask to see the psychiatrist. Tell him how you feel about combat, how you feel about your brother. Tell him some gory dreams, some weird stuff you might have thought about. But show up for the physical. It doesn't mean you're going in, just because you pass. I'll work on it, I'll do everything I can, Simon told him. Then he said he was sorry about Harmon, it was a "tragic waste." He sent his condolences, his sympathy to the family. He was sincere, he really meant it. Bodie thought of the stairs in Simon's house, how well he'd made them, and resolved he'd always work that way.

Waiting in line, Bodie looks around at the bodies strung like picnic ants in and out the side room doors. White-skinned, every one, their ancestries are thick with French and Anglo-Saxon stock. They shiver as their forefathers shivered in drizzle off the east Atlantic.

They wait, bored and restless, arms across their chests, half-naked, cold, bewildered animals herded through the maze. Around them, at the edges of the biggest room they've ever seen, are trucks and jeeps in camouflage, troop carriers with canvas tops across their backs like covered wagons. Cannons, towed behind the trucks, point idly at the next truck's windshield. Four outmoded tanks stand sentry beside a huge overhead door. Everywhere, the dull green metal turns light lifeless, steals its glow. The armory is ringed with the machines of war, and in the center are the mechanics-to-be.

Bodie has never seen so many people his own age in one place. His high school class had fourteen students. Who are these people? Where do they come from? A sergeant prowls the lines with deliberate casualness. Bodie watches him swagger to a table, pause, then hold his hairy fist an inch above the surface for a moment—and *punch* it. *Hard!* Jesus! Why?

The psychiatrist is at the end of the line. A soldier with JARVIS on his uniform name-patch tells the men in Bodie's group to put their clothes back on. Then, if anyone wants to see the "head-shrinker," he should come up front. Otherwise, everyone is free to leave. See youse in boot camp, ha, ha, ha. Immediately, the group is dressed and filing out the door to the parking lot, moving quickly for the first time in three hours. Bodie lingers, tying his bootlaces slowly, waiting for the room to empty. Jarvis is about to leave.

"Excuse me. I want to see the shrink," Bodie says.

"You?"

Simon's voice comes back to Bodie. He can hear the static on the line from Massachusetts. "Yeah. I'd like to see the psychiatrist."

"Name?" Jarvis is annoyed and doesn't mind showing it.

"Bodeman Woodard."

"Which one's your last name?"

"Woodard."

"In this man's army, your name's Woodard, Bodeman. Remember that."

I'm not in your fucking army yet, Bodie thinks.

"Wait here, fruitcake. I'll be right back," Jarvis says. "Woodard, Bodeman," he says again, as he leaves. "I'll get your fucking file."

Bodie paces around the room. The walls are painted poison yellow, bare except for a framed black-and-white photograph of a company of National Guardsmen standing in uniformed rows at the front of the armory. The frame is screwed to the wall. The room has no windows. Overhead fluorescent tubes reflect in the glass covering the photograph. Bodie looks at the faces, rows of them, and wonders who they were and how they felt, looks for somebody he knows.

Jarvis comes back in the room with a manila folder. Bodie's name, birth date and address are typed on a white sticker stuck to the top. Jarvis hands him the folder and motions him to follow. They walk out into the huge hall and stop. Jarvis points to a door near the far end of the building.

"Second door from the end," he says. "Give your folder to the shrink and tell him your sob story." Jarvis looks disgusted. "Second door from the end," he repeats, "just to the left of the exit sign." He sounds like he's talking to a three-year-old.

Bodie says "Thanks," and immediately wishes he hadn't. How did Harmon survive this crap?

It looks like a hundred-yard walk to the other end of the building. Lines of half-dressed men are still snaked in and out of the side room doors. As Bodie walks past he feels awkward for them. They look so vulnerable, like baby chicks dumped out of the nest, like himself ten minutes before.

The folder is light in his hands. He feels the thickness

between his thumb and forefinger: maybe a dozen pages. Of what? He looks back for Jarvis. Jarvis is nowhere to be seen. Bodie slows his pace. His folder. *His* folder? He opens it as he walks. On top are half a dozen pages of the forms and medical information just collected. Next is a carbon of a letter from Bixby Judd—the first letter he sent to Bodie—notifying him he had been "selected." Then, three more letters, all from Judd. Bodie looks up. The second door from the end is still a long way off. Jarvis is gone. No one is watching Bodie. He's dressed, he's not in line, he doesn't fit the description of the people being watched.

He opens the folder again. More letters: one *he* wrote, expressing his intentions not to serve, another from Judd to the Selective Service requesting help in the matter, and another from the Service to Judd. They advise him to "handle it locally" and offer to help only in the event that his efforts should "prove unsuccessful." The last letter—from the draft board—was the letter that prompted Bodie to call Simon, the letter that brought him here today. Bodie's history with the draft board is documented in one thin folder. The pages in his hands turn heavy; the folder suddenly weighs a ton.

A dark-haired recruit in a blue down vest stands waiting outside the shrink's office. He steps aside as the door opens and another candidate comes out. The blue vest hesitates, then disappears inside. Bodie pictures the psychiatrist and tries to imagine what he will talk about, but the shrink's remarks will go unheard. Instead, an image of the Catamount bridge suddenly arcs across his mind, a rainbow . . . and then as quickly, it disappears, leaving Bodie staring at the exit sign twenty paces in front of him.

Still walking, he turns around to look again for Jarvis, sees instead the waiting lines—shoulders, arms and legs, ribbed torsos strung into an interminable body. He turns back; a huge brick wall with a dull gray metal door is now less than a dozen steps away. To his left, a psychiatrist listens to a recruit's story and yawns.

Later, when he thinks back on the turning point, Bodie will remember the startling image of the bridge, how his feet never stopped; how they carried him unhindered through the exit door and around the building to the parking lot. He will remember how tightly he held his folder, how he never once looked back to see if anyone was following him. He will remember putting the folder in the kitchen wood stove and watching the fire through the open door, watching his "official" existence forever altered by the orange and yellow flames. And Darlene. He will always remember the surprise in Darlene's face when he told her what he'd done—her smile, the widening of her features, how her pupils dilated, opened up so black and deep.

Thirteen

March 21 was circled on Darlene's 1968 calendar. Not because of spring's arrival—she had lived in Catamount too long to hope for spring in March—but because that was the day her baby was expected.

Since the news of Harmon's death Darlene had spent her time in waiting. She was an expert, she decided, at waiting. There was nothing she had ever done with such determination: waiting, every waking hour spent in waiting, waiting, waiting for that hour to be gone at last, and with it, parts of her she knew she must discard—or wait forever.

At first, she tried to formulate her waiting into categories: waiting for the pain of Harmon's death to pass, and waiting for the joy of the baby's birth. One would cancel the other, she hoped. The baby's arrival would make up, in part at least, for Harmon's absence.

But it refused to work that way. Waiting for both required day-to-day, hour-to-hour, minute-to-minute courage—deep rockbound reservoirs of courage that made her wonder: where did it come from?

Vera waited with her, waited with the same resolve. They sat at Darlene's new kitchen table, talking, playing cards and watching television. Waiting. They talked about their memories of Harmon as if they were taking inventory in a grocery store. And with each item dusted off and polished bright with scrutiny, they returned it to its proper shelf, hoping it would stay there, not tip off and crash between them, broken and unfit for further use.

They spoke as mother, wife and witness to a life whose seasons would be forever incomplete, stuck fast between the rising sap and hardening off of summer's growth. They traded secrets they had never told before, secrets about themselves. As Harmon's presence had brought them closer, his absence unified them.

The unborn baby waited out the storm that whitened all of northern Vermont on the twenty-first of March. It held back almost two weeks more—so long that by the time Bodie and Vera drove her to the clinic, Darlene had seen an early crocus pop up through the snow on the south side of the farmhouse.

By the time spring comes—this year, in the middle of May—Darlene is too busy with Esther to preoccupy herself with Harmon. She thinks about him still, but the terrible sense of waiting is over and her thoughts, at last, are familiar and patterned after themselves. She can use the past tense, she can say "he *was* such-and-such." She can think of herself as a widow.

The baby becomes the receptor of Darlene's need to give, the center of Darlene's consciousness. When Darlene can't be next to Esther, Vera is. They glorify each tiny knuckle, praise each fold and lobe and toe. At night, Darlene dreams of her daughter's miniature pink body, dresses her in gossamer. Esther becomes Harmon's reciprocal; the love he can't receive she gets, the pain he knew is spared his daughter.

Darlene likes hearing Leon call the baby "little Darlin'." Perhaps he means "little Darlene." She doesn't ask. She congratulates herself for naming the baby after Leon's Esther. He would deny it, but the name has reborn something in him and, in the process, brought him closer to Darlene than ever before—and her to him, and she is pleased with his uncustomary playfulness. She and Vera have heard him—when he thinks no one is listening—speak to the baby in falsetto. Baby talk. They burst into laughter when he plays "this little piggy" with the baby's toes.

At first, Leon had searched the baby's features for a trace of *his* Esther, but soon admitted he found no resemblances. "When you get bigger, you'll look just like her," he had assured her in a squeaky whisper. "She weren't bad looking, either."

Most of the time, for Leon, baby Esther is an inscrutable pink turnip, almost indistinguishable from the women's cradling hands and cooing voices crowded around her. Still, he comes to marvel while the baby sleeps. In his overalls and barnyard scent, he bends his raspy fingers around the spindles of her spotless crib and stares down at her as if she were a miracle.

The thought occurs to him that here is Harmon's soul reborn. And in the frugal way in which Leon's mind associates, he asks: if Harmon's, why not Purdy's as well?

Leon proposes the notion to his long-departed wife; his late-night reveries with her come often now, and lately are full of ponderings on the succession of souls. He calls it *going 'round and 'round.* For him, two generations stretch the limit of spiritual transmission. Souls get *wore out* and *discombobulated* with age. No use hoping for Amos Woodard's soul to reappear. It would *come through poachy. Crimus! Nothing lasts forever.*

As Leon looks for signs of Purdy and Harmon in baby Esther, he watches for a transformation, something to signal

235

the succession of Woodard flesh and spirit. "See how she done that [waved an arm]? Just like Harmon! See? Just like him. Purdy done that, too." On occasion, he inadvertently calls the baby "Harmon," or refers to her as "Bodie's little sister," or, worst of all, "Bodie's little girl."

When Bodie was in grade school, his English teacher, Mrs. Langley, would keep the entire class after school until the perpetrator of that morning's devilment confessed. It was often a lengthy, stuffy stay inside while out of doors the sun shone down like vapored honey on the baseball field. During those periods of detention (most of which he hadn't initiated), Bodie felt guilty, felt somehow *he* was the one who must have done the forbidden deed, and furthermore, everyone probably knew it. He was always surprised when the perpetrator confessed, surprised that it wasn't he, himself.

When the baby first came home with Darlene, Bodie relived those same feelings of misplaced guilt he had known in Mrs. Langley's English class. But that was years ago. Why was this happening now? What had he done? Who was his accuser? He knew it made no sense, but he lived in fear of being found out; he was convinced a dreadful truth would be revealed, an unspecified truth that he would recognize only at the moment of disclosure.

And so he avoided Darlene and the baby. For the first few weeks, he saw them little, working overtime with Jiggsie on a new house south of Catamount. His schedule and Darlene's were such that she had no idea he was purposefully absent.

For the first few weeks of motherhood, Darlene hardly knew day from night. By instinct, she performed each of the endless tasks required of her. Milk preoccupied her thinking. Even her saliva, she insisted, had turned to milk. For the first time in her life, Leon's holsteins seemed absurd. How could they endure their bodies' daily production of over a hundred pounds of milk, day after day for years on end? Darlene's breasts, now huge, amazed her. Here, on her familiar body, were two great strangers, drooling fluid like running noses, ignoring every circumstance but their need to furnish an endless supply of *milk*. At times, Darlene suspected overflow had backed into her bloodstream, had penetrated her cranium and sabotaged the workings of her brain. So between the diapering, nursing and laundry, the quick catnaps that passed for sleep, it took some time before she realized she had seen too little of Bodie, and she realized she wanted to do something about it.

The baby came back from her first month's checkup with a perfect report. With the written evidence of her baby's health and the doctor's compliments on how well they both looked, Darlene, for the first time, believed in it all; she was finally and fully the mother of Esther.

Tonight, as usual, Vera came over after supper to see her, to help her do the dishes and play with the baby. Vera told her that Bodie had been working late, eating out at the Pepper Pot on his way home. She was worried about him. He was taking it hard. He hadn't seen Loretta in over a month. Maybe he needed someone other than Vera to cheer him up. Maybe tonight. He would be home, she imagined, by eight or eight thirty. Could Darlene talk to him? Vera would stay with the baby; she hoped Esther would wake up so she could play with her.

As they spoke, they heard his truck pull in. Darlene waited at her kitchen window until she saw the light in his room. "I'll go up now," she told Vera. "Let me know if Esther needs me." She closed the door behind her, then reopened it and dropped a hand towel on the counter. They laughed. For the first time in a month she would have no use for it.

Darlene knocked and heard him say come in. She found him sitting on the corner of his bed, where she had sat. She realized they had not been together in this room since the night before Harmon left, back in November. But the night before Harmon's departure was different: it was the first time she and Bodie had ever talked about their feelings for one another, the discussion was dangerous, had limits. Now, such a conversation was permissible, and Darlene felt free to explore it.

Bodie seemed embarrassed by his rumpled sheets and blankets; he smoothed them out quickly, then gestured to the end of the bed by the door and asked her to sit down. He asked about her health and then the baby's. As he mentioned Esther's name, Darlene saw a hint of shame across his face.

"She's perfect," Darlene told him. "Harmon would be so proud to see his little girl."

"What did you say?" Bodie shook his head as if to clear his ears.

"The baby is such a perfect little doll. She's *wonderful.* Harmon would be such a proud papa."

Bodie stared at Darlene. How did she do it? How was it all so clear and simple for her? Harmon's name. She had spoken Harmon's name without a flicker of self-pity, unencumbered, no torment. His name rolled off her tongue like a smoothly polished stone. She had held her eyes wide open, a touch of sparkle even, porcelain-white around the amber iris. She had spoken his name clearly, then made the association Bodie suddenly knew he needed to hear. Harmon would be proud to see *his* little girl. *His* little girl. Darlene should know. It was *Harmon's* little girl!

Mrs. Langley materialized and smiled at Bodie, nodded her forgiveness for what he had never done, then vanished.

Class dismissed! He saw himself racing down the school-house steps, out to the ball field, his lungs exploding with clean fresh air.

"He'd be a regular pain in the ass." Bodie laughed. "Spoil her rotten."

"He'd be passing out cigars until she was eighteen," Darlene said. "She'd have him wrapped around her finger so tight he wouldn't be able to move."

They weren't going to do it, Bodie thought. Thank God! They weren't going to make Harmon perfect in death, pussyfoot around his grave. Darlene was right. He looked at her with a crooked smile, encouraged by her clarity. "He was something, the son-of-a-gun."

"He could drive you bananas," she said.

He watched her shake her head, dispersing useless memories, then focus on him as if it were important. "Tell me what you've been thinking," she said to him. "You've been a moving target since you finished my house."

"I don't know where to start," Bodie said. "It's confusing." But he knew that it wouldn't be, once he began, knew she would know the right questions to ask. "I broke up with Loretta," he blurted. The words surprised him. Until that moment, he hadn't admitted it. Funny he should say it first to Darlene, say it to her before he had said it to himself. "It just wasn't going anywhere, that's all."

"How's she taking it?" Darlene asked.

"OK, I guess. Bad, I suppose. I don't know, to tell you the truth. I haven't been in touch with her since—since we heard about Harmon."

"Betsy said she'd heard Loretta was moving to upstate New York. Got a teaching job over there. Pays better money."

"She mentioned it once, but I hadn't heard she was really going to do it," Bodie said. The idea of Loretta leaving town seemed odd to him—odd and inconsequential and only remotely interesting. He pictured her with her suitcases at the bus depot in a dress too big and wearing wobbly high-heeled shoes. She never wore high heels at home, but she would wear them on a bus leaving town because she thought that's what she was supposed to do—wear Minnie Mouse shoes with a matching handbag, a country mouse going off to the city on a Greyhound bus, alone.

It was a relief, imagining her gone. How convenient, how accommodating of her to detach herself so completely. Should he feel bad? Maybe. But he didn't. He felt relieved. He wanted to thank Darlene for telling him the news. Later, he would credit her with Loretta's timely departure; that Darlene had been the one to tell him seemed appropriate, even portentous.

They talked about Loretta, little bits of gossip: had he heard about Loretta's hair? She'd had it cut short, even shorter than last summer. Darlene had seen her at the Superette checkout counter with an almost empty shopping cart, skim milk and a bunch of cat food. She told Darlene she had found an abandoned kitten. Wouldn't look up when she spoke. Had a big red rash, maybe psoriasis, all over her elbow. Looked skinnier than ever.

Darlene told Bodie she had never understood his attraction to Loretta, that she had always thought he deserved much better—not that she meant to run Loretta down. Bodie nodded and thought of Harmon, then talked about Leon and how he spared his words and curbed his feelings, how he always knew much more than he let on. He told a story about a farm machinery salesman who spent half an hour giving Leon a complicated explanation of how the latest hay tedder worked. At the end of the salesman's presentation, Leon agreed: they did work slick. He had been using an identical model all summer.

They talked about Vera and how Darlene admired her. Bodie admitted he had always been surprised to hear Darlene's praise for his mother. Was she *that* special? Think about it, Darlene told him, think about her mother, Lucile. Or Miriam Bushway, or Betsy's mother, or Jiggsie's mom, Marvel, that squeaky little voice that never stops. None of them could compare with Vera. You had it easy, Darlene told him, you never had to watch your mother make a mess of her life, make a fool of herself over some dumb oaf of a husband who wasn't worth dogshit. You're lucky you had her for a mother, she told him, and he understood that whatever it was she was talking about, she was convinced that she would never make the mistakes those women had made. Then he told her that he saw in her the kinds of strength and resolution that maybe he had too easily taken for granted in his mother. He told her he understood what bonded her to Vera and then was silent when he realized he envied them and wished part of it could be his, too.

"I feel like I haven't talked for a year," Bodie told Darlene. "Am I sounding goofy?"

"It's good for you to sound goofy," she told him. "It's good for me, too."

They talked and talked, from opposite ends of an unmade bed in a room filled with more light than its single bulb could furnish. When they realized it was suddenly eleven thirty, they laughed at themselves. How could it be so late? Darlene apologized, but she had to leave. Vera was with the baby and it was past everyone's bedtime.

She stopped in the doorway as she left and asked Bodie if he would take Harmon's clothes. They were still in his dresser, still over there in the room above the woodshed. She hadn't moved any of Harmon's stuff into the new house. Did Bodie think that was weird? Everything would fit—boots, pants, shirts. It would be a shame to waste them, to give them to the church bazaar.

Bodie looked at her, standing half in, half out of his

241

bedroom. She was saying something about Harmon's clothes. Did he want them? But the words were all bird-song, the kind that awoke him some mornings before dawn, signifying great strategies, plans for the future, signifying pure pleasure in singing. He couldn't be certain why, but they had always appealed to him even though he felt no need to understand what they meant.

"Harmon's clothes?" He looked up at her, smiling, focusing again. "Maybe Dale could use them. I got plenty. Maybe Tinker. He's the same size."

Maybe *they* could wear Harmon's clothes, but Bodie knew he could not. And he knew, with renewed certainty, that he needed to put his brother away, to fold him neatly, like the shirts Vera ironed—and store him away for a while. That was what he needed to do.

At first, Leon insisted he would not attend the service. His baler needed fixing, he said: first cutting coming up— early June—and the cussed thing was acting up. When he unexpectedly found and fixed the problem—a sheared bolt, easily replaced—his next excuse was a calving, due anytime now. Wouldn't it be just his luck to be off the place when the calf was born, needing assistance, and him not there? The cow gave forth that night while Leon slept, an easy birth, a healthy calf.

Vanity was his last resort. "Can't find my monkey suit. Must of throwed it out on me last time you tore my room t'hell," he grumbled to Vera. She left him standing in the kitchen and returned just as he was beginning to worry he'd spoken too harshly—returned, grinning, with his black gab-ardine suit pressed and spotless on a hardwood hanger.

Leon would go; he would have gone anyway. It was the telegrams that made him angry, made him want to fight back. Why couldn't it have been like it was before? Officers. Polished shoes. *Loaded* .45s. By Jesus, they took it serious!

Wore starched neckties, too, stood at attention, damn good soldiers. Mister man, it weren't no fluke them soldiers won *that* christly war. Carried loaded guns to Catamount. No one stopping them! Made it different from a two-bit telegram.

The other thing that made it different was not so easy for Leon to identify. It had to do, somehow, with being right.

In his war, and in Purdy's, it was simpler, wasn't it? Leon searched for ways to explain it to himself but fell back on a few words and the images of posters, Uncle Sam, the stars and stripes, a wounded gunner, the Statue of Liberty. Honor, pride and sacrifice. Doughboys, GIs, soldiers, sailors—they enlisted to the sounds of cheering crowds and came back home to ticker tape parades as *heroes*. What they fought for was *right*. Their enemies were *bad;* our boys were *good*. Their enemies would imprison the world, our boys would keep it free. In Purdy's war, no one had questioned Washington, patriotism, glory, liberty—the words were grand, transcendent, noble, elevated us to righteousness, united all against an evil enemy.

Harmon's war was different. It had none of the old words and spine-tingling slogans, it had no heroes, no Sergeant Yorks, no Audie Murphys, popular as baseball stars. Harmon's war made casualties of its dead and its survivors. Leon saw them on the television, read in the *Valley Herald* about the suicides and bitterness among returning GIs. The old sense of togetherness was missing. There were no posters. The hotshots down in Washington knew it, too. They knew they had made a mess out there. Couldn't agree on anything except to spend more money. They must have been ashamed of what they were doing or they wouldn't have sent a two-bit telegram.

Toward the end of May, Darlene stood at the mailbox with a letter from the army. It was addressed to her, marked

URGENT and PERSONAL. A notice on the envelope warned of fines against its illegal use. She walked back to the house and left it on her dresser while she changed her baby's diaper.

She brought the letter with her into the kitchen and wedged it between the salt and pepper shakers in the middle of the table. As she ate her sandwich, she read the swap-or-sell section in the *Herald* classifieds. She read slowly, deliberately, defying the gummed-shut envelope to rush her. There was nothing "personal" or "urgent" the U.S. Army could ever say to her again.

When she finished her sandwich, she checked to see that Esther was asleep and comfortable in her crib, then went out to the garden to plant a dozen rows of corn, pole beans and turnips. Beside the corn, at the edge of the garden, she planted three hills of Big Max pumpkins; this year, she decided, they would celebrate Esther's first Halloween with lots of jack-o'-lanterns.

Darlene opened the envelope after supper when the baby was back in her crib and the dishes were done. She took the letter to the couch and sat down, talking to it as if it were a naughty child. "All right, what's so urgent and personal, General Muckymuck? Are you going to tell me my husband died to keep America beautiful, and I should be real happy about it? Tell me about his fighting spirit and the cause of freedom, how he proudly sacrificed his life? Save it, General Muckymuck. My daughter and I happen to think you're full of shit."

The letter was sent to inform Darlene of plans to ship Harmon's body home to Catamount—dates, times and places. They wanted to know the name of the funeral home which would (by law) receive the casket at the Burlington Airport and transport it to the cemetery. The letter explained that Harmon's body would be back in Vermont on the fourth of June, 1968. It would be accompanied by two officers who would stay with the casket until interment. They would arrange to have present a trio of veterans from the local VFW for the traditional blowing of taps and rifle salute. The letter went on about a flag, life insurance and a presentation of medals that Harmon had earned for his bravery and sacrifice. Darlene crumpled the letter into a tight wad and threw it at the TV, which it missed. It fell, instead, behind the sofa, dropped down and rested against the baseboard, covered with dustballs.

Harmon's body—now a bag of pallid, rubbery skin and tissue that gives few clues to what he once was—lies dark and cool in an aluminum coffin. His is third from the top in a stack of four, second stack in a line of twelve. They wait in a green refrigerated room at Travis Air Force Base, protected from the California sun until a bored and disillusioned private named Roland Stammers from a copper-mining town in Montana gets around to processing the files. Between the pills and marijuana—Stammers discovered drugs in Basic and has disciplined himself to remain stoned ever since—the processing is slow. Since his assignment began in January, Stammers has seen the stacks progressively increase in height and number. Something's going on out there, he repeats to himself each time more coffins are delivered. Something's definitely going on.

Harmon's coffin has been in storage since the end of February. Its history is of no particular significance to Stammers. The coffins all look the same, and those whose initials are near the end of the alphabet have stayed around longest. At the beginning, Stammers processed his inventory according to official regulations, according to a chronology established by the date of arrival. Had he stuck to that, Harmon's coffin would have been shipped out long ago.

But somewhere into February, Stammers got confused about the official procedure and adopted one of his own invention. Alphabetical priority, he called it. It was only by chance that one afternoon, when a wave of incoherence left Stammers weeping at his regulation metal desk, weeping at something he couldn't name, he promised himself to process every box in the room before they rose up in formation and crushed him. Still using his alphabetical priority system, he mistakenly inverted Harmon's names and, thinking he was processing a Woodard Harmon instead of a Harmon Woodard, got one more file completed before he wandered home at four thirty and forgot everything he had done that day.

Now Harmon's coffin is loaded into a military cargo plane with a dozen other coffins destined for the East Coast, flying to Dover Air Force Base in Delaware, to another green refrigerated room presided over—this time—by a sergeant who goes by the book.

Sergeant Dellums is a lifer who enlisted at eighteen to fight in Korea. He doesn't like the coffins and he's too old to consider Stammers' method of self-preservation, so he does his job as quickly and efficiently as possible. Two days after Harmon's coffin arrives, it's on its way to Burlington in the cargo bay of an Eastern Airlines 727. In the tourist section of the same flight, a Lieutenant Shreve and a Lieutenant Harper sit in adjacent seats, in full dress uniforms.

They've done this before, this honor guard business, and each time they do it they swear it's the last. A week before, in Ohio, the dead soldier's mother attacked Will Harper with her umbrella as the casket was being lowered into the ground. It was raining, and one of the points of the opened umbrella ribs missed his eye by an inch. The scrape across his cheek is still unhealed. And yet, he couldn't blame her. The lady had her reasons, he told his partner, later; she had a right to get somebody back. Of all the things he could say and do on these assignments, absorbing physical abuse was probably more useful than anything else. You tried to explain and comfort and justify and all that regulation crap, but when you got right down to it, being a punching bag was probably the best thing you could offer.

The plane circles out over Lake Champlain as it descends into Burlington. To the west, the Adirondacks spread out under a fuzzy forest green as far as the eye can see. Below and to the east, the Champlain Valley opens wide to dairy farms. Lush pasture grass contrasts with browns and tans of cultivated bottomland, still showing harrowed dirt between the thickening corduroys of corn.

The plane drops down, and over rooftops, Shreve sees the wings' imperfect shadows keeping pace below them. He looks at his watch. Eleven o'clock, right on time. With luck, they'll be back in the air by eight tonight. If past performance is any indication, they'll be as drunk as they can be.

Harper and Shreve look around the little airport lobby for the funeral director. He should be as easy to spot as they are—he with his somber suit and tie, they with their perfect military dress. As they scan the crowd, a long-haired hippie passes them, contemptuous, and not afraid to show it.

"Killing any babies lately?" he sneers, and walks on, barefoot. His ponytail sways from side to side across the back of his embroidered Mexican shirt. The question is rhetorical; the answer is irrelevant. They've heard it before—heard worse—but through some unsolicited agency of uncommon wisdom and restraint, they've never answered back in kind.

They find old Quig Brady, wrinkled parchment, sitting behind the steering wheel of his Cadillac hearse, parked by the chain link gate to the airfield. He's picked up coffins before, he tells them. He's got to drive around to the baggage room door and load up there. They should go back in through the airport lobby and tell the baggage handler to come unlock the gate. Then, they can help him load. He's done it before; that's how it works. It's easy, he says, when you get the hang of it.

The ride to Catamount takes an hour and a half. They are going directly to the cemetery. The family didn't want calling hours, Quig explains, as if the Woodards were heartless heathens. Some people act that way, he tells them. Shreve and Harper nod noncommittally and feel the tightening across their ribs as the two o'clock service draws closer.

From a cloudless sky, the sun rakes down at an almost vertical pitch, scribing a razor's edge to shadows, black and plentiful along the back roads. Quig's route across these hills has stayed unchanged for fifty years. No matter that a new stretch of hardtop cuts a section's time in half; at seventy-eight, Quig stays with the familiar. Along the way, he points out abandoned hill farms and rusted trailers whose owners he has buried. "Clotted blood," he tells the soldiers. "That one died of c'lesterine. Chill-bone fever killed his mother. Buried 'em both. One in 'forty-seven, the other, must have been in 'fifty, 'fifty-one. Church Baptists. Granddaughter lives down-country, Massachusetts. Paid me cash. Freckled girl. Big-breasted, too. Cried a week when her mother passed. Took it miserable bad."

"You like this work?" Harper asks, knowing the answer.

"Be a damn fool if I didn't," Quig replies. "Been doing it all my life."

They drive in silence, low gear up a steep and winding dirt road with a deep ravine on the right-hand side. Shreve imagines the coffin breaking loose and crashing through the rear door, tumbling down the ragged slope and bursting open among the rocks and thorns below.

"You fellas been soldiering long?" Quig asks as they reach the summit. Both Shreve and Harper wait for the other to answer. Quig ends the silence with another attempt. "Beats getting shot at, what you do. Him, he took the radish." He rolls his eyes toward the back of the hearse. "You two, you must like it pretty well, the traveling around and all. Yes-sah, I'd judge you fellas got to be some clever, wrangling *this* job."

"Right," Shreve says. Quig hears the sarcasm. They drive in brittle silence the rest of the way to Catamount.

Leon's pants don't fit; they fall from his hips to the floor without a catch. He pulls them up and calls for Vera. "Christly trousers growed on me!" He hates the day, the stupid suit. "Can't go like this. I'll stay to home."

Vera comes into his room and finds a pair of black suspenders in his closet. She fastens them to his trousers from behind, then lifts them over his bony shoulders and hooks them to his belt line. Her hands are sure and competent and although no words are spoken, Leon feels reassured. She pats his hips and strikes sharp edges, old bone from which time has wasted flesh and muscle—uninvited, rude erosions.

"You look swell, Grampy." She holds his shoulders with outstretched arms. "Can I do your tie?"

"I don't care," he mumbles. For all the fixings and intricate manipulations of a lifetime spent working with his hands, Leon has never tied a necktie. (In over sixty years he's worn one once a decade.) "Don't choke me, now. Ain't ready for hanging yet."

"You're a handsome rogue," Vera says as she ties a Windsor knot.

Leon pulls away when he feels she's done, like a dog after a brushing. He'd trot away and roll in something nasty if he could, but instead he wrestles himself into his suit jacket—and buttons all three buttons as if to leave no misery unaccounted for. With his hair raked over and parted neatly, his shoes shined, shirt starched, suit pressed and his only necktie—blue with alternating red and yellow diamonds—tied around his throat, he has all but disappeared inside his wrappings.

"Be waiting in the car," he says. For now, the car will hide him. Later, at the cemetery, he'll huddle close to the tall young soldiers, not so much for comfort, but for his idea of camouflage.

Darlene drives. Beside her, Bodie holds the baby. Leon and Vera sit behind them in the Pinto, bobbing up and down as they cross a washboard patch of the Jordan Center road. A mile before the turn to Catamount, Darlene turns left, up a one-lane road with grass grown thick between the wheel ruts. Banks of poplars line the roadside, crowding in to touch the slowly passing car. Waves of silver flicker through the boughs as breezes turn the dangling leaves to sun-struck pendants, luminous against dark rows of spruce. Ahead, the roadway opens to a modest, tree-lined field where half a dozen cars are parked on new-mown hay. The cemetery lies beyond, shaded by a grove of giant white pines planted before Leon's father was born. Granite posts hold up a wood-rail fence that surrounds the burial ground. A black iron gate is rusted open; the grass between the gateposts grows in healthy disarray.

Quig Brady's hearse and a long black Buick are parked off to the west side of the cemetery. Quig was the first to arrive and, with his assistants from the funeral home, completed the graveside preparations.

As Darlene parks the Pinto, Leon looks across the field into the shaded place he hasn't seen since he left Esther

250

there, more than forty years ago. The pines are bigger—jeesum, could they grow so much so quick? And the graveyard darker, no sun at all among the tilted stones. Back then, at Esther's service, how the sun beat down! October, maple leaves turned fiery, Indian summer, sweat rolled down inside some of the same black suits collected here today—rolled down like running water, rivers of it! Without a trace of pity.

Leon squints through the window glass. Quig's there, christly turkey buzzard, talking to the preacher, Vilas Hall. Both were there at Esther's burial. They plant everyone in town, those two. What in hell would make them choose their line of work, Leon wonders, the vulture and the Bible thumper?

He knows that money accounts for Quig's choice. Quig owns two other businesses, a laundromat and a used-furniture store, and he hires out as auctioneer whenever the funeral work allows. Quig's always been a hound for money, sniffs it out where others miss it. He was working as a bow-tied salesman part-time at the Pike Ford Agency when Leon bought his first farm truck in 1928. Wouldn't bend a nickel on the price, and six months later when the engine seized—main bearings crumpled into sand—Quig told Leon it was Leon's fault. Leon kept the truck at home, replaced the bearings and never bought another Ford—as if to teach Quig Brady a lesson.

Vilas Hall has run the Catamount Congregational Church since he came home from World War One with symptoms of mustard gas poisoning. His faith outlived his symptoms and he serves today with the same undaunted, undiminished myopia that drew him to his calling fifty years ago. He married Leon and Esther, then he married Purdy and Vera, then Harmon and Darlene. He buried Esther, held a memorial service for Purdy and now will bury Har-

251

mon two plots west of Esther—forty-six years, ten feet, two generations apart.

"Sanctimonious psalm-singing saint," Leon mumbles at Hall from the backseat as Darlene and Bodie open the car doors. Vera pats Leon's arm and straightens his tie. Except for the brief exchanges at weddings and funerals, neither she nor Leon has ever spoken to Hall. For Leon, Hall's identity is too much part of the cold gray marble marker etched with Esther's name. He knows he ought to, but he can't forgive him.

For Vera, Hall's assurances offer little comfort; his assumptions regarding God's love and mercy require stronger evidence if her missing son and husband are to be accounted for. Her notion of love and mercy can't reconcile their deaths with Hall's version of a just Creator. Her brand of acceptance is simple and obligatory: she believes in random misfortune—and making the best of whatever follows. She believes the Creator meant it to be that way, and the rest is a fairy tale to help the poor boobs who can't imagine a God so mean.

Darlene takes her sleeping baby from Bodie. She looks across the cars and trucks at friends and relatives who seem embarrassed by their unfamiliar clothes; their movements are stiff and jerky, dreading the expectations of the occasion. Her parents amble toward her, graceless, self-conscious with the fear of misplaying their parts. Behind them, Tinker and his parents shift uneasily from one foot to the other, uncertain of where to allow their eyes to wander. Jiggsie and Betsy, O'Dell Stinson and Taylor Gandy stand by O'Dell's pickup. Strangers. They count on time and luck alone to pull them through the next half hour, to take them home to familiarity, to a blue-sky afternoon.

Darlene's mother hugs her and begins to weep. Her father rubs Darlene's shoulder, then pulls his hand away, confused at how to touch the embracing women. He glances around, as if to find direction, then picks at a sliver of wood buried in his callused palm. The removal of the splinter becomes suddenly urgent, a legitimate project, and he tends to it earnestly.

Bodie takes Vera's arm and begins the walk across the field to the cemetery. He's seen it in movies—the son helping the grieving mother, steadfast, strong—except he knows that Vera has resolved her son's death, grieved her piece, and she will steady him more than he will steady her. He nods to Jiggsie, nods to Tinker and the Bushways, smiles a dry, pale smile to O'Dell and Taylor. Loretta, thank God, won't be here.

Off in the trees at the far side of the cemetery, he sees a figure glide behind a hemlock tree, a lanky form in dusty workclothes, toothless—Dale. Not to be seen by anyone but Bodie today, but here, close by, invisible, until long after the last spadeful is patted down.

As Bodie and Vera approach the open gate, the others gather in behind them. Leon walks with Darlene and her parents but suddenly moves ahead when he sees Harper and Shreve and the honor guard beside the casket.

"Soldiers, by Jesus, *soldiers!*" he whispers to Vera as he limps by. "Loaded guns and flags. They finally went and showed some gumption." He scurries through the tombstones and stands at attention by the soldiers, trembling in his suit.

Hall's words spill out in brief formations: invocation, prayer and eulogy are delivered in the terse patois that comes of eighty winters six months long, of flint and granite and early frost. Bodie listens hard at first, then hears

253

the words as only sounds, a foreign tongue with no translation. He stands between Darlene and Vera, gently holding each to him. In turn, each is the comforter and comforted. The baby sleeps on, innocent of mourning. In front of them, a flag is folded into a triangular pattern, centered on the casket top, thick, like a cushion, its stars eclipsed by diagonal folds. At the end of the service, before the rifles are raised and fired toward the eastern flank of Woodard Mountain, Shreve will present the flag to Darlene, who will tuck it under the infant Esther and mumble thank you, feeling confused about the meaning of her gratitude.

Across the casket, Bodie watches Hall's parched lips form stingily around each syllable. No wasted vowels, no extraneous consonants, each phrase is budgeted to convey the Lord's word with the greatest economy possible, as if undue expenditures of language would somehow bankrupt His Kingdom's coffers. *This is a crock.* Why won't Hall mention something real, like Harmon's skill at tracking deer, his baby girl, Darlene's house mortgage? He looks past Hall's white-bristled head into the trees, searching for Dale, and wishes he were with him, out there, hands around the crinkled bark of a yellow birch, black flies swarming, woods sweat glistening across his brow like holy water, blessing him.

Bodie moves his eyes past Hall—past the two impeccably dressed officers to Hall's left—then on, to Leon, small and stubbornly erect inside his suit, his tie askew, his jaw thrust out. *He's doing good,* Bodie says to himself, and he pictures the yellowed snapshots Leon brought home from the war in France, pictures of Leon in uniform.

To Leon's left, three veterans from the VFW post in White River Junction stand at attention, rifles at parade rest. All strangers. Two appear to be of Leon's vintage, the third from WW Two, no doubt. Their uniforms are not quite right, their bellies push too hard against their buttons; wattles hang from their too white chins. One wears a massive ring—could it be a diamond?—wears it on the hand that holds his rifle barrel. Harmon would have laughed at this, would have said this whole thing was bullshit.

The others stand behind Bodie. Although he won't turn around to count them, he knows they're there. The grave divides the mourners from the strangers as the center aisle at a church wedding separates the bride's family from the groom's. Except for Leon: he stands with his hob-nailed hands curled inward, the shoulder over his lame leg dipped and his gaze directed straight ahead, focused somewhere beyond this shaded grove, beyond the dessicated intonations of the Reverend Hall. He stands among the strangers, among the soldiers and the cleric who are, oddly, more like him than anyone present—and still, he stands alone. Behind him—he could turn and touch it—Esther's stone sits stout and square. The earth beneath his feet will someday pack around him, hold him to his resting place between his wife and grandson. Perhaps that's why he elects to stand with strangers, marking his private territory, defying time to follow its inevitable course.

Without looking, Bodie knows the tilt of his mother's face, the upward lift turned slightly to one side, listening, hearing, understanding more than is given to be understood. He knows her eyes are opened, invitations to receive. He knows when she looks down at Harmon's casket she sees an empty suitcase. She makes no mistake about her dead son's whereabouts. For her, he has transcended matter; in front of her, the wood and metal and lifeless tissue are easily objectified. Harmon is elsewhere, everywhere. Vera will be almost smiling, knowing what she knows.

Hall finishes abruptly: Ashes, Dust, Have mercy, Amen. The veteran with the gaudy ring blows lonely notes through a dented bugle. Three rifles fire in unison; smoke drifts off into the underbrush, the echo fades and the day resumes. Quig and his assistants appear from nowhere and release the mechanism that lowers the long box into the hole. What's down there doesn't matter, Bodie tells himself. What *matters* is up here. He squeezes Darlene's hand and feels her lean against him for a moment. She lifts Esther to her face and awakens her with kisses, saying, "I love you, Kitten. Don't worry. We'll make it up to you."

What matters is up here. Hands touch him, friendly faces blur by—sympathies, regrets are murmured. But no one wants to stay for more than that and so they leave, their duty done, they move off slowly, gathering haste as they reach their cars and start their engines, looking back through mirrors only.

Bodie stops at the iron gate and watches Leon limp along behind the soldiers, watches as they speak with Darlene, speak of medals, sympathies, condolences. Darlene politely shakes their hands. Leon salutes as they leave for the Burlington Airport in their rented car.

Other cars are leaving too. Was Jiggsie here? Of course he was. And Tinker and O'Dell and Taylor. Bodie looks along the forest edge for Dale but sees no one. Instead, between two bull-pine towers, he sees in the distance the Catamount bridge, taut and smooth, a pale rainbow.

This afternoon, when he saw the bridge from the cemetery, Bodie knew he would climb it tonight. Accordingly, the balance of the afternoon and early evening seemed to take forever. Most of that time was spent in the farmhouse kitchen with Darlene's parents, Vera and Esther. When the

McAllisters finally left around five, Darlene went for a walk, alone, up the hill toward Bigboat Rock. Leon decided his cows should be looked after, and Vera put away the various dishes of food that had been dropped off by neighbors and friends, baked and boiled gestures of a kind of caring impossible otherwise to convey.

They ate supper unusually late, without much conversation. Vilas Hall was mentioned briefly—Leon said that Vilas was "tighter'n the bark on a beech tree," and stirred a round of laughter and agreement. Vera inquired why Loretta hadn't come. Seeing Bodie's face turn stony, she immediately regretted her question. After supper, Darlene helped Vera wash dishes while Bodie and Leon went outside to pull the first weeds out of Darlene's garden. Side by side they walked the rows, stooping now and then for blades of witch grass or tender shoots of pigweed which Leon noisily nibbled.

"Used to was, they put this in the salad bowl," Leon said. "This here and dandelion greens. Eats real good with vinegar topping. Lamb's-quarters is what we called it."

"You see Dale up at the service?"

"Dale? I thought we was the only family there."

"In the woods. I saw him slip behind a tree. Injun Joe. He must of walked in from the Boyce road, left his rig at Trombley's barn."

"I wouldn't have thought it, not from him. Not from one of Weymouth's."

"Still, I give him credit," Bodie said.

"Full moon tonight. Planter's moon." Leon looked up at an eastern sky grown soft with hints of dusk approaching. "Them soldiers came from California, rode with Harmon all the way." Leon turned to look at Bodie. "You think they knowed him, friends of his?"

"Harmon? No, I doubt they knew him," Bodie said, then

asked himself—*did anyone?* "Tell Mother I'll be home late. Tell her and Darlene good night for me."

"I know," Leon said, "it all takes figuring. Where you headed, Jiggsie's place?"

"Yeah. I don't know, just out. Drive around," Bodie said, suddenly anxious to go.

"I'll be in the barn if you ain't too late. Full moon. Can't sleep against it, never could. Part wolf, I suppose, part coyote."

"Don't howl on me. You promise, Grampy?"

"Done all my howling, years ago. Now, all I do is growl."

Bodie drives toward Catamount, but takes the long way around, the Boyce road, past Jeanrette's. He slows at Trombley's abandoned barn and looks for signs of Dale. Wheel tracks in the foot-high grass show where a vehicle has pulled in, turned—perhaps parked—and pulled out again, headed toward Catamount. Quinntown bound?

Although Bodie wants to see Dale, he is uncertain why except to prove to himself it was Dale in the woods. Once he knows that, he will finally believe in Dale's example, of finding a way to do what counts, irrespective of style.

Except for the Superette, the stores are closed in Catamount. Bodie passes a car with out-of-state plates at the turn from the highway to the bridge. He sees no one in his rearview mirror, no one approaching, as he cuts a hard left into the empty parking lot behind the freight depot. He gets out of his truck and closes the door quietly, then stands still listening to the night falling in, to the sounds of a village preparing for sleep. Somewhere in the distance a lawn mower drone descends to silence as a backyard becomes too dark to mow. A dog barks at a screen door, hungry. The

Superette's ice-machine compressor hums steadily from the side porch cooler. Bats zigzag, barn swallows ricochet through the thickening dusk in search of bugs. Across the river a yellow halo precedes a moon-in-waiting, floating behind a ragged ridge.

As Bodie crosses the parking lot, he looks up at the arches he has climbed so often—great brawny friends, accomplices, protectors and confessors. Mentally, he rehearses the journey through the iron access panel, up inside the long arched tunnel. Picturing himself at the top, he imagines the wooden bench, the humid darkness, the faint rectangles of light from below. He reconfigures each detail, smell and texture, hears the flutter of pigeons' wings as they fly in and out around him. It's all so safe, familiar and attached to everything that's gone before, a place *between* that has always somehow given direction when none seemed elsewhere evident. It reminds him of his brother Harmon, of a sack of bloodied feathers left behind the Catamount Grange Hall. He walks to the road and turns toward the bridge.

At the base of the arch, Bodie finds himself moving his lips into rubbery shapes, his mouth imitating Dale's when Dale is concentrating. Bodie looks up at the arch and laughs out loud at the obvious. He imitates Dale's toothless lisp: *Th-tupid bathtard. Climb the* top *thide. Look off clear to Canada.* Bodie glances over his shoulder at an empty street and climbs the guard rail to a concrete abutment.

He has heard of people climbing the tops of the arches, but because, as a schoolboy, he always did his bridge climbing during daylight hours, he did it *inside* where he wouldn't be seen, where the risks of being caught or plunging into the river were minimal.

The top of the arch is wide and smooth with the chalky residue of sun-bleached paint. By grasping the edges with outstretched arms, Bodie pulls himself easily up the steep curve at the beginning and soon finds himself walking upright as the arch flattens out toward the top. He doesn't look down, but follows the girder until he reaches the apex. He stands at last at a point exactly above the wooden platform where he and Darlene once lay naked.

The view astounds him, even in shadow. All the landmarks are familiar, but from this angle each element is somehow simplified, stuck in a storybook setting. Rooftops, steeples, roads and fields unfold to woods and mountainsides. East of Pike, the moon fulfills her promise, now a milky ball, a full diameter above the ridge and rising fast.

Still without looking down, Bodie turns slowly to face each point of the compass. At last, his focus comes to rest between the riverbanks, looking south, to night water swollen upward against a film of silvered ripples. He watches as little breezes blow the ripples into scudding shards, then lies down on his back to count each star across the hemisphere.

The moon pursues her scheduled course while Bodie lies with limbs outstretched and plans a life with Darlene and Esther. He slips in and out of sleep and dreams. He plants a garden, stockpiles firewood, teaches Esther to ride a bicycle. They build a garage, connect it to the house with a screened-in breezeway where they sit and watch red summer sunsets. Bodie works in his basement shop, making wooden toys for Esther, making a picnic table. On balmy summer nights they invite friends over for cookouts, load the table with sweating pitchers of iced tea, bowls of potato salad, platters of cold cuts and little dishes of piccalilli and corn relish, homemade mustard and mayonnaise. After dark, Esther and her friends run through the grass collecting fireflies in mason jars. Then, at bedtime, they sprinkle them free across the lawn in tiny galaxies.

In and out of sleep, of dreams, he awakens for the final time to watch the moon slide into Woodard Mountain, into the land where he will live out the rest of his life. The rising sun, as if to imitate the moon, precedes itself with sepia, then burns an edge into the horizon and floods the valley with amber light. Bodie turns and looks over the arch's edge, a hundred feet down to water, wide and deep. A glint of ocher animates the muddy chop. A log floats by, revolving slowly as the current carries it along. The log is Harmon, going, going, around the bend, out of sight. The river flows on, dawn evolves, lowland mist collects and melts, the villages begin to stir.

He hears it, down the valley, headed toward him, and he knows the sound. At first, it is disembodied by the distance and confuses him. He tips his head as if to focus, a ground-bird listening for a worm. By the time it reaches the Jordan road, he knows the source and sits up, waiting. The growing whine becomes a fury as the truck gains speed on level ground along the Catamount Flat. From up above the dawn-lit cliffs that crowd the village to the river, thunder echoes down across the rooftops as the overloaded rig shifts down and down and air brakes hiss *why-ain't-you-up-and-working* at the little clapboard houses lined up close against the road.

Now the wheels swing right and wide in front of the depot dock, bump hard across the tracks and aim for the Catamount Arches. Bodie feels a shudder through the bridge's bones as the thirty tons of truck and liquid concrete roll across its cambered span. He looks down at the yellow drum, the cab top black with diesel soot, its running lights a Christmas twinkle. Taillights blink as the truck begins to brake for the clanking iron plates that marks the bridge's eastern end, then the stop sign at the highway. He hears the

261

final downshift for the intersection, hears hissing, turning sounds. And then he hears the driver changing up and up through fourteen gears, hears him bull and jam his way northbound until the sound is finally gone, to other country, full tilt, flat out, running into rising sun.